I0671008

A Game Of Red

James M. Thomas

JAMES M THOMAS

Copyright © 2019 James M. Thomas

All rights reserved.

ISBN: 978-0-578-44126-9

DEDICATION

To my wife, thank you for supporting me in all you do.

To my readers, thank you for taking a chance.

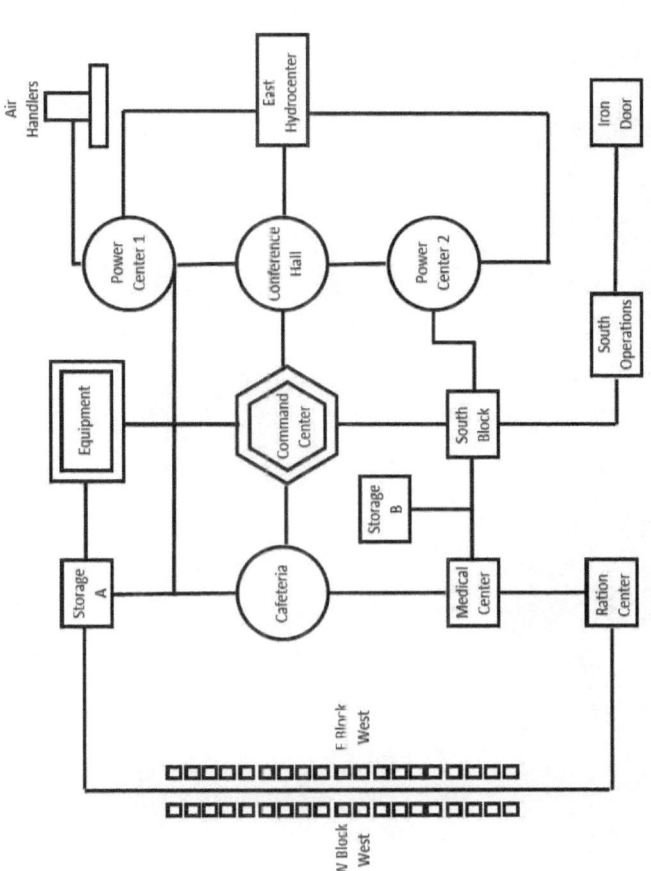

"The dark is merely the absence of light. Without light, the vibrance of color is drained. Our amygdala fires, increasing our anxiety, for we do not know what might come out of that darkness. We, as humans, can sometimes hide in the dark. But in this realm, what might be hiding in there with us can be truly terrifying."

1

Tommy heard the drips.

Soft.

Serene.

One after the other.

Slow.

Even though his eyes were closed, his ears and brain were still active.

Dripping. Viscous. Red.

Blood.

A horrific image was in his mind. Grotesque. Blood spattered on his face from some unknown direction, jolting him to close his eyes and retreat from the splash.

Tommy awoke with a start. His mind racing, eyes darting to see the attack coming, but as he looked around, there was nothing to hurt him. As his breathing slowed, he still heard the familiar sound.

Drip.

Drip.

It took a few more moments to realize where he was. The water from the leaky faucet continued to fall. His breathing normalized and he relaxed knowing it wasn't blood, but a worn out seal from the valve of the faucet.

"Mm, yeah," he said out loud, remembering where he was. *I'm underground.* A familiar sinking and depressing emotion invaded him. Then, an annoying physical pain became apparent.

"Ugh, great." *Another headache. Damn! How many days now?* He shook his head thinking it might be a good way to clear it, but he instantly regretted it. *What a wonderful way to start the day again,* sarcasm laced the thought. *Last week...did I have a headache?* His brow furrowed as he concentrated.

Blank. What the heck was up with that?

His first thought was that crazy bloody nightmare. The second was robbed by the headache, and the third soon followed, thankfully. Her name was Dahria. His mood slightly improved as the negative thoughts were flushed out by her. The girl had a way of making him feel stupid in a room of geniuses. His stomach would swirl with strange sensations when she favored him with a look. He was usually pretty calm and spoke well in front of people, but that all changed when she was around. His body just did not function properly when she smiled or touched him.

Beauty, love, companionship, loyalty, and a few other emotions flooded his mind, but were strangely hazy. Feelings were there, but past images and memories, not so much. The further back he tried to think, the fuzzier the images were.

But it didn't matter that much. Other images *were* clear. She had survived, *they* had survived. The contamination of earth's surface was now a permanent fixture of life having to be relocated underground. Dahria was his main reason to push on. He had to be there for her, protect her. They needed to survive, move forward, anyway they could.

The springs squeaked and strained from his moving mass as he rolled out of bed.

Drip.

Drip. That sound kept pounding his ears, triggering his mind to focus back on the nightmare.

He tasted copper.

Blood. He swirled his tongue around and recognized the source. A sore in his mouth.

Eyebrows raised, "Geez," he said. "Freaky." *Must have bit it in the night.*

He glanced around his room, noticing the light behind the window shade. *Another bright sunny morning,* Tommy half-smiled, but it was hollow. And he knew why.

Wind spoke as it flowed outside. Other natural sounds resonated into the room, communicating that it was a wonderful day. His eyes came to rest on the table. It was smooth. New. Shiny and strongly grained wood looked amazing.

He moved closer and touched the table. It was cold, rough, and splintered. Old and worn. His touch argued with his eyes.

Tommy sighed and moved in front of the image deluder, cutting off the beam of light protruding from the 3d holo projector. His shadow revealed its true reality, turning it into a corroded, worn, discolored version of itself. As he kept moving out of the path of light, the table reverted to its beautiful color and shine. He drifted to the window shade. The image of a bright sunny day and gorgeous forested area outside instantly disappeared as he pulled it up.

The housing units were small with only minimal items for survival. He dressed and ate a modest breakfast at the worn table, trying to think only of Dakria.

Calmly, Tommy walked to the small scratched mirror and looked at himself.

"Okay, let's get going."

Opening the door, he looked at the yellow paint on the wall.

'E-Block West.' The directional arrow pointed the way.

2

Tommy learned the station like a rat in a familiar maze. He explored the dark, humid tunnels that were barely lit with lantern-type lights crudely hanging on the rough stone walls. Cords stretched the length of the tunnels, giving the lights power.

He passed several living-quarter rooms and after a few turns and stairs leading up, he came to a junction. A staircase led both up and down while tunnels and ladders went in other directions. The stairs, the only way out of the living cell block, were cast in shadow and claustrophobically tight. Another maze of turns, more flights up, and a couple times bending over to make sure the obstructions didn't hit his head, he arrived at the operations center's outer rim. The dented and partly-rusted door echoed as he knocked. A piece of metal slid over to reveal a small peep strip. An eye blinked behind it, looked at Tommy standing in front of it, and closed. A lock creaked and banged, the metal door grinded open.

"Tommy," Kevin, a six foot six gangly man, looked down on the newcomer.

"Hey Kev," Tommy nodded, but passed quickly. There was some intimidation to the intellect of Kevin, who was given the title brainiac from time to time. Tommy was smart, but Kevin was on a whole different level.

Once through the door, the path moved to the core of the Command Center. It was a big chamber where delicate information was shared and delivered to various group leads. Tommy happened to be one of them.

Personally, Tommy had no desire to have the responsibility for a group. All he wanted to do was hang out with his girlfriend and other friends, but he didn't have a choice. He was the head of the response unit within the compound. His tasks changed daily. It was a lower level job, but that's the way Tommy wanted it. He did his duty and reported back as necessary.

"Mr. Townsend?" Tommy stood beside the commander and waited for his assignment.

Townsend's face was grim, but he always seemed to look like that, scowling like his mind was heavily engaged in something. Tommy could imagine the stress of the position. People's lives depended on him. Townsend was a solid man, wearing drab and worn clothes.

Without even lifting his head from the two data readouts, he said, "Tommy."

Then, something unusual happened, he lifted his head and his gaze caught Tommy's.

Tommy squirmed, uncomfortable with the hard stare, the awkward silence lasting a little too long.

Then, "I need you to do a run on the station two air handlers today. There seems to be an efficiency problem. It's cranking out air, but the O2 dropped to nineteen percent. We need to find the cause. If the O2 levels don't get at least twenty or twenty-one percent, hypoxia…" he didn't finish as if unsure Tommy would know what he was talking about.

"Yes, sir." Whatever Townsend said with the hypoxo-stuff, the only thing that made sense was about station two. Tommy's heart sank. *Damn, I hate Station Two. That tunnel's nasty.* Dark, far to travel, ducking underneath obstacles, tight squeezes. He wasn't claustrophobic, but the tight places could turn even the hardest man into becoming spineless. Being sealed underground with only the 3D projected images to simulate open spaces was bad enough, but in there, fear crept into a man's soul like some kind of weird game. He sighed. This was a one-man operation too, no sense pulling someone else off duty just to keep him company. He had to keep his imagination in check.

Tommy left the Command Center and headed to the first turn on his way to Station Two. He was already on edge.

Walking out of the command center down a tunnel, something popped out from around the corner. A dark shape came at him from the air like some type of monster out to grab him.

Tommy froze for a split second, stopped breathing, and braced for impact as if some unknown object was about to clobber his skull.

"Ho, Tom!" Jones's huge smile wrapped from ear to ear. He giggled.

Tommy relaxed and gave a sigh of exasperation, the built-up adrenaline faded. "Urgh, asshole!" but a smile formed on his face. "All right, you got me." He nodded. Tommy liked Jones, one of the few people that could make him forget about this precarious place.

"What's the old man got you doing now?" Jones asked quietly, making sure his voice didn't carry far.

"Oh, just checking out a lower oxygen level in station two air handling area. I'm assuming it's just air quality that somehow went down...hopefully just changing some filters." Tommy said.

"Ughh, that place sucks. It's like you're in a frigging B-rated psycho movie and you're traveling down a long dark tunnel," his voice got quieter and slowed down, "and the psycho keeps gaining on you when you're running at full speed and they're limping." His eyes opened larger, and he brought his fingers up to his face and wiggled them while whistling a bizarre theme.

"Yeah, creepy and definitely not my first choice." Tommy grimaced. "Well, we all get shit duty sometimes."

"It's almost *all* shit duty here." Jones chuckled. "Well, here goes my crap-shoot, let's see what Townsend has for me today. Have fun in your solo adventure. Oh, don't forget to give Dahria a nice sweet long juicy kiss! For me." He smooched the air, making an exaggerated kissy face. "Muah, muah, muah." Being the goofball that he was, he laughed and slapped Tommy on the back in a show of friendship.

Tommy laughed with him and shook his head.

Jones was a taller than average boy, nineteen too, they fit together here. He was slim, almost gangly with darker skin. Younger than Tommy by a few months, he had a slight goofiness about him as his face looked like he didn't take life too seriously. It was refreshing.

Tommy scoffed as Jones walked away, but his joy faded quickly as he turned to leave for station two.

3

Drops of water smacked and splattered off the large round pipes and stone floor. The delicate sounds entered Tommy's ears from different directions making it hard to place the location. The echo of the drops and his breathing were loud compared to the surrounding silence of the air.

"Well doesn't *that* just bring back some nasty memories." He groaned, remembering the nightmare. "Easy, it was just a dream," he told himself, exhaling slowly.

The shadows were vast. The dark was pitch black, and the mounted lights only allowed minimal visibility. Musty aromas from the humidity mixed with the rusting iron and other metals weighed on Tommy's chest, making it hard to breathe. Even with a ventilation system, it couldn't keep up with the moisture and metallic aroma.

As Tommy entered the open chamber, he clicked his flashlight on and the beam illuminated the area.

Have I been here before? The familiarity was evident yet he couldn't place it. *Yes, yes of course, I know this station sucks, but something seems…different.* He shook his head and furrowed his eyebrows. *At least my headache is better,* He noticed.

His footsteps were loud as the crunch of dirt and grit suffered under his boots. *Let's get this shit done,* he decided, letting go of his hesitation. He followed his light and proceeded along the chamber. The shadows danced like a ghostly party from his moving beam. As he sauntered on, the walls became narrow and formed a tunnel. A tighter fit, he had to move around giant pipes placed vertically projecting through the top and bottom of the tunnel. Other massive twenty foot diameter pipes ran horizontally disappearing into the vast darkness.

Wonder where these go?

A cold draft hit Tommy on the back of the neck and made his hair stand up. He paused sensing something. He didn't know what. Listening with concentration, he only heard the tinnitus in his ears. "Damn." After a long pause, hoping his mind was making things up, he relaxed and continued. Walking another hundred yards weaving the obstacles, he brought out his checklist. Handwritten, he read the first item. *Check the interlocking system grid and make sure all systems are green.* The ground started to downslope as he walked, forcing him to lean back slightly as gravity was trying to make him walk faster.

His flashlight cut out, pitch black appeared and his inertia kept him moving forward. Losing his balance, he slipped and tried to catch himself, but the slippery and sloped ground overcame the force of friction and he fell on his back. The dancing routine would have won an award, but no judges were present.

"Urrghh! Damn it!" he groaned. The jolt of the fall knocked the flashlight from his hands and it turned back on.

"Piece of crap!"

The dust reflected the light like stars hanging in the air. His elbows and back were wet and it soaked into his shirt.

"Great," he said to himself without enthusiasm, "muddy water. Damn it."

He grabbed the light and got up. Tommy felt the wet shirt stick to his back and rubbed his elbows to make sure there wasn't an injury. As expected, grit, a little wetness, and a small amount of pain were present. Tommy shined the light on his hand and there was blood.

Got cut. He frowned. *Well, nothing I can do now, it's just a scratch.*

Down the tunnel further, he took note of the location and situation of an area he thought might have a possible leak. *Never ends,* he thought. He found the control box, took a couple more steps and heard something beyond his own movements. He swiftly shined the light in the direction his ears told him the sound came from. The light found only massive pipes, cords, dirt, and rocky type walls. Nothing. He heard drips, their echoes, and the noise of silence. He released his breath not realizing he was holding it. Tense. *I've got to get this crap done and get the hell outta here,* he continued.

At the control box, he went through the checklist and marked everything he found...all ok.

Well   shit, Now   what? He   double-checked everything. Gauges, filters, power, all checked out okay. Oxygen meter gauged at twenty percent, slightly lower than it should be, but better than nineteen percent like Townsend told him. He sealed the control panel and left.

4

"Will you *just* do your job!" Theod yelled. "Why does everything have to be so God-damned difficult?"

The girl raised her eyebrows as she stared right through the person yelling, showing her apathy. It was just another day in paradise.

Theod matched her look and thought '*oh, that's right, little fucking brat doesn't care at all.*' Anger blossomed as the color of his skin turned a few more shades of red.

He was short for a male, late twenties in age, buggy eyes, and reddish blonde curly hair. He was unfortunate in his stature, which he tried to make up for with authority. As most everyone else saw it, he stepped on other people to boost himself up.

Dahria was seventeen, pretty, even with messy hair, patches of dirt on her clothes, and some on her skin. Dirty blonde hair, literally, and a somewhat petite build yet has some muscle mass which gave her an athletic look. Most young men would call very attractive, she radiated it, yet she also had a sophistication about her. She wasn't just a thing to look at, but a capable young woman who loved to help others. Being five foot five inches tall in stature, she still looked up to most of the men, except Theod, the arrogant little prick.

She was late in arriving for her baking job today. Her strange and unexplained morning grogginess made her mix the wrong ingredients while she was preparing food. A few weeks ago, the grogginess came and went. Dahria thought it was just a bad cold, but it lasted unusually long. Her job wasn't hard, but it was important to keep the population healthy.

"There's not enough supplies here for you to fuck it up!" Theod accused. "People depend on us, without food...."

"I know, I know," she interrupted, lifting her hand to push on her temple, some pain in her head distorted her concentration, "without food everyone will starve," she finished for him. She rubbed her head...*why am I so groggy again? And a dull pain in my head for days. Last week was...was...*

Theod sighed, not wanting to show any sympathy. "Throw it out, start again and get it done!"

"Sorry," she said.

He turned and left to get his own work started.

Dahria went back to her mixing and tried to get her head to clear.

A slightly shorter girl with brown hair strolled over to Dahria.

"Hey girl," Alexa said. "He's such a dick isn't he? Probably because no one has ever found it," she snickered while wrinkling her nose.

Dahria couldn't help but laugh.

Alexa continued. "Don't worry about him."

Dahria smiled and couldn't help noticing her nose, small and slightly upturned at the end. Most boys would think it cute. She was jealous.

"He's got a point though," Dahria hated to take Theod's side in anything, "Without us doing our job right, everyone'll starve. You know what's funny?" she asked, changing the subject. "I woke up so groggy again. Headache too. I can't seem to remember last month...or much before. Can you?"

Alexa shifted her eyes back and forth as she thought then said, "I remember some things. The memories are there, but hard to detail." She shrugged. "Whatever. It's probably from all the stuff we've recently been through, but I'm sure we'll have fun today!" Alexa finished.

Dahria looked at her confused but nodded. *She sure is in such a good mood. Happy and cheerful for a nasty place like this...that's interesting. I would love some of that juice.*

They continued to work with the rest of the staff preparing for chow time. Bob, the department head, helped in the final preparation of rations.

Dahria became excited as the day went on. She knew she would be able to see Tommy soon.

There was favorable love between them, she could sense it. Memories of him were there, but fuzzy. He was different from most boys she had ever met. Tommy was polite, hard working, and treated her well. A slim build, but strong, and a little gruff. His deep blue eyes fluttered her heart every time he stared at hers. Their relationship was exceptional, even before the memory of this complex.

She pondered for a minute, *what is this place?*

Dahria remembered explosions, earth shattering explosions. There were small numbers of people in a room somewhere. Someone in there told her there had been some kind of catastrophic event. No one knew what, but the above ground became uninhabitable. Assuming it was a nuclear fallout situation, they were moved into underground bunkers around the world.

She tried to think of more information but the rooms in her brain came up blank. Separated from her parents and assuming they were gone, her life before was hazy in her mind, but she remembered Tommy.

5

The shower area looked like an old gym locker room. The space was open with shower heads popping out of the walls. Tiles were dirty, many were cracked and broken, some missing. Tommy thought it looked well used, or even abandoned for an extensive period of time. Cleaning it was not a priority, survival was. However, maintaining a useable resource was a must, so it got occasional maintenance.

Using the shower, being a limited resource, followed the directive of showering every two or three days. Dirty water took time to recycle. The amount used must never exceed what was recycled. Simple math. However, his slip in the mud needed cleaning.

Tommy's back, arms, and legs were wet, yet he could feel some of the sludge dry. He stood under the shower head, dropped his clothes behind him and stepped forward. Pushing the button, the timed water soaked him for ten seconds, then shut off. He took the soap and lathered his body and his clothes. He pushed the button again to rinse off most of the grime and dirt, but noticed something else. There was quite a bit of red mixed in with the grime and dirt.

Hmm, I must have cut myself a little worse than I thought. He felt his elbows again and they hurt, but there wasn't any blood. *Must be iron rich dirt from the corroded pipes,* He concluded solving the mystery. He couldn't help from thinking of that nightmare, but forced it out.

After the shower, Tommy rung out then hung up his wet clothes. He dressed into the next set of clothes that were in his room. They were worn, but at least they were dry.

Tommy's next thought was to get the report back to Townsend, but he had to see Dahria first. It was almost on the way to the command center, the detour would be worth it.

Leaving the shower area, he weaved his way down a long tunnel, through a junction hall, an airlock, and sauntered up to the cafeteria. As he passed the conference hall, he noticed several people going about their business doing different things, talking.

The cafeteria hall was large, able to fit a couple hundred people. Being only thirty people in this complex, Tommy didn't think it was odd because of how quickly everyone was pulled in.

There she was, her beauty entranced him. It wasn't just her beauty either, Dahria was vivacious, and had a good heart. He observed her in several situations where she went out of her way to help someone else. It was a virtue Tommy was attracted to since as long as he could remember.

Tommy noticed she was focused on preparing food as he snuck up behind her, wrapped his arms around her waist, and picked her up off the ground.

She squeaked and almost spilled a drink as she tried to look behind herself, but Tommy let her fall into his arms in a cradle position. Before she could react he planted a big kiss on her lips. At first she resisted in shock, but her wide eyes took in the sight of him. She relaxed and massaged her lips against his. They broke after a few seconds. "Urgh, damn you!" she smiled playfully.

"Hi baby," he responded, giggling He let her down but kept his arms around her, pulled her close.

She stroked his semi-wet hair as she gazed into his eyes.

"Showered already?" she asked.

"Yeah, got a little dirty from the job already. How is your morning?" he asked.

"Much better now," she replied, although he could sense something behind her eyes bothering her.

"Dickhead again?" Tommy predicted.

Silence was the response, but her look gave it away, affirmative. Theod was the head of many departments, the rations hall and cafeteria was one of them. It was tough enough to live down here, but even tougher when someone made the job more difficult.

"Forget him, what he does, doesn't matter. What matters is what *you* do."

She nodded and smiled.

He knew they both had jobs to do, but she was irresistible, like the sweet girl next door.

"Well, hate to say it, but..."

"I know, time to get back to work. Go get your stuff done, then come back."

A quick peck on the cheek and he turned and left.

She watched him walk away and thought of the next time she could see him. Dahria felt refreshed and went back to her duties mixing and preparing food.

Alexa walked out from the back room with a sly smile on her face. It was like she held a secret. She could see Dahria picked up on it right away. Alexa giggled.

"Shut up," Dahria said.

"I didn't say anything," Alexa's smile never floundered, poking fun silently at her. She started singing a love song.

---#---

Tommy met up with Townsend at the command center. There were several other people working on various matters that needed attention.

"I noticed the oxygen level went up when you were in station two, so I assumed you fixed it." Townsend looked at the report continuing to read, "but your report says you found nothing wrong," Townsend stated.

"Yes sir, I double checked everything."

"Good, but not good," Townsend shook his head. "I was hoping there was a problem with the grid or just dirty filters."

Tommy contorted his face in confusion.

Townsend continued, "We may have a nitrogen leak," he avoided the technical jargon. "That might explain why the oxygen's fluctuating. The nitrogen may be pumping into the chamber at a higher rate than normal. This would cause a lower O2 reading, then the O2 sensors are probably reading the extra nitrogen and kick on harder producing more O2. That would suggest why the ratio is fluctuating."

Tommy now understood. He had an aptitude for science. In here, everyone learned about science, whether they wanted to or not. The station depended on people knowing something of value. And if they didn't know it, they learned it.

"If the Nitrogen leak gets worse or bursts, the O2 cannot keep up," Tommy observed Townsend nodding. "Everyone will suffocate," he concluded.

"So now your job is to find this gas leak as quickly as you can before it spreads to areas we inhabit. We will seal off the area that has the highest nitrogen content, but I was hoping it could be found on that grid in station two. Now we know that's not the case." His brow furrowed and he paused. "You might need extra hands. Get Gebriel and Jones. Go to Jen and get any equipment you need. Find that leak and crank the pipe *before* the leak. Then you can repair it with a pipe sealer." He looked at Tommy for confirmation, eyes had a cold hard stare.

"Understood, Sir," Tommy nodded and headed off to talk to Jones. *Whew, at least I can have some company this time.*

6

Jones was working on some contraption. Skilled at taking things apart to find out how they worked, he learned a great deal and it gave him a superior set of mechanical skills.

"Hey, man, we've been assigned a job," Tommy walked up interrupting.

Jones, like always, strained to pull his mind off of what he was working on. His tenacity was unparalleled, except for John, his department head.

Jones stopped and looked at him. "An assignment? Together?"

"Yeah, it's pretty good too."

"Anything's good when you get to work with me," his white teeth were bright with a smile.

"Yeah, you're special alright. So special in fact that you get to check out station two…with me. We're looking for a nitrogen leak that can kill us."

Jones's eyebrows raised and looked in wonder of adventure. "Sweet," he smiled, nodding his head. "Finally," he raised his hands in the air and clenched his fists in triumph. "Yes! I finally get to do something important around here."

"Nah, nothing to worry about, we could die at any time in here," Tommy joked, but part of him knew the joke wasn't funny.

Jones nodded and laughed. "Yeah, sometimes this is bitter man. I assume we need to find Gebriel?"

"You got it." Tommy changed the subject. "One thing I don't get when I think about this place," Tommy said as he looked around, "Why the hell don't we have radios or walkie talkies or *something*? It sure would make it easier to locate someone or coordinate things. We have all this other technology like 3d projectors and image screens but not those?" Tommy asked.

"Yeah no shit," Jones replied as if he had never thought about it before. "Doesn't really make sense. It could be the radio signals can't work through the walls, but an intercom system would've done the trick. Strange how no-one seems to know what's going on. He stopped and thought for a second. "How long have we been down here?" He looked around confused.

Tommy shrugged. "I don't know man, but it sure is strange. I can only remember a few weeks clearly. Before then.." His face morphed into *I don't know*.

Jones knew what he meant, "I hear ya. I guess everyone's shaken up from the move down here so fast. Well, we've got business to do. Let's go."

They found Gebriel. He was sitting at a table drinking coffee. He was about twenty five, shorter than Tommy and Jones. Tommy met him a few times and thought he was a likable good guy. He did his work without complaint when given orders from Townsend. His short hair reminded Tommy of a person who served in the military. He had a certain aura around him that Tommy respected. A leadership quality. Gebriel carried himself high, no matter what was going on. He was capable, but not too personable or overly friendly.

Tommy and Jones conveyed the task at hand, and Gebriel joined them without question.

The three navigated the dark spaces, humid tunnels, and halls to get to the storage cell. As they trekked with purpose, Tommy and Jones talked like friends, and Gebriel added comments on occasion. Tommy and Jones had the best bond, but Gebriel fit in, even though he was a little older. Being down to earth, Gebriel was easy to relate to.

"...Because the middle finger is what sees things clearly," Jones finished the joke laughing. The other two joined in the humor.

They stepped into the equipment chamber and all three smiles faded. Something was unusual.

Jen wasn't there.

7

"Jen?" Gebriel's voice was loud, but it seemed only the walls were listening. He scanned around the hall but found no one.

The equipment chamber was about eighty feet in diameter and had a large metal cage in the center. The outer area around the cage had general equipment items such as pliers, socket wrenches, and other common tools arranged in various places. Inside the cage, which is locked, had more specific equipment and gadgets that needed to be checked out, usually from Jen. But she wasn't here.

"Well shit," Tommy said. "This makes our job impossible until we can get into…"

"Seriously?" replied Jones looking at Tommy chin down and eyebrows raised, "You think I can't get into that cell?"

He had a confidence about him, that's for sure. It made sense. Picking a lock was one of many mechanical talents Jones possessed. He got to work on it.

Under a minute, Jones had the lock open. Tommy scoffed. Jones had an arrogant half smile on his face. "Shopping lane two is open on self serve," he mused.

Tommy looked at him and then at Gebriel and rolled his eyes and said, "Okay, nice work. Let's do it. When we get this job done we can ask about Jen."

They each obtained an oxygen mask, flashlight, an oxygen sensing gadget, and a couple other tools that might help with this type of repair job. Tommy found a multi-tool leatherman type knife that he put into his pocket.

The three of them walked through a maze of tunnels, down a set of steel stairs, and to the sealed contaminated chamber.

"All right, let's gear up," said Gebriel. Donning an oxygen mask each, flashlight, oxygen sensing gadget, and some other general tools to fix the leak, they stared at the sealed door.

When Tommy glanced at the other two, they nodded to signify they were ready. He unscrewed the wheel and opened the door.

A giant hiss of gasses rushed out equalizing the pressure. They jumped back in reflex from the surprise. Looking through the open door, three lights illuminated beams of dust as they disappeared into the chamber.

"Geez, glad you guys are here to protect me," Jones injected, his mask muffling his voice, but it was understandable. "Go on, you first."

Tommy glanced at Jones who gave him a smile. Tommy was even more amused by the way the mask made him appear goofy, like he was underwater.

"Aren't you a hero," Tommy returned. Entering the large chamber, keeping his eyes open. Even with two other guys with him, it still wasn't easy. He bent down and stepped through.

Gebriel was next, then Jones.

Tommy closed the door, sealing them in.

"Whoa, whoa, whoa!" Jones squealed through the mask at Tommy.

Gebriel laughed. "Take it easy man, we'll be alright." He put his hand on his shoulder.

"Let's get this done and get out," Tommy added.

They scouted for the imbalance of gasses. After some spot checking with temperature and gas sensors, they found the leak. It turned out to be a loose roll screw fitting.

"That's strange," said Gebriel inspecting it, "This fitting requires force and leverage to loosen. There's no way this could've come apart by itself."

"There are no vibrations to rattle it," Jones reinforced. He looked at Tommy and Jones with a serious face. "Someone must have tampered with it."

8

After reporting the pipe might have been tampered with, the boys also conveyed the information about Jen being gone.

"She's probably not feeling well and still in her living cell," Townsend said. "I don't think the screw is of any concern now. It's fixed, which is the most important thing, besides Jen. Make sure she's alright, we won't wait for the population check."

"Yes, sir," said Gebriel.

Tommy and Jones nodded.

Population checks were a pain, like a prison, but someone had to keep track of everyone and everything. The checks, beyond presence, were also medical. Depression, hunger, even scrapes and bruises might become septic without treatment. Damon, the complex's physician, was an older man with salt and pepper hair. An aura of arrogance seemed to follow him, at least that was Tommy's first impression. His later impressions would worsen.

The young men turned and left, headed for the living cells located on the far west end of the complex.

After Jen wasn't found in her living cell, they dreaded that the search might not be so easy. They still had flashlights and they added water, a med-kit, and a multi-tool knife that Tommy found and kept.

"This place is too big to search everywhere together. We need to split up," said Gebriel.

The other two nodded in agreement.

"Jones," Gebriel continued, "you take the central core area, medical center, and conference hall. Tommy, you want to go for the east end?"

Tommy gave a quick nod.

"I will take the storage areas. Meet back here at the conference hall in two hours." He looked at them and nodded.

"Check," replied Jones.

"See you both in a bit, hopefully with Jen," Gebriel concluded.

There's never been anyone missing here before, Tommy thought, but then again, *before* was unclear. They went their separate ways to search.

Tommy scoured the halls and walked past the cafeteria to peek in on Dahria. It was a slight detour again, but worth it. A missing person was a concern, and Tommy needed the piece of mind to make sure Dahria was okay, a mandatory action. She was there cooking, washing, and cleaning with some of her other co-workers. He smiled. *Good.* He saw Alexa there with her. She was Dahria's friend, and they looked out for each other. That was good to have in this place.

He walked through the cafeteria without disturbing her. Tommy came to the south block hall heading east towards the power centers. He passed a couple people and asked them a few questions about Jen. No one had seen her.

Gebriel checked his areas, cells, and offices only to find some people, but no-one named Jen. He headed for the tunnels next.

Jones was covering his ground as best he could. He checked many places but only found an unpleasant face. However, the pompousness was not a reason to be rude.

"Hey Theo," Jones said.

Theod looked up and recognized him. His reddish eyebrows relaxed as he focused back on what he was doing.

Jones thought there was something deeper to Theod that most people didn't observe on the surface. A lot of people didn't like him, but Jones, even though he didn't particularly care for him, penetrated a little deeper. He wanted to give him the benefit of the doubt before he made a judgment.

"Jones," said Theod. He was engrossed in something, but gave Jones his attention, but his eyes remained cast at his sheet.

"What're you doing over here? Aren't you supposed to be in the cafeteria?" Jones eyebrows raised. An honest little question.

"Well," Theod's eyes rolled as if recollecting what had happened and replied slowly, "I came to get something from Damon. He owes me."

"Damon, huh," Jones said with a not too pleasant tone. "Whatever he owes you, you owe him a kick in the ass. So do I for poking those needles in us."

Theod scoffed remembering the inoculations. He stared at Jones but said nothing. It was a little awkward so Jones got down to business.

"I'm out looking for Jen," Jones said directly.

Theod's eyebrows rose waiting for more, "yeah? and?"

Seeing the blank face Jones continued, "She's been missing since this morning. No one seems to have seen her, but she was checked last night." He looked at Theod. "Have you seen her?"

"So, Townsend assigned you as a detective? Quite a step up." Theod said with sarcasm. "Have you tried her cell? I think she lives there."

At that moment Theod's reputation became a bit more clear to Jones, he was an ass.

Theod laughed but stopped his mocking, "I saw her yesterday. Nothing seemed unusual. She hangs out in one of the storage stations in west block sometimes, but, no idea why someone would want to hang out there. Creepy places."

He thought for a moment before speaking again. "Well, she's kinda creepy herself," he muttered to himself.

"Man, your ass is growing as big as your insults," said Jones, "or maybe your head."

"Sss," teased Theod like it was water rolling off his back. *He just wants to be me.*

Tommy was unable to locate Jen anywhere, but hadn't checked station one and station two yet. Remembering station two, his hair raised in sensation and his skin crawled. He had just been there, so he decided to start with station one and save the worst for last. Station one was pretty much the same dark nasty place though, but station two gave him a sour feeling in his stomach.

Tommy opened the station one chamber door. With a heavy crank, the door resisted the effort to open due to its sizable inertia. The hinges scraped and moaned as the heavy door accelerated opening. It stopped on its own friction and Tommy turned on the flashlight and shined it around. Taking a good long look before he entered, the light illuminated many areas and exposed a multitude of shadows, pipes, dirt, and a long tunnel. As he stepped over the bottom obstacle frame for the door, the dirt met his boots in a sound of grit, like sandpaper being scratched with rubber. It was quiet after a few steps. Silent. The smell of musty humidity pumped through his lungs. Tommy took a few more reluctant steps shining the light around.

Alone. He sighed.

9

Eyes peered from the shadows and observed the flashlight shining. Anger blended with pleasure erupted in him. He wasn't supposed to be disturbed.

As he watched, it appeared to him the figure was searching for something, or someone. Maybe him, he didn't know. As the figure passed, he recognized the opportune time. In an instant he jumped out with smooth skill, took one step and hit the person on the back of the head with the knuckle ring of his knife. The blow was precise, aimed at the location to induce a shock to the brain that rendered unconsciousness. The subject fell like a sack of lifeless solitary bricks. The flashlight flung from his hand as he hit the ground.

Perfect, he smiled.

--#--

Blackness turned to gray, then to blurry.

His eyes slit open and severe pain resonated in his head. He felt woozy and nauseous, like he couldn't stand on his own legs, yet he was standing. At that moment he noticed something held him up, not his legs. Blinking twice, it felt like pebbles and sandy dirt were in his eyes. The pain released tears washing away the grit. He shook his head and instantly regretted it. The pain was great, and the shake made it worse.

What the hell is this? He felt like he was rolled up in a carpet. *Am I...tied up?*

Some fogginess drifted away allowing him to see an image of a man covered with darkness materialize.

"Hello?" He gasped, his voice weak.

"There you are." Another man responded. "Thought we lost you for a second." The smile protruded on him. He was covered in shadow.

"Where am I?" Looking around groggy and squinting, he looked at the rope that held him up. His eyelids were almost too heavy to keep open.

"You're in the tunnel a ways from the command center. Looked like you were searching for something," the man in shadow said in a polite, easy voice. "You fell back there and hit your head. I found you and tried to help you stand, but you were useless, so I tied you up to get the blood flowing out of your head."

"Oh, thanks. Well..." He paused while physically and mentally checked himself for any serious injuries, "I think I can stand on my own now. You can cut me down."

"Oh, yeah, just a sec, duh," the man with the knife said. He came closer, held the knife under the rope, and sawed. The rope wasn't cut, but the arm it was tied to was. The blood seeped out. "Oh, shit," he said, "I'm sorry man, I accidentally cut you, Jesus what an idiot! I had the damn blade backwards!" He sneered.

The captive looked at the wound. The sharpness of the knife must have been pristine because the wound didn't hurt. The blood dripped in a nice line down his arm. His frown developed as his mind couldn't place what had happened. The amount of blood spilling raised his concern.

The snicker and laugh filled the air from the man in shadow. "What's the matter?"

The laugh startled the captive, and he looked at the man who slowly appeared out of the shadow. He couldn't speak as some light of the situation came into play. He looked confused.

"Here, sorry, let me try again. Hopefully this time I'll have the sharp side on the rope where it's supposed to be. My hands are a little shaky, this whole ordeal being trapped underground has made me a little nervous," he lied. The smile never left his cool and calm face.

As the second cut was made, the tied man's eyes were darting back and forth and adrenaline pumped into his arteries. The blood flowed faster.

"What the hell are you doing?!" he said frustrated, feeling the pain for the first time.

As the third cut sliced into flesh, fear gripped his heart and squeezed. He yelled and struggled as hard as he could. "Help! Someone!" The ropes held as if he were a dingy trying to sail away but a rope designed to hold a cruise ship was attached.

The killer knew the location was secluded, and the sealed doors made it hard for sound to travel. Still, his captive was forced to scream as intense pain was released through the vocal cords.

The face of the killer was now in full concentration. Swift, precise strokes were slashed into flesh finding their way to arteries and veins with accuracy.

The sound turned into pure agonizing gurgled screaming. Soon the struggling came to a slow close, energy draining leaving only a desire to sleep.

"Whoo, that was pretty. Smile for the camera now." The man with the red knife sounded like a game show host. He studied the dying man's eyes. Pure confusion. "Mm, Lost for words a?" A smile curved up in the corner of one side of his mouth. "That's okay, I'll do the talking. How does it feel to know your life is leaving you? Draining from you like a tire with a leak. Sssss."

The dying man's brows furrowed. Confusion. *Huh? What the hell happened? Who is this guy? Where am I?... Damn it! Where's, Where's? Wait! Oh God, God...* Then his eyes glossed over. The reaper came.

10

Jones finished his search over an hour ago and waited for Tommy and Gebriel in the conference hall. People were at tables having conversations about different things, but neither Tommy nor Gebriel showed yet.

More time went by.

Nothing.

A little more time and Jones became agitated.

Come on, he thought to himself. *What the hell? It's been way more than two hours now. There's got to be an easier way to do things around here.* His mind thought of Jen missing. Now Tommy and Gebriel weren't back yet. He pondered and drummed his fingers onto the table. *This is shit, I can't wait here any longer.*

Jones tried to stay calm as he went to search for them. Looking for Tommy first, he passed through a couple tunnels, opened and closed the door for the electrical junction. Jones couldn't help walking fast even though he was trying to keep calm. It was dark here, alone. Claustrophobic. Fighting to keep the anxiety down, the concern for his friends was greater. He walked down another long tunnel. After a while his steps sounded different, like walking on a sidewalk after a rain. Shining the light down he saw a muddy wet stone floor. *This place leaks too much,* he thought. Moving the flashlight around, he followed the wet trail as it disappeared around the corner. Jones moved around the bend and the light shined on a column illuminating the top of the pipe first.

What the hell is that? He squinted to gain more focus. Paint splotched the column. Some of the liquid streaked down it being too heavy to remain stationary. The paint was a deep dark red color but looked out of place, like some irresponsible kid took a bucket of paint and threw it up on the column, but there were no kids here. No little kids anyway.

Jones followed the red lines down the column with his flashlight. *Is that paint...oil...wet...?*

The moment was surreal.

Jones illuminated a body. Tied to a pipe, the head lolled so the face was not visible. Blood slid down from several obvious wounds, still wet. His face cringed as his brain was trying to process the image without success. Disbelief of reality fought within him. Was it a dummy?

Jones stepped closer with trepidation to confirm that this was not some idiot playing a trick. Why would someone do that? *Real fucking funny.*

Moving closer, his hands trembled as he noticed the body slumping being held up only by the ropes.

There's no way this is real. His stomach scored knots that seemed like someone put a baseball inside his stomach. His throat constricted like someone one squeezing it just enough to make it difficult to breathe and swallow.

As he moved even closer, it was obvious this was not a dummy. Jones froze. His eyes became wide and his heart beat fast.

Who is it? Oh my God! Tommy?

"Tommy!" He looked for identifying marks. Frantically searching, his next thought entered his mind. *Who the hell did this?* His eyes became wide, and he had a rush of adrenaline, *Are they still here?* His body trembled with agitation.

11

He smiled in the dark as he heard the voice yell the name 'Tommy.' His eyes peered out between the pipes and observed the person frozen with fear.

This'll be quick, he thought. He had the perfect opportunity as the guy was in flight mode, standing perfectly still.

Sitting duck.

His already bloodied knife out and ready, two steps...

"Jones?!" Someone screamed down the tunnel.

Just revealed out of the shadows, the man heard the yell and re-entered the cover of darkness.

"Yeah! Tommy? Is that you?" he yelled back.

"Hey man, what're you doing down there?!" came the reply.

Jones said, "Dude come quick, I think someone's...!" The anxiety finished his sentence with silence.

The killer heard footsteps now hitting the ground hard. The other flashlight bobbing and bouncing around from the shock of the feet hitting the ground.

"What is it man? Did you find Jen?" Tommy said, coming into view making eye contact with Jones.

He observed pure terror and shock in Jones' eyes.

Out of breath, he repeated, "What's up? What happened?!"

Jones was pale. This was unusual for him being darker skinned. "I don't know. Something…happened, I think he's…dead. There's blood everywhere, come here." He pointed his flashlight in the direction and shined it on the body.

Tommy's lungs were heaving from the run. His eyes were wide as his brain processed the image. They both ambled closer to the unreal sight aiming the light at the grotesque scene.

"What the hell?" Tommy said in disbelief. His eyes narrowed as if wincing in pain. "Who is it?"

"I don't know yet. I just found him and then you came. Here," he pointed his flashlight down, "look at the boots."

Tommy recognized with a sinking heart, "It's… It's," he had trouble finishing it, but then forced it out, "Gebriel." He stared, trying to comprehend the sight. "What the hell happened? Why would someone kill him…How?"

Tommy looked at Jones, who had no answers either. As he observed him, there was no sign of blood on Jones. Tommy immediately felt ashamed of reflex, but his instinct made him gather the information without realizing it. He already knew Jones had nothing to do with it, but this reaffirmed it. Good.

"Look," Jones said pointing, "the blood's still wet. He was alive just a few minutes ago."

The hair on the back of Tommy's neck stood up. "We better get out of here."

"I think I agree,"

"We'll have to come back for Gebriel later," Tommy was filled with regret, but there was nothing they could do for Gebriel. They had to leave this place.

Dahria…Tommy shuttered.

12

Tommy's heart relaxed. Dahria was there, she was okay. He let her be, not wanting to upset her with the news. He also didn't know what Townsend would do.

Gebriel's body lay on the morgue table with a white sheet covering him. A small crowd surrounded the corpse. Silence permeated the room. A few eyes looked at Tommy and Jones. Were they accusing?

The two boys reported the incident to Mr. Townsend, which is why they were here. He had questions and needed answers. Townsends limited people involved, including himself, Tommy and Jones, the doctor named Damon, the tall and lanky Kevin, and Theod.

Tommy risked a slow look around to observe the others. Theod stared right back evenly, an accusing face? Maybe. Tommy held the stare for a few moments. He hoped Theod would observe he wasn't shying away like he was guilty. Glancing at Kevin, Tommy knew why he was here. Kevin was clever at figuring things out. He was the smartest person in here, so it was natural Townsend had a spot for him. A guy named Nick started calling him 'TK,' for 'tenacious Kevin.' He digs into problems like a tick, hard to rip away until he's done. Damon, the only medical person, was examining Gebriel. He sure didn't dress like a doctor, but Tommy figured the dress and supplies were limited. The first impression Tommy had of Damon was a beady eyed 'better-than-everyone-else' type of person, but he didn't want to label him until he was sure.

"We're going to keep this classified for now people," Townsend commanded with sounds laced with regret. "We need to figure out who did this and how it happened." He looked at each one of them in turn, then Damon. "This was obviously no accident. We have a killer among us."

No one said anything.

"There are now twenty-nine people here in this complex. Unverified. I assume you didn't find Jen?" He asked, looking at Tommy.

Tommy shook his head.

Townsend nodded. and continued, "Let's not assume anything happened to her until we can confirm it. We need to create an inner circle of people we trust and know well. It needs to be a tight unit so we can flush out anyone who might be the killer in secret. We also need to enforce a strict curfew and partner system, where no-one is alone anymore," Townsend conveyed. He looked at each of them.

Tommy was lost in his own thoughts. *Who the heck is it?* There were a lot of good people, but someone did it. *And if we put one person alone with a killer...* "Partners?" Tommy asked.

"It might not be best to put people together with a killer alone," Kevin said, "In larger groups we stand a better chance by watching each other. A killer will most likely want to go off alone. That might be a perfect time to draw him out, or at least observe suspicious behavior. That would make it important that the killer does not know we are in groups for a reason. If whoever's alerted, they will know we're looking for them. The question now is, how do we get everyone in groups and spy without the killer knowing?"

"I'll call a meeting," Townsend decided. "A routine shift of assignments shouldn't arouse any suspicion. We have to move fast because the population check is tonight. We don't want Gebriel's death out, yet."

Townsend looked at Tommy and then Jones. "In the meantime, Tommy, you and Jones group with Nick and Tim. You both know what's going on, so you can secretly lead the team without causing any suspicion. Find Jen, if you can." he said tapping his finger into Tommy's chest.

Tommy thought, *I'm taking Dahria too.* No one could argue against that.

Jones thought, *but what if the killer is one of these people?*

Problems and priorities had arisen.

13

Shock and disbelief gripped Dahria's face as Tommy laid out the situation. She looked like she was turning pale and getting ready to heave.

"I can't believe Gebriel's gone...and Jen? No one still knows what happened to her?" she asked.

Tommy shook his head with a somber face. "The next thing Townsend wants us to do is scour this complex with teams to find her. You, me, Jones, and these other guys named Nick and Tim."

She gazed up into his eyes with worry. "Tim? I've seen him before. Who's Nick?" She asked.

"I've only seen him a couple times. I don't know him, but I guess we'll find out."

She hugged him.

Holding her tight, Tommy said, "make sure you stay extra alert. If I'm ever not there, *never* be alone with anyone unless it's someone you really trust. Okay?"

"Okay," she confirmed.

"Let's do what we can, but I want you to be prepared." He gave her a multi-tool knife that he found in the supply chamber. "If something seems off, don't be afraid to use it," he said.

She took the knife.

He stared into her eyes. There were Serious. "I love you," he told her.

"I love you too."

14

Two people strutted down the hall and talked to the man working in the shadows. They mentioned a reassignment and they acted as if it was a bullshit duty. Neither one had happy faces, but the man working in the shadows smiled.

They were speaking to him, but in his mind he was thinking different thoughts.

"So that's it. Let's get started on our runs." Bill, the man's name he remembered, was obviously in charge.

Bill was taller, about six foot two and had a good build.

The other man, Jeff, didn't seem to care and looked at oblivion. He most likely knew there was no use in arguing. The man in shadow remembered the guy's habit of complaining, but for an unknown reason didn't work that angle today.

"Come on, you ready?" Jeff asked.

Fuck you, but he held his death stare inside, covered it well, "Sure bud."

As they started on their new assignment, Jeff went to check the converter power cables by the opening at the front end of the tunnel. The location was around a short curve in the passage.

"Hey Jeff?" A question came from Bill.

Jeff glanced back waiting for him to talk, giving him an irritated look of 'what now?'

"Wait a second for me to check this end, before you go."

Jeff winced. "It's easier if we do our jobs at the same time. What's the big deal?"

There's the complainer I know, the man in shadow had a half smile, but kept it to himself.

Bill tried, but Jeff shook his head and walked to the end of the tunnel, not even glancing back.

Jerk, Bill scoffed. As he looked down the tunnel at Jeff walking away, the man in shadow made his move. He stood up and stepped backward, pretended to stumble on something, and fell right into Bill. Perfect.

Bill tried to catch him the best he could but they fell on top of each other as Bill broke the fall.

"Urgh!" Bill let out in frustration, thinking the pain was a severe elbow that plunged hard into his side mid-section, but it felt wet.

"Shit, sorry Bill, but thanks," the man said for breaking his fall. "How are you feeling?" He laughed close to him.

Then, the pain felt strange, wrong. Bill gritted his teeth as the blade was ripped out and a hand came over his mouth so fast he didn't have time to speak. The other hand held the erect knife, bloodied, and the killer made the blade disappear into the side of Bill's neck. He tried to struggle, but the pain was intense and his strength was leaving at an alarming rate. The struggling became less and less and the killer held him tight. Bill was strong, but he wasn't able to keep up the intensity.

The killer repositioned himself over Bill to observe where Jeff was. He had to be fast.

He was.

Releasing Bill, leaving him gurgling he moved in position to alleviate line of sight for as long as possible. Concentration and energy were elevated in his system, waiting. Jeff came around the corner...he was easier. *Well, I guess there won't be anymore complaining.* He smiled.

15

The man threw more popcorn in his mouth. The satisfying crunch echoed in the room. Crunchy yet fluffy and soft, the corn was perfect. Buttered and cheese-salted for a crisp taste. Feeling his mouth becoming a little dry, he took a drink and washed down the salty buttery popcorn. He breathed in deep and exhaled, letting it out slow. His glasses beeped. *God damn it,* he thought. "Fuck you," he said to a video image popping up in the corner of his vision. The man wearing the glasses was pissed.

Laughing at the remark, the person in the image responded, "That's another ten thousand asshole!"

"You are one lucky son of a bitch!" the guy with the popcorn accused.

They had watched the ordeal from their comfortable private video rooms. More beeps came in and other people started chatting. The sounds of voices coming out of the surround speaker fabric built into the wall. They were high end sound systems to make sure the gamers were enjoying it as much as possible. Gambling was one spice of the event.

Leaning back in the comfortable lazy style floating chair, video glasses on his head, the man with the popcorn chuckled. "Did you see that guy's expression? He didn't even know what was going on."

"The first two-person kill!" A voice plowed on the line, "Yes! Before week five even! That's two hundred'n fifty thousand!" he concluded with excitement.

"I can't wait to see when all the shit hits the fan!" another said with a large amount of energy.

Someone else chimed in, "Remember when that kid slipped in the blood and didn't even know it," his laugh loud and gaudy, "showered it off!" he howled.

"Yeah, that was ridiculous," someone said. "Stupid moron. I still like the one where the dude was tied up." There was a couple second pause in conversation as they all thought of it.

"Yeah, the real deal. Fucking great!" the guy with the popcorn jeered.

Plenty of people laughed for a long time, echoing in welcoming ears.

---#---

A different man, not part of the hilarious conversation, was sitting comfortably at a large video screen, observing the man with the popcorn. The image of him relaxing on the chair and eating his popcorn was an easy sight. Sound vibrations of his talking displayed visually under his video image. There were nine video feeds on the same large screen, squares in a tic-tac-toe pattern. The gamblers, the players, gamers. He looked at the next screen, another nine. There were a total of five different large screens in his cubicle space. These were the different people involved in the entertainment group. In charge of them, he was known as the cubicle operator, or 'CO.' He wore a headset and had communications equipment close by. The CO's job was to observe the group and make sure everything was operational and proceeding smoothly.

The next cubicle held the same set of equipment with another CO manning five screens, all featuring nine different people each, totaling forty-five per cubicle. Over these cubicles stood a man in a suit walking a path managing fifty cubicles. The 'path-walker' spoke into the small dot microphone in his glasses.

"Master path-walker Dennison on site 3A-GD. Two more confirmed kills. Players are responding and having a good time, proceeding as planned."

The other end of the message, a man received the information. A sinister smile of enjoyment was on his face. Another game, better than ever.

16

Tommy couldn't believe what had happened. It kept playing over and over in his mind. The thoughts of the pure terror Gebriel must have experienced, beat hard on him.

How had it happened? Who the hell is it? Why? Where the hell is Jen? The thoughts pounded in his head making him feel sick. He shook it. *Get out and focus on moving forward, this person is still out there.* Tommy feared for himself. He feared for others. He feared for Dahria and Jones. That thought angered him the most. Blood rage welled in him. *If that guy puts one hand on her...* He shook his head again, *stay out of that!* Tommy glanced at the others one at a time in his small group wondering. First, a guy named Nick, who Tommy didn't know much about. He was about five foot nine and had dark blonde hair. Nick had a decent build and was more thick than tall. In his mid-thirties he seemed capable, but a little feisty, while Tim, the older man, was bigger and stockier and seemed more calm and level-headed. He had darker colored hair and a couple scars on his face like he was in some kind of fight in his younger years. He had darkness about him that ran on his face, like a permanent scowl caused by the scars. At about forty five, he seemed to be okay with the assignment, and did his work too, but wasn't pleased with Tommy relaying the message. Tommy understood he might be upset at taking orders from a kid, but he still followed orders. He thought about one of these guys being the killer and he wanted to be prepared. What would he do if one of them sprang? *Don't let them out of my sight,* he thought, *and if something goes down, be hard and fast, be ready.*

A noise claimed Tommy's attention, and he looked over in that direction. Nick and Tim noticed as well and looked toward the sound. Another group was coming down the passageway. Footsteps. They came closer and one of them looked at Tommy. It was John, a man that Tommy has seen work with Jones before, he led the team of the technical stuff in the complex. Another man and woman looked somewhat scared. They had their heads down. Another guy in their group looked familiar. Tommy met the eyes of Kevin, he didn't look like his usual self. He wasn't smiling and his eyes were hard.

"Come on, all of you," Kevin said.

Tommy's eyes flicked to the others in his group. No one said anything, but he could tell they were as confused as he was.

"Everything might be about to change."

17

Tommy filed into the conference hall with his group. The hall was large, with a capacity for over a hundred people, yet only thirty were ever here minus the victims, plenty of extra space. Tommy always thought that was peculiar.

The low grumbles of people talking bounced around the conference center walls filling the room with noise. The conference center, like some other main areas in the complex, had walls and other features to simulate the upside world. Ceiling tiles, rafters, lights, and other items were in these main rooms. Papers, posters, and pegboard littered the walls, most looked old, worn, and unused. Tables and chairs scattered around with a long table at the front which seats the division leaders of the compound. LED white lights made it brighter than most places in the complex. Outer tunnels, storage centers, living cells, and some halls were lit with sporadic yellow LED's. Townsend was in the far corner talking to some other department heads of the compound.

Tommy spotted Alice, an older lady of fifty-five, and joined her as he noticed a worried face. "Hey Alice, what's wrong?" he asked.

"There's been an accident," she whispered and had some trouble getting it out. "Two men named Bill and Jeff. They're gone."

"You mean...?" Tommy wondered if that meant dead. He saw the confirmation in her eyes. Yes. "What? How?" He thought about Bill, he had seen him around, but didn't have more than a few words of conversation with him. He was a big guy, muscular, an intimidating sight. *Geez,* thinking of how formidable Bill should have been, *this guy's a pro,* Tommy concluded. A rush of adrenaline flushed his system and made him nervous.

"Thanks, Alice."

Tommy walked to the table where his group was seated. He grabbed Dahria's hand and held it a little too tight. Jones looked worried. Nick looked confused and Tim looked apathetic. *Had Tim overheard?*

"Thank you all for dropping what you were doing and coming right away," Townsend commanded in a strong voice. The room simmered down and everyone sat and listened. "We have a situation on our hands," he exclaimed. Everyone's eyes were on him. No one said a thing.

Tommy glanced at Dahria and the rest of his group members. They were in this together. No place to hide, nowhere to go. Trapped...with a killer. He listened.

"Fellow survivors," Townsend began, "for the immediate future I want you all to please remain calm. We have a situation. I know we've only been here for a few weeks. We've struggled in adapting to our new lives and learned to depend on each other. Unfortunately, we must remain here until we can surface..." he paused. "Our very existence hangs in the balance. Without *everyone* this place would fail, and that means we fail, we die." His tone and demeanor boomed. He continued, "We are now facing another serious situation that I felt you all should know about." Silence. "We have had some accidents leaving three people dead, and one is still missing."

The eruption was expected. Some stood up yelling back questions, others chattered amongst their own tables.

"What happened?!" someone shouted. The question was almost inaudible with the commotion and loud demands.

"Who's dead!" someone else screamed.

"People!" Townsend shouted, raising his hands. Even with his booming voice, it took a few moments to get their attention again. "Quiet down people!" Townsend commanded again, "I can't answer anything if you ask a hundred questions at once!"

The room rumbled down. The grumbling and conversations ceased.

"Thank you."

"What accidents?" the impatience of someone quipped, but no one yelled at him, obviously having the same question.

"They were all suspected of being murdered."

No one spoke for many moments.

18

Control and order were difficult. Issues were hashed out and argued about the proper course of action. There were several facts the people were aware of; The compound needs consistent work to run, currently no one knew who the killer was, and groups of four or five didn't work. It was decided that the first task was to obtain the original digital manifest from the entrance computer. That would indicate who physically entered this complex from the scanners. The list could be compared to the physical population count.

Nick volunteered for the job which meant his team would go, consisting of Tommy, Jones, Dahria, Tim, and the doctor, Damon, who sat at a different table..

Meanwhile, everyone in the compound would stay here. Townsend recommended that restroom breaks were with people you trust. When one group came out, a new group entered.

Tommy looked at Dahria, then Jones. His eyes were serious and he wondered how the others felt, but didn't say anything yet.. Soon enough, Nick went off to talk to Townsend, and Sue pulled Tim's attention away. Tommy motioned to Jones and Dahria. The three huddled close and Tommy glanced around the room to see if anyone was listening. He caught one guy at a far table looking at him with a worried face. Or was he looking at Dahria, Tommy couldn't tell, but he understood what he might be feeling, upset and worried. He felt sympathy, they were all in this together with a killer. Still looking into the crowd, he whispered to his friends keeping his fingers over his mouth to mask any type of lip reading, "No matter what...we stay together, we watch every move, of everyone." He rolled his eyes to his friends. "I hate to say it, but even people in our own group could be someone we can't trust."

"How can we defend ourselves?" Dahria whispered.

"Well, for one thing we have a minimum of us three against one," Tommy suggested. "As long as we are alert and careful, we should be able to stay alive. Maybe we can find something to use as weapons."

Each one of them dreaded the idea of losing someone. Even though they had a couple extra numbers, it might not ensure that everyone would survive an attack. After all, the killer took out two men at basically the same time.

They broke up their huddle as Nick strolled back and Tim finished conversing with Sue.

"This killer is trained, and he apparently has weapons," Jones usual playful demeanor was gone. He eyed the others at the table.

"So let's go get some weapons of our own," Nick suggested. "While we get the other stuff. Uh...the manifest."

They looked at each other in silence, suggesting they all agreed. The small group left on their assignment to the equipment hall.

19

The man had a look of concern on his face as he watched the conference take place. People talked, argued, and shouted from the speech by Townsend.

In his mind, he smiled. He knew something others didn't. *I'm the killer.* The stakes of the game went up. That meant his focus and concentration followed. He liked it. The prey, the taunting, artwork, fear, sex, and killing. He can handle multiple victims simultaneously with great odds and he enjoyed the challenge. He was fascinated by human behavior; the confusion on their faces when the realization took place, the blood, lust, and even the gloss when it was all over. He took a deep breath.

While the man in shadow had a secret room, sometimes it was exhilarating checking things out in the mix. He scanned the room observing and thinking. He saw Townsend with a group. Next to that table, people were having their own conversations. Playing the part, his worried face was scared, alone.

The man in shadow noticed the girl, the pretty one. She was talking with a group of friends. Dahria, he remembered her name. Her boyfriend glanced around and spotted him. The man in shadow never flinched, but he moved his eyes from her to him, his face still looking worried. Without a care, the kid huddled with his friends and started talking. *Did he notice anything? Nah.*

She was silky sweet. Her golden hair hung down caressing her shoulders. Her soft lips would bleed when he would bite her. Her breasts were full and round, she had white smooth skin. He imagined cutting small cuts that would leak a brilliant red against such creamy perfect skin. He shook his head to get himself out of his daydream. *Soon,* he thought and smiled to himself. He felt an erection coming on.

20

Sitting among the people gathered, another man who blended in absorbed the scene. He appeared ordinary and never drew unwanted attention to himself, which is probably why he was easily overlooked.

The ordinary man slipped away unnoticed as the conference took place.

He wrapped the wire around the device with precise hands. His heart swelled and grew anxious. He could feel the pulse in his neck as the adrenaline kicked in. A storm was about to hit the complex and the people were the confetti. *Come and meet your maker.*

As his excitement swelled, he thought of his job. Life was good. People housed in this complex were criminals, caught in the act of some horrific crime. It was an honor being selected for such a prolific form of justice, or judgment kill as he thought of it, and the money was invariably a bonus. He loved it... well, *most* of it. Stalking, planning, justice, execution. The last part was troublesome for him, but he understood he was useful in bettering society. The ordinary man was extraordinary in cleansing the world, one piece of shit at a time. From what he had overheard from Townsend just now, there was some particular trash that needed extra attention. And fast. Someone was killing, doing *his* job, stealing from him. Although, a killer killing criminals didn't make him feel much sympathy, he was angry at the intrusion. *I'll get him.*

As he got closer to the conference center, he slowed. The ordinary man listened to the people from around the corner in the tunnel. His escape route and attack plan ready. He held his device in his hand, heart pumping, ready for multiple and quick kills. Sneaking up as close as he could without being seen, he handled his device. With a step forward he aimed at the angled wall and threw the device hard. It flew fast towards the wall and struck it. The device bounced off the hard surface and soared into the crowded hall. Classic geometry and billiard physics. He counted five, four, three, two, one.

The sound was strong and loud. BOOM! There were screams and a sudden rush of movement vibrated around the walls.

He heard the hissing of smoke. Half crouching in a predator type stance, knife held controlled but relaxed, he was ready. The first one appeared running toward him. Timing was everything. His element of surprise was a true advantage. The person wasn't considering where they were going, only concentrating on getting out.

Running out of the conference hall screaming, the person saw a glint of steel, shining like a star, for a split second. The knife plunged into his chest and out again before he even flinched. A second slice to the neck made him slow. His momentum carried him forward as he stumbled and grabbed his neck. Legs giving out, he dropped.

The man with the knife suffered no thought on the fallen man. He was already poised for the next criminal. She came, he killed. Another two came out right after. One after another. The first man was downed, but the second man had a quick instant to react, peering at the man in darkness, stunned. The victim was able to throw up his arms in an attempt to block, but only christened the knife, which plunged into his forearm. The training of the professional killer was superb as his other hand whipped like a bat to the other man's throat, just as he tried to scream. No sound flared but a small choke, cutoff by the blow. Keeping his movement clean, the killer found another target, ending whatever life the guy had. By the time the smoke was entering the corridor hallway, the killer used it for cover.

He noticed another man stop well before arriving in range of him. He recognized John. His terrified look revealed he observed the stabbing. The scared man turned and ran the other way. The man in darkness held steadfast for anyone else who might come his way. He knew the smoke would force everyone out of that room, he just didn't know which direction everyone would run. He waited.

A few moments later one more came through...it was Townsend.

21

Tommy looked at the thing he was holding, *Would this help?* There was not a lot to find. This place was for survival, not war. Still, Tommy noticed there were a few items that may be usable. He found a rope, wrapped it, and slung it over his shoulder.

As a group they inventoried their possessions; flashlights for everyone, a rope, a hard metal wrench, and two more multi-tool type items with small knives built into them. As Tommy studied the area, Jones tested the metal wrench by swinging it into the fence.

"Yeah, you piece of shit. Come get some," Jones said. Then to Tommy, "I'll *fix* you." he had a smile, but the tension couldn't be forgotten.

Tommy gave him a 'sup-nod' in support.

Nick scoffed and Tim was silent. Damon was looking at his own supplies.

Tommy shifted his gaze to Dahria. Knowing this was life and death, he felt for his friends. As for the others in his group, it wasn't that he didn't care, but he didn't know them well. They were still people, human beings. One of them being the killer couldn't help but cross his mind.

The group headed back to the conference hall. As they got closer, there was a strange silence. It was eerie. Tommy's stomach felt as if it was sinking.

"Something's wrong," Tim said, stopping, holding out his arms. "Hold up."

Everyone stopped and looked at him. "What?" Dahria and the doctor asked in unison.

Nick said, "Listen."

They tried to pick up noise, but it was silent. Tommy had a bad feeling. He moved closer to Dahria, glancing back at her. She had a worried look. Smoke was coming around the corner in little wafts.

"Look at that," Tim whispered pointing at the faint smoke.

"What the hell?," Jones readied his wrench.

Damon stayed behind them and said, "Looks like smoke."

Tommy stiffened as adrenaline pumped into his veins. "Let me go first," he said.

"No kid," Tim said. "I'll go." He admired Tommy's courage, but knew he should be the one to take point being the oldest, also the biggest. He held the multi-tool in his hand, gripping it hard.

Nick couldn't decide if Tommy was courageous or just plain stupid. Usually *he* was the courageous one. "So eager to get yourself killed?" Nick said sarcastically.

Tommy didn't answer. He didn't have time for this bullshit.

Tim stepped further.

Jones, Tommy, Dahria, Nick and Damon all followed. Tim eased his way from around the bend and found more smoke and...bodies. His heart pounded.

"Shit," Tim stopped to look around.

"What?" Jones asked curiously and stepped around to gain a view. Tommy right behind him. Blood was everywhere. The others noticed the unsightly scene.

Dahria made a small cry of agony and turned away backwards. Shock enveloped her as she stepped away from the conference center. She heard a faint sound coming from somewhere. It was like a soft bubbling of water with air in a pipe. She looked behind her back into the conference hall...nothing. Turning back away from the hall, black shadows were everywhere. Gurgling. The others continued forward into the hall, but Dahria stood unnoticed and shined her light into the shadows until it hit something...a wet spot of...blood. Her stomach churned. Disbelief kept her light on the blood and she noticed something else. A trail. She was petrified. Following the streaked blood trail, it was so long. The light found the end of the line. A body in a pool of blood. The flashlight shook even more in her hand and her breathing turned into quick gasps. She could make out that the body was a man with a deep gash in his neck and blood was all over his chest area. Her body froze in fear.

Staring at the body, as bad as she felt, she couldn't stop looking. His hands started shaking as the man quivered, the face covered in blood. The large gash in the neck spewed blood, and the body convulsed trying to get air into the lungs but couldn't, making a God awful sound. His eyes had a look Dahria will never forget and then rolled up.

Dahria lost it. Her scream was intense, She shook so bad her flashlight flew from her hand and fell. Her mind forgot all current purpose and situation, and ran away from the body towards the conference hall.

Tommy and the team turned in shock toward Dahria, flashlights illuminating her in a spotlight. She was running at top speed headed right past them. Tommy tried to catch her, but she did not want to be caught and slipped through. She was fast, and this interruption stunned all of them. He wasn't ready, and she ran right past him.

"Dahria! Wait!" Tommy said to her. "Shit!" He ran after her. "Come on!" Tommy shouted, glancing at the others. Tommy bolted and Jones was right behind him. Nick, Tim, and Damon followed as close as they could.

Entering the conference center, there were many exits. The one Dahria was running towards had more bodies. Tommy noticed and yelled again, "Dahria wait!"

Jones also tried, "Dahria!" but it fell upon deaf ears.

Dahria's vision was tunneled. As she ran, bodies flashed at her like an electrified camera. She accelerated and tripped on one and fell hard. She tumbled and rolled with it. Numb to the cuts and pain, the fall barely slowed her, and she scrambled to get to her feet. The fall was enough to give Tommy the time to catch her. He grabbed her and pulled her close.

"Dahria, it's okay, I gotcha." Tommy said as assuringly as he could. "I gotcha, you're okay."

She struggled hitting his chest not knowing what was happening. He held her tight, taking the hits that he hoped would calm down in a minute. She squeaked and screamed. Dahria felt like she was trapped in a web and a million spiders were crawling toward her. A few moments later the whining and struggling toned down to breathing heavily. She couldn't break free. He enclosed her head into his chest and shielded her eyes.

"It's okay. Shhhh." He slowed his breathing down so she could feel it. After a few moments she was able to look up at him. She began to cry and buried her face into his chest again trying to escape the horror. She couldn't. Dahria closed her eyes trying to breathe easier and calm down. The images etched into her mind. "Breathe, babe, breathe." Her breathing slowed, and her crying turned into a sob. Tommy looked at the others.

"This just happened." Tim said. "We've got to get out of here." He tried to be empathetic, but they needed to leave.

"Seems like a good idea to me." Damon agreed.

Nick scoffed and muttered under his breath, "pussy.".

For some reason, none of them moved. Trying to catch their breath, they tried to piece it together. It was too much to process.

"So the killer made a bomb or something?" Damon suggested breaking the silence.

"I'm not so sure it was made to kill," Tommy said. "From what I saw a second ago was more like stab wounds, not blast wounds."

"Who the hell are you kid?" Nick asked. "You know your surroundings, you know about injuries. Were you a frigging mercenary or something? What are you hiding?"

"My father's a veteran," he replied. "He taught me a lot of things."

"Did he teach you how to kill?" Nick asked, pressuring him.

"Leave him alone," Dahria turned her attention to Nick. "Tommy's no killer, jackass." She looked into his eyes.

"Yeah, we'll see about that, love." Nick averted his attention and didn't want to battle with her. He at least gave her some sympathy for what she just experienced.

"This guy's really good. He likes to kill," Jones said refocusing the conversation. He stared at the air, eyes focusing on nothing. "He could've used the bomb specifically to kill multiple people but didn't. He took them out one by one." Jones sighed and asked, "What the hell's going on?"

"Not sure," Tommy said looking at Jones.

Better yet, what're we going to do?" Damon asked.

Tim injected, "We better get somewhere we can see people coming and not have so many ways in."

"Yeah. Somewhere we can also have a couple ways to get out," Tommy added.

"What about finding others?" Dahria suggested. "There has to be someone still alive." Her face became grave. "Alexa." Her friend, why hadn't she thought of that before?

"We can decide that once we're better prepared," Tim said. "Let's go."

"Where?" Damon asked.

"Let's ask the genius." Nick said, referring to Tommy.

"How about the west block living cells," Tim suggested, ignoring Nick. "It's farther from most open halls."

"No, I wouldn't want to be in a spot where there is no way out," Jones replied. "How about the south block hall?"

"Wonder boy? What cha got?"

Tommy thought for a moment. "Jones is right. That might be our best bet. It's a well lit place, with areas to store food. It doesn't have a whole lot of places to hide though. There are two ways to get in, three ways to get out, but one of those ways leads to the iron door." The iron door referred to the control room door leading to the outside world. Restricted area, Tommy had never seen it. "I guess I wouldn't consider it a way out. If we get forced down that tunnel, we're trapped."

"Let's go, and we'll head through the cafeteria hall to collect some food," Tim suggested.

Damon stood around and didn't offer anything, Tommy thought that was unusual. He kept a mental note of it.

As the group ambled on, they had to step over a few more bodies. It was silent, increasing the eeriness. They collected food while Tommy and Jones scouted in all directions.

Somewhere a pan fell. The sound echoed through the kitchen. It shook Dahria, who was already on edge, and she looked like she got shocked by a stun gun. Her nerves have had tremendous use over the last hour, like an ethernet cable beyond its maximum bandwidth.

But a thought penetrated to the top. "That could be Alexa," Dahria said with hope.

"Maybe," Tommy replied. Tommy crept over to the sound, he was the closest to where it came from.

"What are you doing? Shouldn't we be *going?*" asked Damon.

Tim and Jones were ready and followed Tommy. Nick, Damon, and Dahria watched closely.

Tommy looked at Jones and gave a signal count. Three, two, one. Tommy moved fast and flew around the corner to where the sound was. His eyes fell on the kitchen.

No one here.

He listened. A small bead of sweat accumulated and ran down the side of his left temple. He hardly noticed as his eyes found the pan that fell. It was a light pan, but better than no weapon so Tommy kept it and held it ready. A large cabinet was right next to it. It was big enough to fit a person inside. He positioned himself to open the door without being directly in front of it. Tommy looked at Jones and Tim this time for confirmation of his proposed action, nodded, looked down and opened it. He stepped back to allow more reaction time, but the cabinet was empty. Simultaneously, a loud metal sound came from behind them like the slamming of a gym locker. A figure burst out.

"No!" the person cried and was accelerating into a quick run.

Dahria's heart skipped a beat at the loud and hefty sound.

The man was trying hard to get out of the kitchen, but seemed clumsy in doing it. Using his force and momentum, the person barreled right into Damon, sending him flying in the other direction, right into the opened cabinet. He hit the back of the cabinet with some force giving off metal vibrations like hitting a metal locker with a sledge hammer.

Damon yelled in more startlement than pain, "Arrh!"

Nick couldn't help but smirk at the mishap for a split second. He giggled inside.

The man wiggled his way off of Damon and stood up. He stopped, noticing that he was surrounded.

"John?" The speech came from Jones.

Tim furrowed his eyebrows when he saw John.

"Jones?" the man asked and looked at him. A smile. "Aw man am I glad to see you." He took a deep breath and sighed.

Tim studied John's face and there was something familiar about it. More familiar than just being in the complex. A strange moment. He tucked it away.

John glanced at him. There was recognition in his eyes too, but nothing more than a fellow companion from working here. "Tim?"

Tim nodded, but he didn't say anything as he was trying to figure out why he looked so familiar.

"Hey man, what are you doing here?" Jones asked.

"Hiding," John replied. "I saw you guys leave at the end of the conference," he started, then paused for a moment. His mind was racing trying to get the words out. "It was about fifteen minutes after. I heard this loud bang, like a grenade or something, it was crazy loud. Some people were already running out of the room. Then, I noticed smoke started to pour out of this box on the ground. It started to fill the room real quick. I choked so I got the heck out of there too. There were a couple people ahead of me…" He lost his train of thought as if he was searching for what to say, or he had a hard time saying it. He put his head down and kept breathing hard.

"Go on," Tim urged.

Looking back into his eyes he continued, a little slower and more calm after a deep breath, "I saw the first person in front of me disappear into the tunnel. Then, several steps ahead of me and…then…a shadow moved…it was a dark shape, like a black blanket."

Tommy squinted at Dahria and Jones.

"A glinty metal looking thing…a knife disappeared and then reappeared. I…couldn't really tell what was going on, it was like magic. Then…I saw his eyes. They glowed like lanterns and looked right at me. The person by him fell, and I froze. I…stopped dead in my tracks." After another deep breath, "I…I saw his eyes…then…the glint of light of his blade…red."

"You saw him?" Jones asked. "The killer?"

"Yeah," John replied. "I saw him. I was petrified. I turned and ran as fast as I could the other way. I was yelling, but by the time I got back everyone was gone. I ran in here to hide."

"Holy shit." Nick said. "He didn't come after you? We must have moved right past him."

Damon was getting more nervous, he scanned the hall afraid someone might jump out at that very moment. Hair on the back of his neck became electrified.

Nick felt edgy. "Whatever, come on, let's get the hell out of here and get to the south block."

Even though Jones had a new nickname for him, 'Nick the dick,' he couldn't argue with him this time.

They started in the direction of the destination.

What are we going to do? Tommy pondered.

22

"Well hello there," a man said to a small group of people hiding behind a table. He engaged them with a large smile showing a rack of white teeth. However, the smoke was thick enough to only allow some sight penetration.

Three people were holding each other in a tight group. One of them coughed several times, unable to breathe. They were sitting on the floor.

"I'm glad I found you. Are you guys okay?" the man asked. He couldn't see clearly through the haze of smoke, so he waved his arms rapidly to clear some of it away.

Two faces glanced at him. They were women.

The man smiled bigger.

"What the hell happened?" one of the women asked.

"Someone had some fun in the conference center," he answered.

"Fun?" she asked, appalled.

"Yeah, fun. You've heard the word before right, being how *old* you are?" The man's face was cool, calm, and collected. His face contorted. "Gosh, I'm sorry. Did I say old? I meant...well, yeah...old." His face held an expression of pity.

There was a man also on the ground stifling his coughing and looked up at him. His eyes were red and watering from the smoke. A look of disgust was aimed at the insensitive figure staring at him from above.

"Whoa, don't hurt me," the man in shadow pleaded, raising his hands in surrender. "Oh, come on," he continued saying to the three of them, "a few old farts like yourselves won't mind dying, right? You're so close to death already. So what's the worry?" He laughed.

The older man's face had obvious offense. "Who are you?" he asked.

"I'm an artist." He smiled like it was the best line of work in the world. "Would you like to see some of my paintings?" It turned out not to be an optional request.

23

After finding John, the group arrived at the South operations hall. It was a main part of the complex, so it was lit better than the tunnels and larger than most other halls. It had many pipes running through and gauges to go with it. It looked like a submarine hydro control system. There were boxes of electronic equipment with cables and wires running with the pipes. A computer terminal was next to it with a couple of chairs. It looked like it was hooked up to the system as a control unit. A few tables and matching chairs were in the center of the hall. The place even had two small offices, the doors were open.

"Those are the sensors for our living cells," John pointed out. "This is where I monitor information that's gathered from the outside."

That statement drew the attention of everyone else. None of them knew anything about this. Gathering around John, they listened, even Damon, who wanted to get out at any cost.

John, taking a quick look at his interested audience, proceeded. "See this here? It monitors all the gasses coming in and I can see the mixture levels. If something is off, I report it, fix it. Over here," he continued pointing at the computer screen, "Is the outside monitor. It shows the levels

of gasses, radiation, pollution, and weather from out there."
He pointed up.

Tommy looked at the computer screen John had popped
up. The readings were strange. Maybe a little dancing with the
interface and he might figure it out. Jones was ahead of him.

"So the O2 level outside this complex is only fourteen
percent?" Jones asked to confirm.

John looked at the screen and clicked the mouse on some
graph. Old clicking mice were obsolete, but down in the
complex, technology had to rely on what worked, and what
was cheap. "Yep," he said. "However, I have learned that a
part of this complex's purpose is to produce more O2 for
delivery to the outside."

"Must be what the gigantic pipes are for," Tim suggested.

"How much does it need to be…okay? You know, for
us?" Dahria asked.

"At least nineteen point five percent," John replied.

The statement enlightening Tommy, to return to his
home someday would be the dream.

Tommy, born in Colorado, lived a good portion of his
life there. He had a normal childhood, loving parents, and
went to school online like everyone else. Tommy was a good
student with an aptitude for leadership and had an upgraded
level of common sense. He met Dahria and fell in love with
her fast and hard. Above all of her attractiveness, what he
loved most was that she made him feel good about himself.
The relationship was reciprocal. They depended on each
other and grew to have an unusually mature relationship for
their ages. When the epidemic happened, they were both
rushed down into this underground bunker. He remembered
being put into an individual sleep chamber and waking to this
complex's medical center. Next, they were moved into the
central conference hall and told about the fallout on earth's
surface. They must survive underground for as long as they
can until the earth's surface is recycled. Down here in the
bunker, the complex.

It was hard for Tommy to adjust, but at least he had Dahria with him. An advantage he probably had over others. He met Jones, and they clicked right away like long-time friends.

"Hey man," Jones said, snapping Tommy out of his thoughts.

Tommy blinked and shook his head to focus.

"Let's scout this place out," he suggested.

"Alright, yeah," Tommy agreed.

Nick had nothing better to do, so he decided to come along too. Damon wasn't interested and Dahria was exhausted from the ordeal so she took to a chair and rested. Tim was wandering around looking for items that might be useful.

The three of them explored the hall, but found nothing special. It led into two tunnels on the east side. One of them led to the iron door. Tommy, Jones, Nick, and Tim were interested in that since they had never seen it. John was the only one who had ever seen it, so he plucked away on the keyboard for any information.

The group of four set out down the tunnel. About fifty yards later, there it was, the great iron door. When they inspected it, the metal door was large, dusty, solid-heavy, and air-sealed door with a wheel on it.

"This thing looks like it hasn't been used in years," Tommy said.

"Yeah, it probably hasn't," Jones said, inspecting it.

There were several buttons next to it of different colors, a computer screen, keyboard, and a large red button on the top right. Different color siren-type lights were on the door on one side. The caked-on dirt and spider web confirmed it sat a while untouched. Jones pushed a key on the keyboard to see if it would fire up. A clean spot was made on the enter key. A second or two later the screen turned on and a script ran across the screen one letter at a time.

DOOR SEALED...>

They looked at the script. The square cursor flashed on and off waiting for a command.

"Huh, I think it says the door is closed," Jones said with a mild retardation enactment.

"No shit," Nick said, playing along. "I wonder if those readings on that computer are accurate?"

"What do you mean?" Jones asked.

Nick glanced at him with pitiful eyes and said, "Really kid? I can't be the only curious one here. Haven't you ever wondered about this place? I don't know about you, but I can't remember my life very well at all before last month. He stared at them for a few seconds more before adding, "Headaches too. This is a conspiracy."

"Yeah, you may be right Nick," Tim nodded his head. He thought about it before, but never understood it. He also considered never having the time to ask anyone else. "It's like trying to remember when I was younger. I'm there, I can feel the memories, but can't see it. I'm old, but I shouldn't have lost my mind just yet, but..." there were two names in his head. Dee and Olivia. Emotions of love were there too, but he couldn't place much else. He looked around at the walls here remembering the tragic scenarios, "I probably have a few marbles running around now though." Tim, being in his forties, was concerned about the information. He kept it to himself thinking it was just a fluke. Now he realized it wasn't. And John, what was up with him seeming familiar?

"Hmmm," Tommy chimed in. "Well...it looks like things may not be quite what they seem here."

"Yeah, it sounds obvious, but what does it mean?" Nick asked. No one had any answers.

The lights went off.

24

Several weeks ago a man stood wearing a white lab coat looking down at the person in the sleep chamber.

Poor sucker, he thought. He didn't like this part of the job, but it was a job. The company paid him well but the cost was his integrity. He stared at the younger girl in the pod with sympathy. Staring at her, he wondered what she did in life to be a participant. The pod manager kept thinking of her unpleasant future and the things that would happen to her. She would be chased, hunted, and killed. He couldn't help but think how innocent she looked. It was hard for him to visualize her as a criminal. Someone who could hurt someone else, destroy their lives, kill them. He lifted his eyebrows and pondered on the fact that sometimes even innocent looking people could be killers.

The society had devolved into greed, becoming its driving force. Criminal justice became overwhelmed with the crime rate, unable to keep up. Prisons grew overloaded to the point where they couldn't admit anyone anymore, allowing criminal networks to gain even more power. The law had to take quick action to regain order. A company emerged offering help with providing swift judgment in reducing the population of criminals and also providing a lucrative avenue of entertainment. And where there is money, there is corruption.

The corruption grew.

Over time, citizens prioritized their wants and desires, but forgot their needs. People wanted more and more. The hunger of possessions grew, like a drug. Depression and anxiety followed as most people struggled to keep up with everyone else, working themselves to mental breakdown. Hate and anger became even more popular as most people could hide behind some media device with no consequence of facing someone. True colors, glowed like a lantern, no filter. No morality. The colors were vibrant, evil. What was left of so-called 'decent' people were forced to move into remote areas leaving behind the carnage of idiots.

The games of red, often dubbed 'blood games' by the commoners, started in the middle of the hateful corrupt cities. The games grew so big they gained their own jurisdiction; they were their own law. As focus grew on the games, giant cities could no longer run properly and started to wear. Plants became overgrown, buildings weren't maintained and parts of the structures even started breaking off. The people didn't care, they stayed. There was nowhere for them to go and no place they would rather be. The games dominated people like an addiction that was incurable. It was the relief of a hard day of life, the extreme entertainment everyone needed and couldn't get away from.

Life was tough, but maybe it helped everyone feel that their lives weren't so bad knowing people were being hunted and killed. Maybe others loved it for the sport.

Transients grew at an alarming rate, littering the buildings and streets like locusts. Only a select few lived well, if one played the games and bet well, one could live like a king. It was the new world. The peak of society had been reached and then broke. Today was the downfall, and it would be a long hard fall.

The pod manager looked around at the numerous people sleeping. He went to each pod and hooked up connections and performed the routine diagnostics. All the pods had a set of wires attached and electrodes placed onto each person in appropriate spots. The pods were placed in a large circle of thirty, all with their heads facing the inside of the circle. Their feet aimed to the outside perimeter. There was a machine in the center attached to robotic lines on the ceiling allowing it to travel precisely to all the pods. Computer screens were in front of each pod, displaying vital information of each participant. Blood pressure, heart rate, brain activity, and other readouts.

"Okay, everyone," he said out loud to himself. It was a lonely job, so speaking out loud sometimes kept the mind sane. "How do you like your eggs? Over-easy, over-hard...or scrambled." As he stated the last word, he flicked the final button starting the machines.

While the technology was deficient in erasing memories in full, it was good enough to scramble them. It turned out to be a superb component, discovering that erasing memories in full would render a vegetable. Sometimes a person could read or write, or even speak, like a baby, but it would render no usable subjects for the games.

After experimentation, the trick was taking the memories and swirling them, like a magnet to an old disk drive. The participant remembers things, but can't quite place everything or link anything together. It disoriented them, but didn't ruin their character or the essence of who they were. It was like having a milkshake with melted vanilla and chocolate in it and then swirling it all up. The vanilla and chocolate are still there, but mixed.

After time passed, the memories would fade back by linking other memories together, re-establishing the connections of the neural net, but by that time it was usually over.

The machine moved with swift precision to the first participant, labeled T64-1645. The pod manager looked at the screen name, Tommy Knight. It delivered shocks in different areas and then took pictures of his face. A long drill with a super thin needle appeared and drilled into his skull.

"Oakie, doakie," the pod manager said. "See you guys la.." he caught himself mid sentence, knowing he wouldn't see them later, "well maybe not." He left the room and let the machine do its job.

25

"Son of a bitch!" Damon exclaimed with dread. He was nervous. Everyone looked up at the lights that had suddenly turned off. It took a few moments for the emergency lights to flicker on. They were dim and far apart. Shadows appeared everywhere, tall and dark covering the room, making it hard to place where anything was. A couple of flashlights flicked on and flashed around, making the shadows shimmer and move.

"Oh, my God," Dahria gasped. She breathed heavier, feeling her adrenaline kicking in. Then, she felt Tommy's hand find hers. Their faces dark from lack of light, but she found comfort from his touch. He could make out the fear and uncertainty from her shaking.

"Hey, it's okay," he said. Although, he wondered if he could even protect himself much less her.

"Well," Tim said as he sighed. Referring to the flashlights darting around he said, "We can't keep shining the lights constantly or they'll run out of power. They should last a while, but we can let our eyes adjust and conserve them. Only use them when needed. I can try to work on getting the power back on. These computers are still on. They might be linked to part of the emergency system."

"They are," John said. "I can give you a hand. I've worked on these before."

"What the hell are we going to do?" asked Damon.

"We kill anyone who comes down that hall we don't like," Nick answered.

Tommy rolled his eyes.

"Don't be ridiculous," Tim replied. "It might be just a normal power outage. If a person did this, it could be anyone, except us now I guess." Tim lifted his eyebrows. "Let's keep watch. We'll set up shifts of two. There are only two ways in here. We put one man on each tunnel."

Dahria listened and then commented, "What do we do if we see someone?"

"We each have a flashlight," Tim continued. "Shine it to the other watchman, and flash it three times. They can then wake everyone."

Eyes darted around the group looking for answers. Nick nodded as if he liked the idea. Damon didn't disagree.

Tommy said, "Guys. What about the people down here? Alexa is still out there, Theod, Townsend. This guy has spread us out into different sections...I would think that's what he wants. We've got to find other survivors and try to stick together."

Tim sighed and his head fell. "You're right, but the problem is we don't know who's killing," Tim said. "But what do you have in mind kid?" Tim was intelligent enough to welcome any ideas.

Nick scoffed and shook his head.

26

Her eyes opened, foggy. She was lying on the floor. Her head hurt. Consciousness faded in like a digital image materializing on a screen.

Hazy.

Crackling.

Her thoughts quickened as she remembered what happened. The smoke, everyone running, Townsend telling them people were murdered. It was all so new and hard to comprehend. Her eyes grew wide She gasped and turned her head. Looking around she didn't recognize where she was.

A soothing voice vibrated from a distance. "Hey there," he said.

She peeked over to the person sitting in the dark. "Where am I?" Her speech required effort. She could see a faint outline of a person, but couldn't make out any details.

"We're in the east tunnel, just out of the conference center. You fell and hit your head running from that God awful explosion and smoke. I pulled you out of the main walkway so you wouldn't get trampled. You never know who might run out and step all over you."

She started to sit up, weak, and pain was in her head. Her hands played around the area and her fingers felt the bump. It hurt as she eased her fingers over the mountain. "Who are you?" she asked.

"Don't worry, I'm not gonna hurt you," he reassured her. He could see she was shaken. "Are you all right?"

She darted her eyes around to access multiple parts of her brain, like a systems check for a machine to determine injuries. She focused on different parts of her body, but only her head seemed to hurt. Her body was hard to move and felt strained because of it. "Yeah, I think so."

He got up slowly, walked closer, and offered a hand.

"Thank you," she said, "but I think I've got it." She sat up on her own. He didn't seem to mind and took a step back.

"I'm Art," he said with a small smile. His bright eyes shone through the dark. "I'm the guy that works on the water treatment in this place. See here?" he said pointing at the several large water containers close by. "Here is where the water passes through several types of filters. Then, it moves on..." he caught himself as he noticed that he already lost her.

She said, "hmm," but she didn't care. She recognized the name, but not him, although it was hard to see him clearly. "I'm Alexa."

"I know," he replied. "I've seen you around in the cafeteria. Everyone has to eat," Art said with an awkward laugh.

She gave him a soft smile. "Where is everyone else? Have you seen anyone?"

Her eyes detected a sad look. "Yeah, two people over..." He pointed with his thumb, "unfortunately they are...were, not alive," he managed to get out. Eyes focusing on the ground, he sighed. "Crazy what's happened." He said. Sadness was evident, but he popped his head up and stared at her again. "Man...just glad I found someone...alive." He said and gave her a half smile.

She returned the smile, "yeah...me too."

Her smile penetrated him. Her smile was genuine.

Sweet.

Innocent.

His mind captured a picture of the moment. Her smile proved to be too much. He stared at her too long. He wanted the moment to last longer, but knew he slipped. Gazing into her eyes turned his groin into hot lust. He could feel the tingle of an erection. Hard, engorged to the point of bursting.

Ferocious.

Okay...that's kinda creepy, she thought. His eyes penetrated her, like an arrow going right through the target. She felt naked and tried to cover herself up even though she was fully clothed. Alexa removed her eyes from his. She felt like roaches were crawling all over her body but she couldn't move. She tried hard to keep from showing fear, but it ruled her. Something was wrong. She could sense it. To make matters worse, her realization of being alone with him shook her.

"You know," he purred, "We're alone right now. I'm a man and you're a beautiful woman, the fairest one of all, I'd say." His eyes invaded. The light was dim but they seemed to glow with fire. "I can't wait to see what's under your clothes."

Her face contorted, *What did he say?* Confused, she couldn't comprehend it. The hair on the back of her neck raised like old spike strips for ground cars. Adrenaline pumped into her and spread throughout her body giving her anxiety.

"Okay sweet thing, you're gonna need this," he said, holding out a flashlight. He was cheerful. The tone was very different now, like someone transforming from nice and gentle to someone playing a game and giving orders. "Take it," he said holding it out.

She was a stone statue, petrified, but her body vibrated from trembling like a tuning fork that struck a hard surface. There was a strange compassion as he put it on the ground and stepped back. He watched her and waited.

"Trust me, you'll want this for our little game," he said. "Go ahead, get it." She didn't move. "Look, you were out cold for a long time. If I wanted to kill you, you wouldn't have woken up."

She knew that was true. Taking a few steps forward, she grabbed the flashlight terrified by what his 'game' would be. She tensed for him to pounce. He didn't move, just stared at her with that half smile on his face. She grabbed it and quickly stepped back.

He continued, "Good. See? Don't worry, we're gonna have a lot of fun together. Okay, here's how the game's played. You're the little mouse. Try to run and hide..." he wiggled his fingers in a running motion.

She was already on edge but now breathed even heavier and turned a little pale.

"...honey, honey, calm down," he soothed and stepped back, giving her some room. "If you don't listen," he continued in a cause-and-effect way, "you will not understand the rules on how to win." He paused.

The man in shadow looked at her with patience, but the gentle taunting drove her to madness. No one would disturb them. Her adrenaline from the fight-or-flight reflex now flooded her entire body. She had to get away.

"Shhhh," he soothed, he seemed full of patience, like he had all the time in the world. "Now, your goal is to search and find the lucky treasure hidden somewhere here in the East end of the complex. Try to find it any way that you can. This hatch," he said pointing in the direction of it, "leads to a long tunnel with a good deal of water pipes running through it. Try not to break these pipes," he said with concern and humor, "If you crack one, it will contaminate our water," he gave a small chuckle.

She didn't respond.

"Anyway," he continued back on track, "If you find the treasure it has a combination for the code to exit the tunnels on the far end. If you find it before I find you, you can escape and win!" He raised his arms in triumph. "All you need to find the treasure is...to look carefully, my queen. Find the beautiful treasure, my fairest one of all." Then his smile disappeared, and a sense of pure serious lustful pleasure entered his face. His eyes were stabbing her, "If you lose…" he broke into a giant grin. "Well now, that's just gonna highlight *my* day. You, however, might not be able to walk…or talk very well though."

Her face settled into pure disgust and terror. Alexa could put up a fight, sure, but he was a man, much bigger and stronger. The only thing to do was run. Panic enveloped her, she screamed. It was loud and determined.

She opened the door and ran into the tunnel.

He laughed. "That's it, you go girl! Weee!"

27

Alexa pondered, *where can I go? Where the hell can I go?*

She tried to slow down the panic, but it was difficult. She felt clumsy as she lost some of her fine motor skills. *Any hiding places?* She wasn't aware of where the tunnels went, but she kept going to strengthen the distance from him.

She risked a look back to see if he was chasing her. There he was, covered in darkness. She could only see his black shape. And those eyes. He stood, not moving.

"Keep going!" The man in shadow shouted.

His demeanor frightened her beyond anything else. He was too calm, too controlled. She was desperate and frantic. Her mind raced to think of something she could use to defend herself as she ran. These tunnels were barren, nothing useful.

She noticed it was getting even darker down this tunnel but remembered she had a flashlight. Alexa fumbled around trying to flick the switch on, her thumb found it. The light popped on and it bounced around in front of her as she ran. Breathing hard, she turned left then right. She didn't know how far this tunnel went, but kept going, anyway. It seemed to go on forever, and she became tired. Her lungs were running at full capacity now and she noticed that she couldn't breathe fast enough to keep up with her muscles. Looking back again thinking he would be right there, he wasn't. The only sound was her breath beating in her ears. Her legs slowed down to conserve energy. She was trying to catch her breath and noticed the tunnel ended up ahead. She glanced left, there was a tunnel. Flipping her head right, another tunnel. It overwhelmed her mind processing which direction to choose. She only hesitated for a second, chose left and galloped down the hall.

What am I going to do? Where can I go? pounded again and again. *Fairest one of all, what's under your clothes, treasure.* That triggered a thought, *Yes, yes, this treasure, I gotta find it! No! No! That's bullshit! He's just screwing with me. There is no stupid treasure. A combination?*

Her eyes darted around the area as she moved along the tunnel. To her horror, there didn't seem to be anywhere to hide. Finding nothing resembling a treasure, she came to a chamber. She flashed the light around. There was a dim emergency light in the room's corner.

The flashlight touched many pieces of the room, revealing machinery. The chamber had a tiled floor, rolling metal carts with electronics on them. Wires attached to devices littered the ground. The chamber looked used on a daily basis.

She didn't have time to waste, her heart thudded. Her throat was constricted.

He's coming.

She shined the light down the tunnel to where he would be coming from...nothing. Shining the flashlight around, she found the switch for the chamber. Flicking them on, nothing happened. She flipped them off and on again rapidly...still nothing.

"Come on!" she immediately regretted the sound. She went back to her search. *Would he really make a way for me to win?* She doubted it, but looked around anyway. Some chance was better than none.

"Hey baby!" came a distant howling that echoed around the area. He sounded like a kid playing hide and seek. It was muffled but still made her shriek in terror. He was coming!

She froze. *Oh my God!,* she thought. *He didn't give me any time!* Frantic, she tried to find something to defend herself with. Looking around, nothing came to mind. *Hide!* She was feeling faint. Scanning more, she exposed a few large lockers. She didn't think about how obvious it might be to hide in them and moved closer to them.

"Come on sweetie! Show me what you got, show me where you like it," he said. He started humming and singing like an opera. "Oooohhhh, you are so sweet to meeeee...baby! Where are you?" he taunted singing, over-exaggerating the vibrato.

He was getting closer.

It was the lockers or nothing. Opening it, her image stared back at her. A mirror. Only for a split second, she observed the sheer panic in her face. Her hair a mess, her face was flushed, and tears lined down her cheeks like small glistening streams. She had seen lots of reflections of herself, but never like this.

She got into the locker and breathed long and deep to reduce her heart rate. The locker was large. She had extra room to get behind hung up clothes. The locker door had two vents at eye level she used to peer out of carefully. Nothing yet. All she could do was wait. Her breathing still rapid, she focused on slowing it down even more, making herself more quiet. She couldn't believe what was happening.

Trapped.

Backing up, she held her breath. *Did I hear something?* Listening with everything she had, Alexa felt the need to breathe again and let it escape as softly as she could.

Out.

In.

Out.

In.

She risked looking out again. Nothing. Dark shadows stretched over items in the room which were barely visible in the dim light. She watched until she could see a faint light flickering from somewhere down the hall. Her heart beat faster again, but she tried hard to keep silent. She gave everything she had to keep her breathing deep, long and quiet.

She looked out expecting him to be there. His light was shining brighter and moving around as if searching for something...her. Finally, she saw the source of the light...he was there. She backed up behind the hanging clothes, careful not to make a sound.

Images of her phasing through the back of the locker played in her head, wishing she could become invisible even for a moment. No matter how hard she tried, she knew that wouldn't happen.

Holy shit, she thought. *This is it!* She tried to freeze, but her body battled it with uncontrollable trembling. *Go Away!* She screamed in her head. *What do I do? What do I do?* No other alternative, she prayed.

Humming.

He sang a song to himself. His flashlight searched all over the place.

Alexa could hear something else. It sounded like he was moving carts. She couldn't tell for sure, but waited for the door to be yanked open. It was agonizing not knowing what was going on. Seconds felt like hours. Tick, tick.

Waiting even longer, she could still hear movement but it was much more faint now. The humming faded. Eerie muffled sounds echoed in the distance surrounded by the noise of silence. She thought he might not find her. Growing more hopeful, she listened still. Another short while, the noises were gone.

How long do I wait? She thought. *God damn it, I wish I had Dahria with me. I have to find her. He's probably waiting right outside for me.*

The waiting was agony. Not knowing when to open the locker was torture. She let a long time pass.

When to open?

I can't just wait in here forever. She had to find something to use, something to do, somewhere to go. Maybe she could find someone, Dahria, Townsend, anyone...else. Someone she knew and could trust.

She crept to the vent, trying to make as little noise as possible. Her hot breath formed a tiny layer of humidity on the mirror that lay below the vent. She peered out. Only the dim emergency lights illuminated parts of the chamber. Looking around for a flashlight waving, she was excited to find none. She moved her hand to the locker latch, pulled up as gently as she could, continuing to look through the vents. Her hands shook. She was breathing in short puffs bouncing off the locker and hitting her own face. Her heart intensified, beating heavy and fast. She could feel the adrenaline fill her body making her nervous, the intensity rushing back.

The locker door had no squeak.

Thank God, she reflected. Thinking about which way he came down the hall, she headed in the opposite direction. That would lead back to where she started. If she could just get there, the main chambers would be in reach, leading to freedom. She crept in that direction. Without making too much noise, she eased her way back. She felt this incredible vulnerability from being outside the locker, like swimming with tiger sharks without a cage securing her. However, the more she moved the more hope and excitement built as she made it to the large door. That was her escape route, her freedom. However, she also noticed something that was not there when she began, an image of herself. A large mirror was halfway in front of the exit.

Confused, she stared at it, at herself.

The reflection showed a beautiful girl even though she was strung out. She saw her shoes, worn pants, shirt, and face. Her eyes were swollen and her face puffy. Her darker hair tangled and dirty but still pretty as it fell on her shoulders. She walked closer to the mirror. Alexa noticed something around her neck. It sparkled, even in the dim light. It was a necklace, beautiful. She reached up to touch it...

Where'd this come from....?

"Isn't it beautiful?" a voice interrupted the silence. He was calm.

She shook so hard it was like an incredible hulk just grabbed her and shook her. Even though he spoke softly, the previous silence made the sound loud.

Her eyebrows furrowed up, her jaw dropped, but her eyes focused on the man behind her...in the mirror.

He materialized out of pure darkness almost like an illusion from a magician. His white teeth were bright accentuating the smile. His eyes glowed.

28

Tommy stared off into the dark, wondering. There was no telling who or how many people remained.

John was able to catch a glimpse of the killer, but due to the dark, all he could relay was a man of decent build. Obviously a pro, John also mentioned how the killer's eyes glowed, and he might be able to recognize him, if he got the chance.

Nick was a little edgy from frustration, but in light of the situation, was easily ignored and even forgiven.

Lost in his own world, Damon didn't seem to notice people were around.

Dahria remained at Tommy's side and tried to keep as calm as she could.

Tim brought food and water for all of them. They were thankful, but it was hard to eat. He sat next to Tommy. "Hey kid," he said.

"Hey."

Tim was sympathetic. It was a lot to experience, for anyone. "Look, I know I can't say 'don't worry about it, nothing's gonna happen', but at least we're together. I hate this just as much as you, believe me. You seem like a good kid with a shred of common sense."

"Thanks," Tommy said looking at the ground. "I can't stand the thought of some killer hunting us down in here." Tommy glanced into his eyes with concern. He was glad Dahria was safe, at least for the moment, but what about the others? "We need to find others. We need to find this killer. I can't let him get my girlfriend, or anyone else."

Tim grew a new respect for Tommy. "I know, I know." He nodded. "But first we need rest. We need to be sharp if we're going to be able to do anything at all." Tim got up and finished, "You all get some rest, I'll take the first shift with Nick."

"Shit, it's going to be a long night." Nick frowned rolling his eyes at the ceiling. Apparently, he was listening.

29

Theod was shaking. In all his life, he had never been a hero, or courageous. His joy was to be the boss and give people commands, but the second he lost his power, he was nothing.

The flash-smoke bomb had scared some people into running. It was loud and knocked a couple people down in the blast. Theod assumed they were dead. As the smoke billowed out of the device, it forced everyone out of the hall.

There were four exits and Theod noticed a bunch of people fleeing in different directions. He noticed Alexa, the cafeteria worker. She ran with two others out the east end. He glimpsed figures running north and south, but they were too quick to account for who they were. Theod noticed John running toward the west end. Townsend covered himself with his arms and glanced around the hall. Theod thought he would be best to stick with.

The smoke was spreading and as Theod tried to get close to Townsend, Kevin grabbed his arm, "Come on Theod." He was coughing.

The smoke was getting heavier now, and Kevin was pulling Theod with him down a different path.

"No," Theod said, "This way." He pointed to the west exit. "I saw Townsend go *that* way. He's just in front of us."

Kevin glanced in that direction and decided he didn't care which way to go, he just wanted out. "Okay, come on."

Both of their eyes watered from the heavy smoke, but it thinned as they vacated the chamber, clambering into the tunnel. Blinking and coughing, they strained to see through their leaking eyes; they noticed people on the ground not moving. Theod's brain couldn't process it, he didn't move to help. Kevin was quicker witted and knelt down to shake one person closest to him. They were half on their side but their shoulders and chest faced the ground half twisted.

"Hey!" Kevin shook the body. The person seemed to be lifeless. Kevin hoped they were only knocked out. "Help me!" He yelled to Theod.

Theod was stunned and still couldn't move.

Kevin pulled the shoulder back to reveal the face, and he viewed the mortal wounds that leaked blood. The eyes were white, the pupils rolled up into the forehead. Only small parts of the iris could be seen, a grotesque and shocking sight. Kevin yelled, "Holy...!" and let the shoulder go as if they were infected with a deadly virus. The body went back remembering the position it was in. "Jesus Christ!" he hissed and backed up. "They're dead!"

Theod was frozen in horror at the sight. Eyes wide and mouth open, the sight reassured that he couldn't say or do anything.

Kevin looked around for other bodies. There were more. Not caring about anything else he checked each one...all dead. "Damn!" Kevin muttered to himself. However, he was quick to recover. "Hey! Theod!" he shouted.

Theod moved nothing but his eyes. It was like his body was in cryostasis, but his eyes worked fine. His body lost fine motor function as his brain failed to cope. New images of horror ran ubiquitous. He had never seen imagery like that in his life. It mortified him. He could see Kevin's mouth moving in slow motion but no sound was coming out.

"Hey man!" he shouted again. Kevin could see Theod's eyes fogged. He stood up and got right in front of him. Kevin grabbed his arm. "Hey man, wake up!"

Theod's eyes turned glossy again, and the touch startled him. Time sped back up to normal and his ears picked up sounds. He was dizzy.

"Hey, you with me?" Kevin said again. "Come on, we've gotta get out of here!" Without wasting time looking at Theod, he glanced around to make sure the tunnel was clear and moved.

A little further down into the tunnel and around a corner, Kevin began to make out a dark figure in the shape of a person. No...two people.

30

"Oh, sweetheart," the man in shadow acted like he was picking up a date. "Wasn't that fun?" He was gleaming with pleasure.

She couldn't move, yet she also couldn't take her eyes off of him in the mirror, the dark form reflected back. His face had a wide smile that in normal circumstances would be soothing, almost alluring. He had an athletic build, it was easy to tell as he wore well-fitting clothes. Those eyes were shaded, but she could feel them gazing at her.

Penetrating her.

They saw deep into her nightmare. Her body felt like putty. It was hard to stand, like she had no bones to support her weight. There was nothing she could do, and she knew it.

"Alexa," he said playfully. "You didn't use my clue, you knucklehead." His smile never faded as if he was trying to arouse her.

Her eyes moved back to the necklace she was wearing the whole time. *Fairest one of all,* dread flooded her as she knew what he meant from the old fairy tale. How easy it was, but she was under too much pressure to link it together. Her heart sank, and she stumbled, unable to hold herself up.

He glided closer to her. "Careful baby, wouldn't want you to get hurt."

She didn't trust the mirror anymore and turned around as if to prevent an attack by a cougar from the rear. She backed up and stumbled into the mirror which was against the door.

"So..." he began. "You're Alexa, assigned to work in the food area, feeding lots of people. I'm sure you've got something really delicious for me to eat too."

His smile seemed even bigger. It gave her chills.

He didn't wait for any response and continued. "Who else do you know in this complex?" His eyebrows went up in the form of a question.

She couldn't speak.

"Calm down baby," he soothed. "I'm sorry about that snide comment too. I won't do anything you don't want me to do," he lied trying to sound like a respectful gentleman again. "It was just a little game. No harm done. Now, let's talk about who else you know."

She didn't want to say any names, but knew she didn't have a choice. She couldn't form any sounds.

His smile faded. He stared at her for a moment and said, "Do I have to spank you?"

Alexa didn't recall recognizing him from the population, but her memories weren't all there either. She thought she had to keep him going, for he probably knew their names, anyway. From somewhere inside, deep, she struggled. "Theod." The words broke as they were forced out. "Townsend."

He waited for more. "Yes, go on."

She said nothing.

"I said go on. Who's the girl with you in the cafeteria?"

No. No. Not Dahria. She said nothing. He moved closer with death on his face.

"I don't...know..any...," she shook.

The man in shadow put his hands on his hips like he was disappointed.

"That's alright," he said. "Dahria, right? That's her name?" *Yes,* he thought. Beautiful and innocent. Special fun with her was on the docket. "Now you say it." he urged.

"Why?" She asked as nicely as she could.

"Say it!" he shouted loud enough to make her jump.

"Dahria." She managed. A rage was the last thing she wanted him to portray.

"Again, but this time say it loud and say 'Dahria, I'm here'."

"Dahria, I'm...," she said even softer, scared to speak.

"I said shout it!" he screamed at the top of his lungs. She closed her eyes and shrunk back from the outburst.

"Dahria!" She forced out. "Dahria, I'm here!" It took all her breath and energy to get out one single word. She couldn't catch her breath.

"Good," he said, "That's it. Now, scream that you need help. You never know, someone might hear you." His face grew dark and disturbed and he came at her with a quick jolt as if trying to attack her.

She screamed. "No! Help me! Please don't. Help me!" Her arms covered her head to block the attack. It never came.

He laughed, "That was great!" he said. "Now one last time. Say, 'I'm over here'."

She had to play along, it might save her life. "I'm over here."

As he moved closer with a purpose, she tried to shrink away but he placed a small wet rag over her nose. She looked up at him.

He was smiling, "Good girl, I love you." She struggled as he covered her mouth and nose to prevent her from breathing normal air. it happened too fast for her to do anything.

She couldn't hold her breath any longer. Taking a deep breath in, a musty sweet smell entered her lungs, and she became confused. He had a strong grip, and held it in place for what seemed like forever. Everything became very hazy. She felt weak. All of her fight, what little she had left, was gone. In a half-sleep like laughing gas in a dentist chair, her eyelids closed to slits.

"There we go," he said. "Relax babe," he removed the rag before she lost consciousness. "I can't have you fighting me now, can I?" He grabbed her limp arm and slung it over his shoulder and lifted her up with a bit of a struggle. "Urgh," he said. "It is always so much harder when you girls are just dead weight."

Her eyes closed, everything slipped to dark.

31

This was such a delight, an ordinary looking man thought. *The smoke went off, four quick kills.* They seemed awfully easy. *These people seem to have much less experience in killing than the last spot.*

The ordinary man, enveloped in darkness, had watched the exit of the conference hall, smoke poured out from his gas bomb. He had waited for people to come running and sure enough, four met death, there to collect their souls.

Several seconds later a figure emerged.

Townsend came into view. The killer locked eyes with him and smiled shrewdly.

Townsend returned a look, but it wasn't a look of shock, or horror. He nodded once.

The ordinary man had a small amount of compassion for these people, that was the human side. The other side was hatred, fury. These people were criminals. *Brutal* criminals. Usually the kind you couldn't normally tell were killers and rapists.

The ordinary man thought of himself as an avenger. That is part of what kept him going, kept him sane over time. It was also his job. He didn't like the actual killing piece, but he could relate to the avenger part. Thoughts of the damaged people being vindicated was like sweet honey. He was responsible for the justice the old court system couldn't accomplish. People paid crazy big money to have their loved ones avenged, vindicated.

The criminals were hunted down, caught, and detained. By the time they made it to the company they were erased from existence. However, the ordinary man was still killing a human being, but in his eyes the killing was serving justice. He was carrying out a death sentence judged by the system.

Human psychology was one of the largest knotted balls of yarn in the universe. Untangling it was a monumental task not fully understood. Human lives were only worth what society's limits were. One person valued life while another valued nothing. Unfortunately, this meant that a life's value was held to the bottom of society's amount. Where does a person draw the line? What stakes would a person value into killing another person, taking their life into their own hands or giving a life into another's.

Sounds erupted from behind Townsend. The ordinary man put the killing tool away and put his fingers on the corpse pretending to check the pulse. Townsend moved a little closer to him and turned to meet the people coming. He saw Kevin and Theod speeding toward them. Kevin looked concerned and Theod looked freaked out.

"Kevin, Theod," said Townsend in his assertive voice. "Good, you got out of there."

Kevin looked from Townsend to the body on the ground. Blood was seeping out of wounds. Another man was checking his vitals. After a moment, the man looked up at Townsend. Kevin vaguely recognized him. The man shook his head to signify he didn't make it. He stayed crouched and rested his forearm on his knee, his hand was bloodied.

Townsend sighed, looked at Kevin and said, "let's move. Stay together."

"What the hell happened?" Kevin asked.

"Later, let's move," Townsend headed down the tunnel.

Arriving at the rations hall to pick up food, they went to the main command center. No one else was found on their way.

After getting bunkered in and settled, Kevin started a conversation with the unfamiliar man, "Hey. I'm Kevin. What's your story?" Kevin wanted information if the guy had it.

The ordinary man was washing his face and peeked through wet fingers. Grabbing a towel he patted the water off and dried his hands.

"Well, probably the same as you," he lied. He knew this 'Kevin' was no doubt the type to lure in little children then rape and beat them to death, pack up their body, and throw them away like trash. Yeah, they looked harmless, but he knew better. He hid his disgust well, none showing on his face. "I was brought down here," his eyes rolled suggesting a correction, "I should say *pulled* down here in a hurry. They told me it was urgent to get away from the fallout up on the surface." He paused for effect pretending to be thinking. "Then, one morning I woke up, and it seemed like I had always been living here. I remembered some things about...before, but it was clouded. Headaches came with it." He laughed.

"What?"

"I don't know. It's just kinda weird."

True enough. He seems pretty sincere at least, Kevin thought. *But I will not trust anyone until this maniac is caught,* he vowed.

Kevin nodded. It was a little generic. He sighed and started small talk. "So, what did you do down here?" he prodded further.

Nothing like what you did to innocent people up there you fuck. He stared, perhaps a moment too long. Inhaling he replied, "I worked on maintaining the water quality. Made sure the supply, filtration, and generation did not fail."

"Hm," Kevin answered. "Sounds interesting."

"Eh, not really, but it keeps me busy."

Kevin noticed Theod off by himself. He seemed pretty rattled earlier. Kevin opened the conversation and called over to him. "Hey man, you alright?"

"All right? All right! I will never be *all right!* This whole place sucks, man!" Louder. "People are dead! And you know what? We could be next!"

"Quiet down Theod!" Townsend yelled. "Pull yourself together. You might give away our position!" He waited a moment and changed his tone. Townsend figured the best thing to do was keep Theod busy. "Theod, organize the rations. Find out how long it will last, then I want you to get some rest. The both of you too," he looked at Kevin and the avenger. "Go on, I'll take first watch. We can switch off every four hours."

The avenger nodded.

Kevin's face showed apathy glancing at Townsend then Theod, then the avenger. Kevin pried, "Hey. You," he said getting the avengers attention. "What's your name?" Kevin asked.

"Jake," the avenger said truthfully.

Still reserved, Kevin stared at him for an extra moment trying to figure him out. There was something about him. It was well hidden, but Kevin sensed the man didn't like him. Kevin had a gift of being able to peer through people like a window, as children often could, was useful.

Kevin was one of those awkward boys who was chosen for athletic games towards the end. Never having it well with girls being so tall and lanky, he accelerated in other areas. He wasn't an ugly guy, but didn't possess great looks either. The awkwardness led to shyness as a kid, which made talking to girls an alien language, so he buried his nose in books. Reading every chance he could, he consumed fiction for his creative side, non-fiction for his academic side, and technical books for his interest side. It paved a nice path into a career that even higher civilians couldn't obtain.

A little uneasy with so many thoughts swimming through his mind, Kevin tried to get rest. He glanced at Theod, who was sitting curled up in a little ball hugging his knees, his head resting on them, staring off, focusing on nothing in particular.

Nothing more Kevin could do, he watched the ceiling until he relaxed, then closed his eyes. He had trouble letting it all go. He didn't fall asleep, ever, though he was exhausted, but at least it was a rest. His mind was running thoughts processing the information like a computer sorting data.

Jake took the time as an advantage. His training allowed him to be half alert when he slept in these conditions, and Townsend would watch over him, anyway. *Theod is a different type of criminal,* Jake thought. *The pussy type who always cries and blubbers only after they've been caught.* Theod was the type always pointing fingers everywhere else and played the 'why me' card. A true sociopath. He didn't even know he was fucked up. *That's okay,* he thought. *He'll get what's coming to him soon enough.*

As Jake rested, he thought about his mistake. Someone got a glimpse of him. It wasn't extensive, but it increased the risk of the game. It may not have been good enough to identify him, but he wasn't sure. The shadows camouflaged him well, but the man peered into his eyes, maybe even saw his face.

Jake smiled to himself remembering the fear on the man's face. Little bonuses were sometimes worth it. When the smoke billowed out, Jake was too busy killing other criminals to worry about the man who stole a glimpse. It would have been foolish to rush him with the possibility of more showing up. That would be like a trap-door spider leaving the safety of its web.

His smile faded as he imagined the person who stole from him. Killed three of his prisoners. *I'll get you soon. Stealing from me is your worst mistake.*

32

Tommy woke up with a start. He was breathing heavily and his heart was racing. One emergency light glowed soft yellow in the distance. It was silent and dark except for his breathing. Eerie. Tommy rubbed his eyes to get the moisture flowing, but all he felt were dry hard pebbles. He glanced around trying to calm himself. Where was she? He blinked trying to get his tear ducts to work and flush the grit.

He felt around in the dark for his flashlight but couldn't locate it. The silence bothered him. He peeked in the distance to where the dim light shined. Tommy stared hard to find someone on shift watching to protect them, but no one was there.

He felt around again...nothing. Dahria shouldn't be that far away. He got up carefully not making any noise. Now standing, Tommy moved in one direction probing the floor with his foot using it as a blind man's white cane. He tried to find Dahria, or anyone else. Nothing. Nerves fired, and he sighed with frustration.

What the hell? Where...

He continued and turned to search in a circle around where he was sleeping. Frustrated not being able to locate the flashlight, Tommy listened for any breathing sounds. Nothing but the tinnitus ringing in his ears. He risked a whisper, "Dahria. Jones?...

"Mm, m, sstt...cctt," Tommy heard faint sounds far off in the distance somewhere. Holding his breath, he turned his head so his ear could pick up better reception. His face frowned, concentrating on the words. It was strange, like people having a normal conversation but a hundred yards away. He tried to pinpoint a direction trying to follow the sounds. They became more clear as he walked.

"Da...com...but you..."

He followed it. As he became closer, the sounds faded from cloudy to clear.

"Filth....fuc...bitch...did you really think you could escape me?"

Tommy was shocked, it sounded like Theod. There was no response to the question. It was like Theod was talking to himself. Tommy sped up and rounded the corner to see who it really was. His eyes grew wide.

Disbelief. Denial.

Theod's face was unrecognizable, a face Tommy had never seen before. Mean, sadistic, crazy. Foamy drool was running down his mouth like he was rabid. Every time he would speak, a glob of foam would fall from his moving chin.

Theod had a knife and was looking at...Dahria! She had a white dress on that appeared to glow. She looked like an angel. A gentle breeze seemingly coming out of the walls blew her hair and dress. Her skin had a faint iridescence and she had a strange smile on her face, like she knew everything would be okay.

She looked at Tommy. Her recognition of him formed on her face as it relaxed into a loving smile. She reached for him in slow motion.

"Tommy," she wanted to make contact but he was beyond her reach. A small stream of blood appeared and ran down the corner of her mouth. She didn't seem to notice.

Tommy's blood drained from his face, "Theod, no!" he screamed. "What are you doing?!"

Theod saw Tommy. "This is what you fuckers deserve! All the people you hurt!" Back to Dahria, "Die bitch!" he thrust the knife forward.

Tommy bolted toward Theod, but he was too far away. The knife clanked hard against the stone column right behind Dahria...who had disappeared before the knife touched her.

Theod turned and looked at Tommy. His face now different. Sad, empathetic. His voice grim, "I'm sorry Tommy, I'm sorry. You can't save her. He *will* get her." Blood started to flow out of several wounds on his body that appeared out of nowhere. His face now flooded with dark blood.

"Tommy." said Dahria from somewhere. "Tommy," it came again pleading for him to find her.

A short time after, the tears would wake Tommy up. He looked around.

---#---

Kevin popped awake with a guttural sound. He was taking short, but fast breaths. Sweat beads were running down his face like a waterfall.

What the hell? A hundred thoughts ran through his mind. He remembered his nightmare vividly. Kevin saw himself die, but it was the love of his life that killed him. She was beautiful, brown flowing hair and pearly white skin. In fact, he remembered her name...Pearl. He shook as it gave him chills.

Kevin rubbed his eyes. They burned from salty sweat that touched them from his fingers. He tried to blink the stinging away as best he could and calmed his breathing. Kevin glanced off into the far corner and noticed something strange...no one was there. It looked like Townsend and Theod were gone, but the other...

"Good morning Kevin," Jake interrupted. "Did you sleep well?"

Kevin immediately stiffened. He looked over at Jake and saw his smile. That smile looked sinister, Kevin looked distraught. His heart sank, *how could I be so stupid?* He looked again to see if anyone else was here. Regret poured into his body.

"Yeah, you guessed it," Jake said as he noticed Kevin's distraught face. "They're both gone. I'm the only thing left between you and that hot place way down there," he said pointing to the ground. "So, I will do something a little bit different, turn up the heat as they say. Get you used to those flames." He was relaxed and confident in his words. "Let's see if you are actually willing to admit why you're down here, shall we?"

Kevin was not easy to perplex, but his face now wore a confused frown, "Huh?" he asked.

"Huh?" Jake mocked him, making a dumb face. He laughed. "Geez man, you sound like a dumbass guilty kid trying to get away with a lie." He crossed his arms like he was the authority. "I was expecting more from you. You seem pretty intelligent." He lifted his eyebrows. "Guess I was wrong."

Kevin, who was quick, was still confused and unable to speak. All he could do was shake his head a little.

"Oh Kev," he sighed. "To be honest, usually it *is* much easier. Normally I have files on all of you. I would know your past actions," his face disgusted, "your gross, nasty, despicable fucking brutal actions." He looked around for a second before turning his pleasant demeanor back on, "your past jobs, friends and what not." He paused. "You know? I've always found it odd that some people like you could seem so likable, so innocent." He paused again. "Strange though," he continued, "this time I don't have anything on you people."

Kevin was shaking. Something was very wrong. He managed to get something out. "What are you talking about? I haven't done anything gross or nasty to anyone...and what files?"

"I've heard this all before," he said nodding his head, "You people will deny your crimes forever. It's classic sociopath, you don't even realize that you have a problem. Well, if that's the case it doesn't make any sense to continue the conversation. It's really a pity," he finished looking at Kevin like the game was over.

"So...*you're* the one who's killing people?"

Jake smiled. He stood up and laughed. "That's funny. I was gonna say the same thing about you."

"What did you do with the others?"

No answer. The pleasant face and demeanor were gone.

"Hey, wait a minute," Kevin injected, "You don't have to do this. You're making a mistake."

"Am I? Am I *really* Kev? You mean to tell me that you didn't rape, kill, or murder anyone?" He had an apathetic look on his face. Jake didn't believe anything Kevin said.

"What!" Kevin said with a nervous laugh. "Are you kidding me?" he shifted his questions. "What the hell's going on here? Who are you?"

That is always the part that Jake loved. Watching the confusion, the wonder of how the hell they were caught, the revenge, and he *was* the avenger.

Jake pulled two knives, one in each hand and spun them around expertly.

Kevin's adrenaline kicked in and rumbled his body.

"I'm the avenger Kevin. Judgment has already been passed on you. I'm here to collect." Jake got into a combat position and started backing up ready to come at him.

Kevin put his hands up as if to hold Jake back with an imaginary force-field. "Hold on, man! Hold on!" Kevin pleaded. "I'm not a killer, I'm not a criminal!"

"Of course you're not," Jake said calmly. "Here." He threw his knife right at Kevin's face so fast that Kevin couldn't even react. The knife flew perfectly past it and stuck into the pegboard behind him. The thud on the board made Kevin's eyes flinch. "I want this to be a fair fight." Jake finished knowing he was full of shit. He smiled anyway.

"Yeah, real fair," Kevin added sarcastically. "You're a trained killer and I am a technology geek."

"There you go, now getting all smart," Jake congratulated him. "Of course, this makes you an even more clever killer to unsuspecting people." He stared at him for a moment, his curiosity getting the better of him. "Who was it? Tell me? How many Kev? Were they kids, your wife, someone else? Did you like it?" He taunted Kevin as he started to move forward. "Better get that knife," he warned. "It'll be better defense than nothing."

Kevin was frantic, "All right! Stop! Let me get it!"

Jake stopped and waited patiently.

"Hey, let me ask you something," Kevin said desperately trying to obtain some information and keep Jake talking. He already assessed that Jake loved to talk, and it seemed he needed a reason to kill. And Jake wanted to have him confess to something. "You said you usually had files on us, but not this time? Why do you think that is?" He let that sink in for a split second before he continued hoping to buy some time. "So how can you *really* know who I am? Maybe, just maybe, I'm really not a criminal *or* a killer." Kevin hoped if he could present a reasonable doubt, he might be able to survive.

Jake responded in a light manner, "Well, I must admit, it's not the best way to do business, but this isn't my first game either. I know what I'm doing and I know the company I work for." Then his face frowned. "You know, it *is* a little disturbing and frustrating when you pricks try to do *my* job." His eyebrows raised and mouth made a half moon frown as he remembered the conference hall disclosure from Townsend. "Most of the time you all are just trying to survive. Usually, you don't think about killing down here. No one can run the station alone, so you have to keep everyone alive. One of you here is a real twisted fuck that just can't seem to get enough." He looked at Kevin, "Is it *you* Kev? I honestly consider it stealing, from me."

Kevin did not see that coming. *Is he telling the truth? What is with this company he mentioned? His job? A game? What the hell's going on here?*

Kevin didn't know if Jake was truthful, but he was proposing that there was more than one killer here, and a crazy one at that. Kevin couldn't help but think of everyone else in this place he knew. Tommy, Jones, Dahria, Townsend. They can't be killers.

Kevin prodded further. "Well guess what Jake," he projected, "you seem to despise killers and criminals, which you think we all are, but what does that make you? You're a killer yourself, no matter how you slice it! I saw what you did to Gebriel. Tied him up. Hung him upside down. What's with the missing finger? Pretty sick."

"You know, trophies are wonderful to look at later." Jake replied evenly, a little disgusted.

Kevin was intrigued. The man had a slight pause. There was no missing finger. *He didn't know about Gebriel. He only seems to kill who he believes are criminals.* Kevin thought furiously on how to save his life and keep Jake going. He replied incredulously. "So you don't think it's possible that we are all just regular people...innocent people, just trying to survive? What have you got to lose to wait and find out?"After a time of moving slowly backwards, Kevin finally hit the wall. He was cornered.

Jake thought the people here didn't seem to fit the profile at all. It made him question. Was the company this good at picking groups of people now? People that were extraordinarily hard to tell their character? He considered for a moment what Kevin was saying. Then, shook it off. "Nice try, Kev," he said, "I know you're clever and intelligent, but I also know you deserve to die. How do I know *you* didn't kill this Gebriel guy? You're guilty. Otherwise, how would you know all that detail? It's time to play."

Jake closed the distance and from what Kevin observed with Jake's handling of the knife, it would be over in a few seconds.

Kevin was desperate. He realized the man didn't kill Gebriel, but he had no idea how to convince the man *he* didn't. "Come on man, reach inside your mind. I can see deep down you're a decent guy. You want to do what's right. Don't you? You don't enjoy killing real innocent people, do you?" Pleading his case, he was trying to produce any kind of empathy he could. "Doesn't it bother you to know that if I happen to be right, you're not an avenger anymore, but a murderer? You will be guilty of all the things you despise." Kevin had nowhere to go, he couldn't run because Jake was too fast, too professional. He definitely couldn't fight because he knew Jake was a well-trained killer. He had to keep his mind going.

Kevin remembered something. "Let's play a game."

Jake stopped, his curiosity aroused. He gave Kevin a moment. It was good for the show.

That did it, Kevin thought. *But what game, what game?*

33

A hand grabbed Tommy's shoulder and shook it. He wasn't asleep but wasn't awake either. Tommy's face was wet from his streams of tears. His nightmare hung, in a daze.

"Hey kid, wake up," Tim said.

Tommy assessed his surroundings and looked for Dahria...she was right there next to him, sleeping. He relaxed and sat up. The grogginess was taking a toll. Dark and eerie halls with eyes seeming like they were everywhere, watching. The dim lights were still on and showed objects shadows. He rubbed his eyes and asked Tim, "How long?"

"About six hours," he replied.

"Mmm, thanks." Tommy saw Nick and Jones were already up moving. He leaned over to Dahria and caressed her hair. His hand moved down to her shoulder and gently shook it. "Hey babe, wake up."

She moaned with frustration as if being nudged by her mom when she was late for something. He rubbed her back, glad she was here.

Tim, letting them wake up on their own, walked over to the others. Jones walked up.

"Good morning Mr. sunshine," he said with a grin. "Are you ready for our trek to catch a killer?"

Jones' sense of humor was uncanny, but Tommy appreciated it. Rest influenced his mood. "Let's tear it up," Tommy said, not as enthusiastic as he wanted to feel.

Jones got serious for a minute, glanced around and made sure no one was within earshot. He huddled a little closer. Tommy's brow furrowed up in curiosity sensing the secret about to be told.

"I've found something strange," Jones said just above a whisper. "Just pondering around the computer, you know?" Tommy nodded his head. "The computers have cameras right?" Tommy was still nodding his head. "Well, normally these cameras are built into the computer, right?"

Tommy studied him. His facial language read, 'so'?

"This camera had a separate cable, and it didn't go into the computer." Jones let that sink in.

Tommy now looked with interest, raising his eyebrows. "What? Where'd it go?" Tommy asked.

"I'm not sure, but it definitely wasn't plugged into the computer."

"We've got to trace it, but we need to keep it quiet until we find out more," Tommy said.

"I agree," Jones concluded, glancing behind him again to make sure no one was listening.

Tommy noticed Dahria awaken. He gave Jones a nod. Tommy hugged her as she came close.

"Morning, babe."

She smiled.

Jones smiled too and hugged them both. "I love you guys too," he said with a fake cry.

Dahria couldn't help but give a soft chuckle and Tommy smiled. They accepted their friend with open arms.

"Oh, you know we love you, Jonsey," she said.

After a few moments they mixed in, Tim started, "We stick together and search this place one room at a time for survivors, but the first piece of business is to get the main power back on. One good thing," his eyes were serious, "that just happens to be part of my assignment working here."

Tim looked at John. "You're good with technology right?"

"Yes, my job is computers. And before I was here..." his eyes darted around trying to come up with something "I worked somewhere up there...monitoring," he finished.

Tim frowned. *What? What is it about him?*

Before he could put more time into thinking, Damon interrupted. "What if we can't get the power back on?"

Tim looked at him without an answer, "We'll just have to do the best we can, figure it out as we come to it."

"I don't like this. We can't just go around in the dark, hoping to find someone who we don't know is killing people," Damon urged. "I can't stay here. I've got to get out. We're all going to die in here!" He was getting hysterical. "He's going to come after each one of us and...!"

"Shut up old man!" Nick said. "Stop being a pussy!"

"Knock it off!" Yelled Tim. He peered at Damon. "Now hold on, nothing has happened to us yet! But if we don't act, then we just wait around here and run out of food and water and die, anyway."

Damon calmed down a little, but he was still visibly shaken. The doctor proposed, "What about the iron door? Could we go out the hatch, aren't there suits we can wear?"

"Dude, shut up, No. There aren't." Nick said. "You're just causing everyone to get all stirred up. Grow some balls."

While Tommy thought Nick's testicles were bigger than his brain sometimes, Nick made a point, but he sympathized with Damon. "All right, let's look at what we need to do," Tommy said, getting to the point. "We need to get the power back on. That's in power centers one and two."

"How do you know all this?" John asked, stealing what Nick was thinking. There was a hint of nervous accusation.

Nick glanced at Tim with his eyebrows up as if to say 'see, I'm not the only one.' "Did you run around and map this place out, what, just to be more efficient? Or to stalk and kill?"

Dahria frowned, but before she could say anything...

"Lay off," Tim cut in, "Yeah, he reeks of killer instinct," he added, rolling his eyes. Tim had grown to like Tommy, but in the back of his mind he knew John and Nick could be right. He had no way of knowing who was who.

"All right, look," Tim said. "Let's stop wasting time. We do have two power centers," he stated, confirming Tommy's words, "each on opposite sides of the conference hall, north and south." Tim drew a crude map in the dirt of these places and pointed to each one. The map was incomplete. Tim didn't know the entire facility, but had the two stations marked accordingly. "Each one has to be turned on sequentially, within two or three minutes, otherwise there will be a circuit failure. We need to split into two teams." He looked at the three friends. "I know you three are close so I will go with Tommy, Jones, and Dahria and hit the North center. Nick, take John and Damon for the South. The North center must be switched on first and it's also more complicated, so I'll take that one." He stopped and looked at everyone. "Okay?"

"Great, I get the scared old man," Nick said under his breath.

The others nodded and proceeded to get ready. They gathered water, food, flashlights and any weapons they had. A few minutes later they got back together before they dispersed on their tasks.

Tim looked at John and said, "Give us about five minutes. Then follow the tunnels and get to the South end of the conference hall. That power center is close. If we get the power back on you should see the main circuit breaker light up red. When that happens, turn on the main switch, then turn on all the individual circuits. The red LEDs should turn green. Got it?" John nodded and the other two responded accordingly. "Then we meet you in the South center. If we're not back there in thirty minutes..." he pursed his lips together. Without finishing he said, "ready?"

The task was risky. Tommy was distracted with that computer camera. It was strange, but he had to force the thought out of his head and focus. When they had time later, if they had time later, he and Jones could examine it.

As they stood up, Tommy leaned over to Jones. All other heads were facing away. Nick and his team walked back toward the tables and chairs to sit and rest for the five minutes.

"We're just going to have to wait a little longer to check out that camera," Tommy whispered to Jones.

"I know, It's probably nothing anyway," he said.

He was so wrong.

34

"Where're we going?" asked Theod following Townsend down a tunnel. "Why'd we leave Kevin and Jake there? What's going on?"

"Calm down Theod," Townsend said, a little more irritated than he meant. "We didn't. We're going back as soon as I get some information from my terminal. I need you to watch my back."

"Oh. What information do you need sir?" Theod asked, swallowing the orders.

He just keeps asking questions, can't shut him up. Townsend thought. It was draining. "I need to look at the manifest. If I can get my hands on that, we can determine who might be responsible."

Townsend didn't like Theod anymore than any of the others, but he was a good worker, not that Townsend cared. He had to string him along until he could feed him to the sharks. He would be glad to get rid of him. As morbid as it was, he viewed this as a job, nothing more. He put no energy into feeling, none into empathy, but this spot was a little different, better than the previous spots. He couldn't help but feel something for them. Maybe he was just getting old.

After countless games, Townsend was so rooted into the system he was almost like a robot. It was now hard for him to produce feelings of sympathy even if he wanted to. It was like people passing him by in the heart of New York City just going about their business, living out their lives. Many invisible faces staring six inches in front of themselves, yet looking at nothing. Walking like zombies with no purpose. One day they would die. One day everyone dies. So what does it matter if it's now or later? Or by what hand? The only difference is the path we carve for ourselves during life, but in the end all roads come together into one destination. Townsend thought it was too late for him to change.

Townsend kept his pace and made a little noise to pronounce his presence, appearing to Theod like accidents. Townsend wanted to make sure he wasn't accidently hurt. In fact, he met the killers, but separately. He thought it was strange that this particular game had *two* of them. That was the first time Townsend had experienced it. He thought it was overkill, no pun intended. However, he was trusted with the information that only one killer would be aware of the other. The company told Townsend to keep this quiet, and to let it work itself out naturally. Many extra bets on each killer's competition would be placed. That leads to more money, and citizens love it, and of course, the company profits.

Townsend knew this complex well. He had detailed knowledge of every part of it.

They navigated to the command room. Townsend had an office inside the center. "Wait here Theod, I'll be back in a minute. Be careful and keep a sharp eye." Townsend ordered. It was a confidential office that no one ever entered but Townsend.

Theod nodded, "Yes sir." He looked around. The hall was empty. He had been here many times yet never noticed all that was here. The hall was a circle that had a large table in the middle with various paperwork cluttered on it. The perimeter walls consisted of a couple computer terminals and tables with readouts and wires going off in different directions. Emergency lights were dim and shined only in a couple areas around the hall. Desks and chairs were scattered around but they were missing people.

It was dark.

Silent.

Inside, the office lacked windows allowing no one to view anything in or out. A computer terminal was off to one side. Townsend sat down and peered at the monitor.

Theod heard the noise of silence and felt alone. It was loud, ringing in his ears. He swallowed as if to give his ears a sense that they still worked. Each minute dragged, making it seem much longer. It was dreadful. He felt like he couldn't let out a breath anymore, like something was holding his chest up and he couldn't relax it. The gloomy walls seemed to be floating toward him from all directions. Slowly. Were they? Panic leaked into his blood, he stood, and shook his head. His heart was thudding in his chest. A sinking fear circulated, growing in his arteries and veins.

Calm down. It's okay, he tried to slow down his breathing. *How long has it been?* Sweat formed on the back of his neck and brow. Theod tried to focus on something else. He observed a poster on the wall. It was of a girl. The photo hung above a desk. Lots of skin was revealed as her clothes only covered tiny private areas. She stared at Theod with a welcoming seductive and playful smile. All of his concentration was on that image, lost in that inviting fantasy.

Theod remembered parts of his youthful past; girls not wanting to be friends, too many times rejected for dates. For some reason, these thoughts played in his head as if it were yesterday. Something strange about it. It was like he wasn't able to see it before, but now they flowed. He thought of other events that came swirling back…

"Click!" The sound of the door opening was loud in the silence. Theod jumped out of his skin. Ripped from the ill dressed woman's image, he looked at the door that Townsend just came out of. Theod hurried away from the photo, almost like he didn't want to be caught staring at it.

"Urghh!" Theod let out in relief. "Geez, man, you scared me."

Townsend's hard character let the comment bounce right off of him. "Okay," he said, holding up the clipboard of the manifest. "Got it, let's go."

"Where?" Theod asked. His curiosity never lacked.

Townsend sighed inside his head. "Back to the conference hall. There we can see who needs to be crossed off this list. Maybe even find some survivors," Townsend finished.

Theod became horrified. His heart pounded and he could feel the pulse in his chest and neck again. Theod did not want to go anywhere in the vicinity where bodies of people he knew were lying dead. He envisioned himself staring at them in twisted positions, waiting for them to show some sign of life, but none ever would. He shivered.

Townsend's movement snapped Theod out of his daze. He didn't want to be alone in this place, *that* he knew for sure.

Arriving at the conference center was difficult. Entering from the west, Townsend blasted right by bodies that Theod couldn't help but notice. There was a faint rancid smell in the air, but it wasn't overbearing, like a dead rat. Theod tucked his face down trying to hide it into his chest, but his chin and neck only let him hunch down so low. His shoulders crept up in a shrug to create a barrier between him and the bodies. He shied behind his appendages trying to act like a racehorse, looked ahead, and continued to follow Townsend. He was led to the east end and arrived at a table. Townsend's demeanor was efficient but to Theod it was just plain cold.

Man, how does he do it? Theod thought, wondering how it didn't seem to bother him at all.

Townsend set down papers and the clipboard with the manifest on it. He took a seat and organized the materials. Theod sat across from him being silent, letting him do his thing. After a few minutes, Townsend peered at the west end of the conference hall as if alerted by something.

Theod moved into adrenaline mode. "What?" Theod whispered.

"Shhh," Townsend replied and lifted his hand in a show of a 'hold on' signal. He stared at that area for a few more moments without moving a muscle.

Theod could see his jaw muscles clench and loosen as he listened.

A few more seconds of nothing, he seemed to relax, "I guess it's nothing." He sat back down and continued looking at the papers.

A faint hissing sound coming from the west end breaking the sound of silence. Townsend didn't even seem to notice it this time, but Theod did. His ears felt as though they shot up like a deer and focused on the noise. It grew slightly louder now, like the hissing of a flat tire.

"Listen," Theod said, growing nervous. "Do you hear that?"

Townsend set the papers down and listened.

"I don't like this," Theod said in agitation.

Townsend frowned. "Come on, this way."

They moved out of the conference hall into the east end tunnel toward the hydro center door. Townsend picked up the pace as he came closer to the door. "Hurry," he said.

Theod didn't have to be told twice. As Townsend turned the wheel and opened the door for Theod, he ran through it. Theod took a few more steps to allow Townsend to step through. The beautiful sound of the door closing echoed in his ears.

"Whoo, that was close," Theod smiled and glanced back at Townsend. "What the heck was th...?" he didn't finish as something seemed odd, Townsend wasn't there. "What the? Townsend?" Theod asked himself. He tried the wheel on the door but it didn't budge. He didn't want to be alone again. "Townsend?" Theod asked, "Townsend!"

Unable to budge the door he turned away from it to look the other way and observed a shocking sight.

"Well lookie what we have here," a cold voice emerged out of the dark. The person was trying to hold back a laugh with some failure.

Theod's eyes became huge round circles. Hairs on the back of his neck stood on end as erect as one of the skyscraper city buildings. He stood frozen like a thief who had been caught red handed. He now wished he was alone.

"Come on in, come on in, join the party" the voice sauntered to Theod. The man in shadow laughed and almost couldn't get the words out. "You...should've...seen your face," He laughed aloud, "When you turned around." He patted his own leg in amusement and took a few seconds to gain back his control. He couldn't help but giggle a few more times. "You know, if you came a while earlier, that would have been quite an inopportune time, might have made me angry." His face lit up, and he scoffed. "And you won't like me when I'm angry," he added, referring to a classic green creature. A huge smile showed bright white teeth.

Theod yelled and bolted past him.

The killer watched and laughed, shaking his head. "This is just too fun." He said to himself, and he imagined the audience was having fun too.

35

Dean was an honorable man. A compassionate man. Someone who goes out of his way to help anyone in need. Very few retained these character attributes in the city anymore. He also was aggressive with justice. The pain of watching the world break down was overwhelming.

The cities, over the decades, reached a peak of performance, then declined. The causes were pure numbers. Productive families would have an average of two or three children. Parents, who loved and were committed to each other, would try to raise their children in the best manner possible, holding their kids' futures above their own, teaching them values, morals, respect, and proper responses to situations. In contrast, broken families would produce several children without any plans to raise them, or teach them. Lacking proper guidance, these children were raised by the worst parts of society. Not knowing any better, they were lazy, greedy, offensive, hooked on what was popular, which hardly meant what was right. Drugs, alcohol, single parents, computers and devices to entertain them would envelope that generation. They were called the 'T-generation' or 'turn' generation by the wiser people of society. 'Turn' meaning the turn of the downfall.

The United States of America was the frontrunner in technology, but also the first to fall. They called it the 'birth of the death.' The great height of the American country would also ensure the fall would be hard. The corruption, mixed with the need of belonging to something, birthed the new entertainment, the brutal hunting of people. Today, years after the start of it all, the world clung to the games, needing more and more.

Dean was lucky, being raised in a reasonable family. He had two brothers and a sister. One brother passed away from influenza and the other went to live a somewhat normal life. His parents both passed from natural causes, but Dean was old enough to understand and accept it. His sister married and moved away to Costa Rica where they talk from time to time. She was smart to move away from the carnage of this country. Most good people did. He admired her for that. Sometimes Dean didn't know why he stayed, but it wasn't so easy when your life is so rooted. He was also the type of man to work on problems rather than run from them. Dean was forty-five but still fit and sharp minded. At one hundred and eighty-five pounds and six feet, he had muscles, yet was slim and tone. His demeanor was polite and respectful, always doing his job to the best of his ability. Clean cut and dressing nice for the job, Dean took pride in the way he looked. He cared.

His latest gig was to cash in on the greedy and distrustful nature of people. He worked as a private investigator. Work was busy. Work was good. It seemed like everyone had something to hide from someone else, or so-and-so is cheating, insurance frauds, and secret lives. Tax evasion was a huge problem these days, however the government was so corrupt that they just went after the top offenders and erased them in secret. There were too many people involved and the government didn't have the manpower for everyone, so they let the little ones go.

Dean got up and dressed into his usual attire for a comfortable day off. Dean never liked just lounging around, so his days off were still productive. The last assignment, already forgotten, he strolled over to the coffee machine and spoke, "Mr. coffee, French Carmel, light cream." The pot started its job. His mind was at ease. He was one of those rare individuals that could forget his work when he was off. It was an important characteristic to have. It helped keep your own sanity.

He walked over to the mirror, rested both hands on the sink counter and looked at himself. Dean noticed the ever growing age with a few more gray hairs and lines around his eyes. There was one more beginning on his forehead too. He looked young for his age, but nothing can keep time from eating away at the free moments left on earth.

This is gonna be a good day, he deluded himself, *I can do whatever I want.*

He sat on the couch while looking at the wall TV. Detecting his stare and blink, it flicked on. It played a slideshow from his life. The first image was of him and Jenny on the beach, a love interest that ended due to Dean always being on assignment. Having no children, they separated easily but still loved and respected each other. Dean smiled at the memory and then another image appeared. His brothers. Memories flooded back and he let out a soft chuckle as he looked at them. They were in their teens all standing at the shore of a colorful lake with fishing poles in their hands. Smiling at the camera, one brother held the fishing pole between his legs protruding outward in a way that suggested he was not trying to catch fish. A timed camera caught his wild face capturing the moment while the other two were cracking up. He stared at it for a moment longer taking in the memory.

Life was easy back then, he smiled and shook his head. He was envious of those times. Isn't that always the case?

He got up, went to the computer, and cleared backed-up emails. Just as he started deleting junk mail, a new message popped up.

"Nice to be loved", he said out loud. He looked at it and blinked twice. The computer obeying the command opened it up, and he read it. It didn't quite register the first time so he read it again. He stared at the words trying to contemplate. His brow furrowed. He read 'IF YOU ARE READING THIS, I WILL PROBABLY BE DEAD.'

"What the hell?" he asked the air and squinted his eyes. He checked the sender address. No sender. He kept reading.

'I AM SORRY TO GET YOU INVOLVED, BUT I NEED YOUR HELP. I WORK FOR THE COMPANY, FOR THE GAMES. MY POSITION ISN'T IMPORTANT, BUT I AM TRYING TO DO THE RIGHT THING FOR ONCE IN MY LIFE. I CAME TO YOU BECAUSE OF YOUR BROTHER.'

Dean looked at that word in shock. 'BROTHER.' His mind became extra sharp and focused. He continued.

'YOUR BROTHER IS A GOOD GUY, EVEN THOUGH HE AND I WORK FOR THE COMPANY. I DIDN'T REALIZE JUST HOW BAD IT HAS BECOME. THE COMPANY HAS CHANGED. I KNOW, NOT THAT IS WAS EVER GOOD, BUT THEIR PRACTICES ARE MESSED UP MORE THAN EVER. THEY ARE NOT USING HARD-CORE CRIMINALS ANYMORE. THEY'RE USING INNOCENT PEOPLE! AND THEY'VE TAKEN YOUR BROTHER. IF YOU ARE READING THIS, IT MEANS THEY HAVE ME TOO. PLEASE...HELP.'

Dean stared at the words on the screen reading it again and again. He blinked, and it began to register.

"Jesus," Was his mind was playing tricks on him? He closed his eyes and opened them again. No tricks. The message was still there. Dean thought if the guy's writing were true, there is no telling what the company will do to him.

He thought about calling the police, but quickly realized that wouldn't work. He was not even sure they would believe him even with the email as evidence. The police had a nasty reputation of overlooking the company in the past with obvious cover-ups. They couldn't be trusted. No, he had to do it himself. Dean looked up the ip address from the email. He found that it was located in the city of Los Angeles, coming from a general location of a town called Culver City. Dean looked at the surroundings and studied them well.

Of course, right next to Beverly Hills and Hollywood, home of the rich, greedy, and twisted, he thought.

He packed a bag and grabbed useful detective gear; Audio devices, cameras, some recorders, GPS trackers, and other items. He pulled out his Sig Sauer P320CAR and four extra magazines. He was no stranger to firearms.

Putting on his watch he spoke to a machine somewhere, "Buy a one way direct ticket for LAX from here."

A moment later a female voice answered. "What time would you like to depart?"

"About two hours."

A few moments of computing and the voice responded, "One-way ticket from Colorado to Los Angeles confirmed, departing from Denver International Airport at 11:00AM and arriving at Los Angeles International Airport at 12:38PM. Best price four hundred and forty-eight credits. Confirm?"

"Confirm."

"Thank you, confirmed."

"So much for a day off," Dean muttered to himself.

36

Kevin was staring at death. The moment reminded him of a childhood memory. It came flooding back into his mind like a lost coin found by pure accident.

Playing in the woods, the leaves had fallen so the trees looked like dead sticks, reached into the heavens for help. It was getting dark, and he found a clearing that looked interesting. As he headed for it, a small black pond, peaceful and serene, shined like a mirror. As he walked up to it a soft wind blew, and the leaves rustled with a coyote or two howling here and there. He peered over the water and saw himself. Staring at the image for a long time, Kevin studied his features. He could see into his own soul. Then the image morphed into a creature not of this world. Something horrid and rotting reflected back. Kevin's heart raced as he couldn't rip his eyes away from the image until it became clear. Grotesque, it was an image of death, smiling back at him with a rotting face. As it grinned at him, a piece of wet necrotic flesh fell from its face. Kevin screamed, pulled himself away, and ran back to his parent's house. That memory shook him for as long as he could remember.

That same face appeared to him now.

Fear covered Kevin's face. "Let's say we play a game of 'truth or step'." He struggled to say, knowing it sounded awkward.

Jake laughed, "What? Truth or step? How about truth or die?" He laughed and looked at him with pity.

"Let's just say for game's sake, that I might be able to convince you that I'm innocent. We start twenty paces apart. I ask you a question. If I'm right, you take a step back. If I am wrong, you take a step forward."

Now Jake understood and finished the next line, "And then I am supposed to ask you a question, but no matter what I ask you will obviously just lie and step back."

"As I am trusting you to be honest also, I will step forward if you are right." Kevin countered.

"I'm not sure this is gonna work." Jake added, but he knew it was great for show, *and* he might be able to get what he wanted...a confession. "Okay," he agreed. "But when I'm within reach...you're mine." His eyes narrowed in seriousness.

Kevin nodded in agreement, but his mind was already trying to generate questions. "All right, twenty steps," he directed.

Jake backed up facing Kevin, not allowing himself to break his sight in case he tried to run. Kevin was terrified, Jake was excited and eager.

"Go ahead, it's your game, you first " Jake urged.

Kevin thought hard. He didn't want Jake to become angry and ask a ridiculous question. He figured he'd better start with easy questions. He stated, "You killed people here in this complex."

"You can't ask questions you already know the answer to in your favor."

"I don't know if you personally killed anyone? You didn't directly answer that."

No answer.

"Fine. Did you kill Gebriel?"

Without a word, Jake stepped forward.

Kevin's hunch was confirmed, the man had no idea about Gebriel. But was it the truth? The only problem with this information was that Jake was now closer. *Shit.*

"You didn't expect that, did you?" Jake asked easily.

Shit. True. Kevin had to take a step forward. "If you didn't kill him, who did?"

"That's not a yes or no question,"

Fine. Kevin said, "You enjoy killing people, not because you enjoy the killing, but because you believe they deserve it."

Jake took a step back. True. After a moment, he said, "You held a regular job outside these walls."

Kevin took a step forward. *Damn, this is easy for him.* "You've killed an innocent person before." It was a risky question, but possibly worth it. Kevin watched Jake's demeanor. He appeared upset. Kevin gained useful information as he noticed Jake step back, like he was exhausted. *How do I convince him I'm innocent,* but Kevin's thoughts were interrupted.

Jake's voice was more serious now. "Be careful now Kev, if you lie to me, I can cover this much ground before you can blink." He let that sink in before he spoke again. "You've hurt people in the past."

Kevin knew this was a risky step. He didn't agree with this statement because of the word 'hurt.' He knew Jake meant injured, killed, raped, or whatever, but he had to take the chance and agree with it by means of emotional hurt, which he *was* guilty of.

He stepped forward.

Jake's smile grew larger as if he caught Kevin red-handed doing something bad as a kid.

Kevin fumbled for his next statement. His mind was cloudy. He didn't have enough time to think. The pressure of the situation weighed on him. "Who hired you to judge us?"

"Nope, must be yes or no."

Dammit! "Umm."

Jake stepped forward. "Penalty! Too long to come up with a question."

Kevin was frustrated.

Jake added, "you're scared shitless about what's gonna happen."

"Don't you already know the answer to that?" Kevin belted out.

"I don't know who you are. I've seen many people look innocent on the outside, but inside they are...real nasty. Now make your choice."

Kevin had to take a step forward. He thought with desperation to save his life, "You will not be able to run this complex alone if you kill everyone."

Jake stepped forward.

Kevin's heart beat faster. *What? Damn it!* His mind was whirling. *That has to be a step...*

"You can't seem to remember your life vividly before last month," Jake said.

What the hell? How did he know that? Kevin wondered. His mind spinning, he became light-headed. Wobbly.

"Don't worry Kev, I can see you can't walk anymore, so I'll take your step for you."

Jake moved closer, chuckling.

Kevin's lightheadedness made him unbalanced. *What the hell's going on?*

"You were told that the living conditions outside were uninhabitable. You had to remain here and...fix the earth." Jake had a nasty grin on his face, he already knew the answer.

How did he know this? Kevin wondered. *Christ, what am I going to do?*

Jake stepped forward again.

Kevin noticed that Jake got out a blade from somewhere concealed. He put the tip of the blade into his palm, curling his fingers around the blade, and gave it a spin. He opened his hand wide and performed some elegant maneuvers and flourishes. He gripped the handle, glanced at Kevin with an arrogant smile, like a little boy showing off his skills.

"What the, how did you...?" Kevin was frantic, confused, and wasn't thinking straight anymore.

Jake laughed. "I almost gotcha!"

The stress was just too much. He panicked. Kevin lost his strength and the knife fell out of his hand. His wobbly legs gave out.

Just as he fell, the lights flickered on, illuminating the area. The extra bright lights shattered the previous darkness, making Jake squint. Down the tunnel, the door wheel behind Jake turned as if by a ghost on the other side. It made a squeaking noise as the metal scraped against other metal. At the same moment, Jake threw his knife at Kevin with lightning speed. The game was over. He had to end the current confrontation fast and prepare for whatever was on the other side of the door. The blade glided through the air at Kevin, but he was already falling.

The blade cut into Kevin's trapezius muscle right above the clavicle. It sliced and kept going as the hilt hit his body and then bounced off. Kevin hit the ground and was trying to catch his breath. Death knocked but only claimed a small cut. As pain hit from the fall, Kevin watched Jake. He already turned and ran for the door. Kevin used the opportunity. He tried to get up by planting his hands on the ground, but the shoulder area refused to accept any weight. Struggling with the uninjured hand Kevin got his legs under him and pushed himself up while accidentally kicking the knife. It slid far away. He grabbed his shoulder with his free hand and ran the other way down the tunnel, away from Jake. His next thought was about the poor soul coming through the door. He turned a little sideways and yelled back as he was running, "Hey! Watch out! Don't come through!" It didn't help. The door opened fast, and he recognized Theod burst through. Kevin tried to stop, but his momentum kept him going and he stumbled forward as he slowed down. "Theod! Look out!" He watched from afar. Stepping forward to help, it was too late.

Theod already had a terrified look on his face, like he was running from something...or someone. Theod looked at Kevin. Then his face turned to confusion. A gut wrenching sound came out of him. Theod stood for a moment longer as if he didn't know if he should care about anything anymore.

Kevin saw the loss of life. Mortified, Kevin turned and ran knowing there was nothing he could do. *Damn it!* He thought.

Jake withdrew the knife and let him fall. Theod's knees bent like they were made of toothpicks holding four hundred pounds. He fell hard and made a tiny movement as if trying to curl up into a little ball from the pain.

Jake looked at Theod and knew he was finished. Glancing back toward Kevin, he could see drops of blood, but no Kevin.

Another voice echoed from the tunnel Theod just came through, "Yoo-hoo! Dude, where are you?" It sounded like a man was playing hide-and-seek with his own child.

Jake tightened and needed a better position. The person beyond the door would stop at the sight of Theod's body and Jake was not within striking distance. He backed off and moved along the wall to keep out of sight for as long as he could.

"Hey bud, you ran off so fast I couldn't..." the voice cut off in mid sentence.

Silence.

Jake knew whoever it was just saw Theod.

"What the hell happened to you?" The man asked. "Did I really scare you that bad? Did you run too fast and hit your poor little head? Aww man," he said, complaining like a child who didn't get to play the rest of their game. "That sure was no fun." He used his foot to nudge Theod. "Come on, wake up."

Jake couldn't see anyone yet. His line of vision was obstructed by the door. That meant the person chasing Theod couldn't see Jake either.

Theod moved, but only from the foot that nudged him. Then the man saw the blood coming from a wound. Not one he did.

Jake rushed him, but the man, lightning quick on his feet, backed up before he could reach him.

"Ho! We've got a live one here!" The man's voice was jolly, like he was at a party.

Jake realized his advantage of surprise was gone and stopped. Jake eyeballed him. "So you're the twisted shit who's been doing my job."

"Excuse me?" the man asked, raising his eyebrows in pity. He noticed the bloodied knife in the other man's hand. "Ah, my competition." His voice was slow and indicated awareness. "Yeah, that's right,' but Jake didn't know what he meant.

"Oh, I've been longing for this. I'm the one who's gonna kill you," Jake said with confidence.

The scoff of ridiculousness that came from the man infuriated Jake.

"Pffftt. Uh-huh, you obviously have no idea who you are dealing with." A knowing smile of arrogance shined on the man's face. The killer stared at him for a moment. "You really don't remember?" His voice had pleasure in it. "Or…they just didn't tell you." His eyes squinted.

"Guess not." Jake had no idea what he was saying, but would not be distracted. He came at him.

37

Dean gazed at the city looking out the large window of the mass transit system car. While he didn't like what the cities became, it was still a spectacular site, even though they were run down. The huge buildings towered over smaller ones showing off some intricate and beautiful architecture. Some towers were quite miraculous, demonstrating how well the physicists did their work. They created magnificent structures that looked like they couldn't stand on their own, almost hovering in certain areas. The sun was a large golden-orange medallion in the sky as the light bent through the pollution making it glow.

More pollution meant an increase in beauty and intricate details. How ironic. Life followed the same suit. Many of the large buildings were rough around the edges, many with noticeable cracks and broken windows. Most were vacant giving the city an eerie, desolate look, like a ghost town. Natural green foliage grew on them giving an unkempt, but natural appearance. They stood there in their glory, reaching for the top of a mountain but just shy of reaching the summit.

Dean envisioned the crowds of booming societies now plagued with no one to admire their lost glory. Other countries, especially third world countries, maintained their stability because they already live in minimal standards. They escaped the fall because they never had a rise.

The vibrations of wind on the hover car shook it, but it was a normal movement. The car glided along without the need to touch anything; the wind being the only resistance.

Dean thought about his plan. The previous call to the company played out in his head. He got an interview for a position using a fake name and created files to present as identification. An electronic trail usually provided enough evidence that someone existed. Technology had its good uses, and Dean was excellent at utilizing them. The position was low, but at least he found a way inside. Could he find his brother? What about the person that contacted him?

The red light near the top on the inside of the car turned on with a sound showing the passenger to take a seat and buckle in. After a few minutes the car started its reverse cycle to decelerate. The high speed bled off and the negative inertial effects were felt, wanting to send his body forward. The belt held him in place.

The car reached its destination, slowed to a stop, and lowered to meet the ramp. Dean grabbed his belongings and stepped off.

Dean had time before his interview. He began the surveillance from his hotel, which he booked close to the source of the signal, around Culver City in California. The hotel was dilapidated and old, but all he needed was a place to sleep. The staff were apathetic and minimal, enough just to keep the place going but it was apparent that the owners were not interested in making a profit.

Dean had noticed, on the outskirts of the city, there wasn't anyone on the streets. Here in the center, it was much more congested. The games were here, the action, the money, the greed. The only place for people to go, and they flocked.

The noise was intense, even from his short distance away.

As he walked, Dean absorbed the scene, looking around at the madness outside. A game was on the air, happening now, Dean worried about his brother. He had to get started.

The noise became deafening as he walked closer to the crowds, like an ocean swaying in different directions. People were loud, drunk, and didn't seem to care about anything else but the game. It was a good distraction from what he was doing.

Dean picked up information from trash programs on the ground, fliers, and some wandering people as he made his way over to the entrance of the company. As he neared the company skyscraper, he gazed up at its vast overwhelming appearance. He became dizzy as the building looked like it would fall on top of him. Looking much nicer than most other buildings around, it had a large front courtyard with lots of trees, exotic plants, flowers, and they were all kept clean and trimmed. Several intricate water features and fountains were flowing out front. They displayed a beautiful frenzy of choreographed water matinees.

His plan for his Sig Sauer was to bring it in one piece at a time, breaking it down into smaller parts that were easy to hide. As he got closer a security guard eyed him. Dean looked right back and nodded, the security guard pointed. This wasn't a request, it was a directive. 'You go here or you get out' type of command.

Inside, Dean noticed a beautiful lobby unlike any he had ever seen except online in history searches. Shiny marble floors, great Roman looking columns standing forty feet tall, wall waterfalls on both sides rushing down grated media. Golden trim along borders with intricate and detailed mural artwork on the ceiling. A few massive chandeliers hung down and sparkled.

He came up to a window and spoke to a clerk about his appointment interview. After a maze of hallways, more security, and paperwork, Dean found his destination, a waiting room.

"Right over there," the guard announced, pointing to the person in the window. Alone in the waiting room, Dean walked over and smiled at the clerk.

"John?" A receptionist spoke clearly.

He nodded using his brother's first name.
"We've been expecting you," she smiled.

38

John was scared. He had seen his share of rough times, but down here he had been through much worse. He learned from Nick and Damon that someone had killed more people than he thought. The killer, his glowing eyes pounded in John's head. When he caught a glimpse of him, something was familiar about it. He had seen him before, or had seen the situation before. John couldn't shake it. At the time of the encounter, an image appeared in his mind the moment he saw what was happening. The killer murdered the person right in front of him. It was as if he was watching it happen from a computer screen, but he was there in reality, watching it live. John just couldn't seem to make it out clearly.

"Hey, you with us?" Nick asked, interrupting his thoughts.

John looked up. "Hmm? Oh, yeah. I'm with ya."

"Good, keep an eye out man. I don't want to be ambushed while you're off in your own world," Nick told him.

"All right, got it," John tried to ease the frustration and tension he received from Nick.

They arrived at the South center and were waiting as instructed. After a couple of breaths, the lights on the panel turned on.

"Nice!" Damon said, noticing the panel lights.

"You two keep a sharp lookout," John said as he concentrated on the panel. The other two nodded their heads and looked in different directions.

Soon enough the flipping of switches was complete, and a turbine whined and increased in pitch, like an airplane engine accelerating.

Nick and Damon grew a little uneasy as it sounded as if something would explode. Nick backed away from the panel.

"Take it easy fellas, that's just the generators firing up," John said.

The sound of 'click' 'click' 'click' echoed in the hall as the lights flicked on, one by one.

"Yes," Nick said with a grin sounding triumphant. Nick looked at the other two men, they returned the smile, but as soon as they did, Damon's smile vacated his face.

"What is it?" John inquired, staring at Damon. His tone was soft. It looked like Damon was trying to listen intently.

"Shhh," Damon responded. They both remained quiet. "I heard something." He turned his head to focus his ear toward the sound. He heard it. It was faint, but it was there. As the silence continued, Another sound echoed, and they all heard it, but it still sounded muffled and far away.

"Thaa, ook, ou!"

John's face contorted. It was a cry for help! His eyes grew wide.

"Oh no," Damon said in fear. He couldn't take much more excitement. The adrenaline pumped in making him shake. He cowered and hunched his shoulders knowing something bad was about to happen.

"Come on!" Nick said and started maneuvering in the general direction of the sound. "Someone needs help!"

"Wait! Let's not be too hasty!" Damon said. He didn't want to admit that he was a coward, but didn't want to be left alone either. He was a doctor, not a hero. Damon was meant to save a life *after* someone became hurt, not before.

"Are you kidding?" Nick said slowing down and turning around to Damon. "If someone's in trouble as we speak, you're the one who can help most." Nick said. "Now come the fuck on!"

Damon took a deep breath and pulled himself together and nodded in agreement.

"Don't worry Damon, there are three of us," John reassured him. "If someone's there, they can't take all of us out." He said, hoping that was actually true.

Nick ran and led the way down the hall, John right behind him. Damon was a little slower.

39

"Are you really that eager to die?" The man in shadow asked. He let out a small laugh and shook his head, "This is going to be fun."

"You're going to pay for those kills you piece of shit. I'm the hunter and judge here." Jake said, using careful steps to line up with the man. It surprised Jake studying how this other guy moved as he took a position. *There's something different about this guy,* Jake thought as he watched him having knowledge with positioning. *He knows combat.* Jake paused, eyeing him. He knew most people in the game had killed before, or worse, but most killed out of passion or craze. None of them had the slightest sense of being a professional hitman. This one did.

"Judge, huh?" He laughed. "Don't worry, your death will be just like the others...long, slow, and," he took in a deep breath as if smelling a sweet fragrance that enveloped the room, "amazingly artistic," he finished, giving a shiver.

Jake squinted. *Serial killer,* he thought. *Good. He belongs here. This guys special.* However, Jake knew there was something else. Things he said were strange. It was almost like insanity and genius put together simultaneously. He looked at his face and studied it. It was like he was drooling with anticipation.

"This will make the games really entertaining," the man in shadow said. Then he added, "huh, Jake?" His smile grew to show a set of bright teeth.

What? Jake wondered with bewilderment. He was caught completely off guard. *How does he know my name? Did he say games and entertainment? How the hell did he know this was a game? Coincidence?*

Before Jake could solve it, the man in shadow continued, "What, did you think *you* were the only hunter down here dude?" He laughed as he observed Jake's face of confusion. "Not too bright are we, even with the lights back on." He laughed louder.

Jake was furious. The guy was somehow able to see right through him, like a window. A hundred thoughts entered his mind, and he wasn't able to sort anything. Jake thought about the people he killed coming out of the conference hall with his smoke bomb. Kevin popped in head. He...*might* be telling the truth? The company told him he was the law, the avenger to close criminal cases. He gave their loved ones some peace. *Was it all a lie?* His face turned a little red. It was beyond his control and he started sweating with rage.

The distraction was perfect.

Jake was exposed and was not ready for the confrontation. He thought about two possibilities. He could run and calm his nerves and clear his head, or stay and fight. Running meant risking a knife in the back. Jake stood his ground and observed as the killer came at him with measured steps.

Once in range, both on the balls of their feet, the man in shadow gave a quick lunge and then retracted. A fake move to tighten up the opponent, make them commit to a false defense. Jake didn't fall for it. The man in shadow came again, this time committing further than the last lunge. It was sufficient for Jake to counter the move, just in case it turned into a completed attack.

The man in shadow reached in with his free hand trying to cover as much of Jakes' vision as possible to hide his knife hand. His free hand was in Jakes' combat zone, so Jake side-stepped away from the knife hand. As Jake side-stepped, the man in shadow pivoted with amazing speed and his free hand opened in front of Jake's eyes within range of his knife.

Jake stepped back, avoiding the bait with ease.

"You recover quickly," the man in shadow praised. He had an admiring tone. "Good moves too, patient, alert, but man are you dense. I think I'll call you...baka." A large belly laugh erupted like it was an inside joke that Jake didn't understand.

Jake said nothing. While he didn't understand what the word meant, he was sure it wasn't good.

"Don't know the word? I guess no Samurai combat training for you. So," the man in shadow said, changing the subject, "How many people did you manage to take out baka?"

Jake still said nothing.

"Aw come on. Don't you remember that this is just a game? Come on, let's play the game together. You're a pawn and so am I. The others are the chips that are spent. Did you kill more than me?" His eyebrows raised in question, then continued as there was no response. "I'm guessing so because I love to make mine last. I like to play with the paint. I like to tease every inch of their bodies. Their tears embrace me."

Jake despised this man. He had a new mission. Kill him. Kill the killer of innocence. He turned his attention to the lust of hammering this guy into oblivion. End his reign of terror. The players remain the same, but the objective to win has changed. Jake was now the avenger for the people down here, for himself, for the good soul.

Jake gazed at his glowing eyes and a memory touched his mind, nothing substantial, just a name, Phoenix.

"All right asshole, tell me more," Jake spit out and was now turning the game into his own. "What did you see when you stuck it in? What was the best part?" Jake could feel the adrenaline fueling his nerves. It was firing like a metal fork in a microwave.

The man in shadow let out a good laugh. "Ho, man! Now we're talking, let's play baby!"

They kept stepping around each other moving in a small circle. Neither one yet committed to any moves.

Jake had recovered. The man in shadow made a small mistake, but no matter, he would rely on his superior skills. He continued to play along. "You must admit, the adrenaline rush and exercise is great for the heart. Just before a takedown, your heart is beating out of your chest. You have all this energy feeling like you can fly." He shivered. "There's nothing like it. And to take all that built up energy and then release it through one channel of your body. Mmm, cumming in all kinds of her orifices...and then there's the blood, oh man! The blood is beyond words, booyah!" he said emphatically, laughing and rocketed his pelvis forward.

"Mmm," Jake purred, but his lust was his own pleasure of killing this criminal, "It will be the same joy for me when you're looking into my eyes wondering how the hell I beat you."

"Whatever baka.."

"It's Jake...Phoenix."

Right as Phoenix was about to speak, Jake thrust forward and then striated to the side, knife held close to the body, free arm protecting the blade like a treasure. Phoenix stepped to the other side, avoiding any attack range, but Jake double hopped and brought his strong foot forward to gain a larger distance faster. Phoenix's left side was in range. Jake's knife sprung from its hiding place in a reverse edge-out grip.

Phoenix leaned back.

Jake's blade missed, but at the last second Jake twisted his wrist upward giving the knife a few more inches of extension. The tip of the blade struck flesh but penetrated the skin, but only on the surface. A small red line was left by the sharp blade. After the move Jake took another bold step forward with surprising speed and whipped the knife hand around in a circle, but Phoenix blocked it with his knife hand.

Phoenix completed his countermove by hitting Jake's arm with the free hand deflecting it backwards. Phoenix then took an aggressive step forward and tried to step on Jake's leading foot, not allowing him to retreat. Jake saw it coming and lifted his foot off the ground. Phoenix's foot stepped into the vacant spot and Jake extended his leg back down at an angle toward Phoenix's knee. Jake's foot struck the hard patella, and Phoenix let out a scream.

"Awrgh!" It was more frustration and anger than pain. Phoenix's attack circumvented with Jakes kick threw him off balance.

Jake came at him again from the top, stabbing straight down expecting a check. He got it.

Phoenix blocked the blade and slashed through the midsection of Jake. The action left Phoenix's right shoulder vulnerable for a moment.

Jake came down with the knife going for the trapezius muscle. It came down hard, too committed to adjust for any sudden change of movement.

Phoenix leaned forward just enough where the knife would hit behind him. Jake's wrist hit Phoenix's shoulder hard. He curled his wrist and the tip of the knife penetrated maybe an inch into Phoenix's back shoulder area...not enough. The hard blow made Phoenix's shoulder shrug up to his ear.

Jake was feeling wet at the front of his stomach. *Damn it!,* he thought. He took steps backward and disengaged to assess the damage. He was bleeding through the shirt, the cut was bad enough.

"How are ya?" taunted Phoenix. "Eww, looks pretty bad." He winced at Jake's midsection and saw blood seeping through. "Mine's okay...thanks for asking." Smiling, he took a finger to his shoulder and wiped one drop of blood and put it in his mouth. "Mmm, love that taste," He smiled as he pulled his finger out with a sound of a kiss, "but sweet girls are much, much better," he finished. His eyelids relaxed like they were in dreamland.

They continued circling each other. Jake had the open door to his back, Phoenix the long tunnel.

"You're fucking insane," Jake accused. At least, Jake thought he had some form of honor, courage, and knew where the line was drawn. This guy had no line, he stepped wherever he wanted, ice cold in the middle of fire, and he could put the fire out.

"Geez, man, make me out to be the bad guy," he said with joking sarcasm. "Listen, you and I both kill, I just enjoy it more, but you're no saint. You killed people here didn't you? Didn't Towns..." he cut off his own comment. Phoenix didn't perceive what Jake knew about this place, and who might be in on it. He kept the rest to himself. "So let me ask you this baka. Were you working on someone as I came up?" He was wasting time letting Jake bleed a little more.

Jake responded, "There will only be one more kill in here. You."

Phoenix didn't even acknowledge what Jake said and continued, "I only ask because of the trail of blood here leading down this tunnel." Phoenix pointed to the ground and flicked his finger down the hall. "Lookie here, you wounded someone, bet you were upset about being interrupted." He chuckled. "Man, I was almost interrupted too! Just before I came in here, that guy," he said pointing at Theod lying in a puddle of his own blood, "came into *my* house. I was banging this girl, then *he* popped in. You believe that? I wasn't done with my artwork." He shrugged, "Maybe I'll get the chance to finish later. Paint a Picasso, no, better...a Phoenix!" He laughed.

Jake wanted to kill this man so bad he could taste it. He never felt like a true killer before, but now it filled every vein. It was bitter in his mouth, like an old worn-out piece of metal. His wound needed attention, but he had a little time before he would feel dizzy. That required about fifteen percent loss of blood. However, the wound *was* leaking.

Jake started to say, "Or maybe you won't..."

Phoenix bolted at him in a fury of strikes shutting him up. He came fast and hard. One strike to the face, block, the other hand used for a shove.

Jake was backing up in defense. He knew these were half attacks with the ability to change a bit in motion.

Phoenix was smooth and switched grips to a hammer grip with his thumb on the hilt for another quick four jabs and Jake was running out of room to back up.

Jake waited with patience and focused. Observing the moment of a committed stabbing thrust, Phoenix aimed at Jake's heart. He changed his momentum from backward to forward abruptly. Phoenix was left with a vital open area in the front. The distance between them closed with rapid obsession, and Jake had his weapon unleash fury. It connected. Phoenix twisted to relieve some damage. The blade sunk into flesh, but the twist allowed him to retreat and didn't allow Jake to make the wound wider by turning it.

In the twisting motion, the action allowed Phoenix to use his free hand to push Jake hard away from him. As Jake took a few steps back, Phoenix also took steps back retreating. He held his wound and looked up at Jake with a tinge of worry in his eyes. *Fuck,* Phoenix thought. He was no longer having a good time. The humor gone, the smile gone. Anger now engorged it.

Jake turned toward Phoenix. "Little by little, I will drain your life one drop of blood at a time. Your soul will seep out on the dirty floor and be washed away...down the drain to hell."

Phoenix stumbled backwards where the tunnel curved, hit the side wall, and sunk down to one knee.

Jake noticed Phoenix's eyes glance behind him. Following his gaze, he saw a pair of curious eyes look in from the open door. They gazed at him, then at the bloodied knife and then back at Jake's eyes.

"Don't you fucking move," the man in the door chided.

Jake stood, "I'm not gonna hurt you." He took one step closer toward the wall.

"I said don't move," The man repeated harshly.

"If you're not going to hurt us, then drop that knife." The eyes belonged to Nick.

Jake was at a loss. He wasn't going to hurt these people anymore, but he didn't want to give up his weapon either. He had no choice and let the knife fall and kicked it away. Jake would try the path of reason.

Before Jake could speak, Nick asked, "Who are you? What the hell's going on here? Did someone yell? Who else is here?" he used caution and moved into the tunnel to make himself more visible, and Jake noticed another guy followed, then one more. The last guy locked eyes with him.

"Holy shit!" the last man said with nervous excitement. "It's him! It's him! He's the fucking killer!" John recognized him.

"No, No, No, hold on!," Jake pleaded. Shit. How can he say he's not a killer when he was? "I'm not...I wasn't hurting...I was fighting the killer. He's over there, look for yourself." Jake felt stupid ranting this way.

Nick said, "Don't move!" He walked out into the middle of the hall to peer down the tunnel. "What the fuck are you talking about?"

Jake glanced for Phoenix.

No one there.

Damn it! Jake thought and exhaled deeply.

40

"Thank God," Dahria said with relief as the lights flickered on. She sighed and looked at Tommy, who returned the smile.

"Kick ass," Jones said. "We can see," some joy leaked into his voice.

Tim continued working on the panels. "All right," he said, jamming the doors shut. "That should at least make it difficult to open."

"Good," replied Tommy. "At least it's an advantage, but I wonder why whoever it is didn't put the lights out permanently?"

"Shit!" Tim said. He lifted his head. A grim look appeared on his face. "I wonder if it was to separate us into smaller groups."

Tommy and Jones were speechless. Worried.

"Let's get back to the others and head to south operations," Tim suggested.

Tommy nodded, eager to get back into a larger group. Jones and Dahria followed close.

They moved through the tunnel to the conference hall. As they weaved through disarrayed tables and chairs, the place had an eerie peacefulness about it, like an abandoned old mine that was populated only a few minutes ago. Some water dripped in the background, echoing as it bounced off the walls and entered ears. A piece of paper lifted and wrinkled from the air blowers catching under it, added to the anxious ambience.

Jones broke the silence. "What're we gonna do with everyone?" he asked, concerned about the bodies. "Can't leave 'em here to rot? Can we?" There was a rancid smell, but nothing anyone couldn't handle.

"No," replied Tim, giving him the answer he wanted. His voice was somber. "First though, we need to make sure we're safe in this compound. Then, we can worry about putting them to some kind of rest."

Tommy came close to Dahria as she looked like she was getting sick from the memories again, or the smell, probably a combination of both.

After crossing the conference hall, they plodded through the tunnel connecting the south power center. When they arrived they observed something all of them feared. No one was there.

Oh no, Dahria thought. She could feel her nerves acting up.

"Nick?" Tim asked in a soft voice. He didn't want to speak too loudly yet. "John?" He looked around and stepped, trying to be light on his feet. "Damon?" He glanced at the others when he found nothing. "You guys spread out and look over there," he said, moving his hand motioning the locations.

They spread out and checked the center. There was nothing. No one.

"Where the hell are they?" Tommy asked. "They had to have beat us back, it's a shorter distance."

"Shit, do you think?" Jones questioned.

"No, no," Dahria said trying to delude herself.

"Hold on now," said Tim, sounding like he was hopeful, "There are no bodies," he looked at Dahria and felt bad about bringing it up, but didn't make it any better when he finished, "I mean, no one here is dead," he fumbled. Then added, "Maybe they went back to the south operations without us."

"There's one way to find out," Jones said.

They stayed a few more minutes hoping they would come back. No one showed. The group eased their way back into the tunnel leading to the south block hall. As they were walking, they kept their ears open and their footsteps as quiet as they could. Tim was in front and Tommy slowed down to have a quiet conversation with Dahria. Making sure she didn't go into shock, Tommy tried to make her feel as secure as he could. Her mind was on edge, stressed, fragile. Tommy's stress was high too, but he was better at hiding it. He wondered how Jones was holding up. Tim seemed to be dealing with it okay at least.

Arriving at south operations, the search turned up nothing. They checked the entire place including the tunnel to the iron door. They scouted and confirmed no one settled in here while they were gone.

"Damn, what do we do now?" Jones asked.

"They were supposed to wait for us there," Tim suggested, trying to piece it together. "Being that they didn't...could mean anything, but it doesn't mean anything bad happened. I think we should wait here for a while and see if they show up. If not, then we may consider three choices. One, we go look for them and others. Two, we look for the killer, or three, we stay here and try to defend this area." He glanced at each of them. The look on Tim's face suggested he liked none of the scenarios.

Jones volunteered a choice. "Let's wait here for a little bit. There's something I need to do."

Tommy knew what he meant.

The camera.

Jones could read the clarity on Tommy's face. His eyebrows rose. Tommy was asking Jones if they should let Tim in on the secret. Jones nodded. It was a risk, but they weren't sure if it would even amount to anything. Having another brain might prove to be useful.

Taking the cue, Tommy said, "Tim. Jones found something kinda strange on that computer." He pointed to it in the corner of the hall. "We haven't had a chance to check it out, but we are curious about it."

"What's that?" he asked.

Tommy looked at Jones for him to take over and continue, "There is a camera by the computer, like all computers have."

"So? The cameras are there for all kinds of reasons."

"Yeah, but this one isn't plugged into the computer."

Tim looked apathetic and shook his head. "You two go ahead. I'm gonna rest and get something to eat. Let me know if you find something."

Tommy looked at Dahria, "It's up to you if you want to check it out with us or not."

"I'll stay with you," Dahria said.

"How sweet," Jones joked with a smirk. He regretted it as he saw Dahria not smile at all. She was distraught. His eyes went down and the look of apology crept into his face. "Sorry."

"It's okay, I'll be fine," Dahria conveyed.

At first appearance the computer seemed normal. Jones fired it up and looked at the screen. He could log on. They inspected the camera itself. It was a normal camera, and the wire was bunched into a set of other cables. The terminals were archaic technology, but were appropriate in the complex. The wires ran to the back of the computer and appeared to be plugged in. However, tracing the line, as Jones had already done, it broke into two sets of cables. One set into the computer and the other set ran into a box in the wall.

"Can you tap into it?" asked Tommy.

Jones looked at him, "I don't know. I would need a cable and a way to splice it. Then I could plug it into the computer." A moment later the computer made a notification sound interrupting their conversation. They looked at the screen. An application opened as if the computer had a ghost controlling it.

JAMES M THOMAS

"What the?" Tommy asked astounded.

Jones looked at the screen in fascination as a message in a window typed all by itself. It read 'KIDS, YOU ARE IN DANGER!'

41

Dean sat at a terminal inside the company. He escaped the attention of personnel, finding it easier than he thought. Most workers were concentrating on the game or wrapped up in their own personal tasks. After his interview, Dean was directed out of the building, but as no one escorted him out, so he never left. From the time he entered the building for the interview, he had gathered information, recording everything. Finding a dressing room, he donned a wardrobe, and gained an identification tattoo tag.

Finding a secluded terminal, the screen showed basic information icons, but he couldn't access anything beyond general information. He looked for John's name as an employee but it wasn't listed in the company's files. Dean found this most likely a purposeful deletion. He wasn't surprised. However, after scanning the files he found a way to create an employee file. Excellent. That should get him back into the building after he left.

After navigating around the myriad of systems, he stumbled onto strange video feeds, and lots of them. He scanned them but most just showed empty various rooms, tunnels, and halls that looked somewhat regular. Dean discovered that the feeds were categorized and coded to location, so he could find his way around with the cameras easily. Thanks to his brother John, Dean had learned a lot about computers and electronics, and he had the gear, so hacking into the system wasn't too difficult.

Hmmm, where is this? He wondered about studying the feed images. After thinking about it he considered, *probably some hidden chambers underneath this building. Is that where these games are?*

He later noticed that there were red dots on a few of the video feeds. By clicking on them he discovered they signified movements. He opened the first one. The screen lit up with a figure holding a knife and Dean could see blood running down from the man's midsection. Then, Dean noticed a body lying right there on the ground a few feet away.

Christ!, This is entertainment? What the hell have we become? There was a bitter taste in his mouth. *Jesus.*

He watched for a moment more. It was morbid, but he needed intel. There was a figure on the screen as three men came through the door. Dean's jaw dropped. He watched the last man in shock.

He was a familiar face. It was him!

John! His brother was there! His heart pounded and the adrenaline flowed. His attention turned to the man with the knife. *Shit! He's gonna kill all three of them!*

He watched in horror. The moments seemed like hours and sweat accumulated on his brow. Dean was helpless. He grabbed the sides of the screen frame with force, but not enough to break it, eyes glued. The sweat ball was wiped away with the back of his sleeve before it could enter his eye. The figure on the screen dropped his knife and kicked it away. Dean let out a deep breath. A different man picked it up. There was no sound so he couldn't hear what was said, it was like watching an old silent movie. He could tell John was anxious as he jumped up and down and pointed at the figure. The three men surrounded him.

After one man peered down the long tunnel as if looking for someone, they spoke more. The man who was surrounded walked in front through the door while the three others, including his brother John, walked behind him. The man with the knife was a captive. *There's the killer.*

Dean followed them into the other tunnel by opening the feeds that just turned red and corresponded to the code categories. He followed them all the way to the medical complex where it looked like one of them was trying to administer first aid on the wounded killer.

Why would they be doing that? He wondered.

Dean had to get a message across, but how? He checked out other feeds, but only a few had movement indications. He tried another. There was a guy, one he hadn't seen before, and it looked like he was searching for something, or someone down a tunnel. Nothing seemed of interest.

Dean tried to hunt for schematics that indicated where terminals were located in this area. That would allow him to check if someone was on one, and then he could communicate.

Opening up another red signaled feed, Dean found a few kids messing around with the terminal. *That's it!* The kids looked like they were in their late teens. Dean typed a quick message.

The kids were transfixed at the message on the screen. It worked!

42

All three of them looked at the screen and read the text, 'KIDS, YOU ARE IN DANGER.'

Dahria was shocked. "Where? Who do you think this is?" Dahria asked, turning her head to Tommy. She was excited.

"I don't know. It could be someone else in this complex just playing with us," Tommy suggested being skeptical.

Jones pointed to the screen. "Look. There's a cursor."

They stared at what he pointed to, and sure enough, it was blinking. It was a command private chat window. Jones put his hands on the keyboard.

"What should I say?" Jones asked.

Before Jones could type anything, letters appeared in sequence forming a message.

'MY NAME IS DEAN, I AM HERE AT THE COMPANY ON A TERMINAL. MY BROTHER JOHN IS IN THERE WITH YOU.'

Tommy, Jones, and Dahria looked at each other in surprise. Could it be? Was this the killer trying to put false information into their heads? Jones took it upon himself to type a response. 'COMPANY? WHAT ARE YOU TALKING ABOUT?'

A few seconds later the message appeared. 'THE COMPANY IS RESPONSIBLE FOR THE

GAMES. THEY ARE IN COMPLETE CONTROL OF THE CITIES NOW. IT IS BEYOND CORRUPT.'

Confusion. "Do any of you know this?" asked Jones.

They looked at each other and shook their heads.

"I wonder if this has something to do with the headaches." Jones suggested.

"Yeah, we all have had trouble with our memories, haven't we?" Dahria asked.

Tommy's face showed agreement.

Jones typed, 'WE CAN'T REMEMBER. TELL US MORE ABOUT WHAT YOU KNOW.'

The response followed. 'THE COMPANY IS CONTROLLING A GAME THEY SET UP BY COLLECTING CRIMINALS AND PUTTING THEM IN A COMPOUND LIKE THE ONE YOU ARE IN. BUT, THIS COMPANY HAS BECOME EVEN MORE CORRUPT. I FEAR THEY MAY BE USING INNOCENT PEOPLE FOR THEIR GAME…YOU GUYS. I KNOW MY BROTHER IS INNOCENT. I CAN ONLY ASSUME THAT EVERYONE ELSE IS TOO. MY BROTHER HAS CAPTURED THE KILLER. THEY ARE IN A MEDICAL CENTER RIGHT NOW.'

Tommy, Jones, and Dahria were all dumb founded.

"I can't believe it," said Jones. He typed. 'THIS IS CRAZY. HOW DO WE KNOW YOU ARE TELLING THE TRUTH? AND YES, WE ARE ALL INNOCENT.'

Tommy looked at Tim, who was lying on a bench.

"Tim! Tim, come over here!" Shouted Tommy.

Tim, who was resting, pulled himself up with a grunt. His lack of urgency was written all over him with frustration. He looked at the screen and read the messages. His jaw dropped. "Holy shit," he said in awe. "Where'd this come from?"

"Don't know," replied Jones, "It popped up when we were checking out this camera."

"Mind if I have a look?" Tim asked.

Jones got out of the chair and let Tim sit and take over.

'HI, I'M TIM. YOUR BROTHER IS JOHN?'

'YES. MY BROTHER WENT MISSING AND I CAME TO THE COMPANY TO FIND HIM. I HAD NO IDEA THEY PLACED HIM IN THE GAME.'

'YOUR CAN SEE US?' Tim typed.

'YES. I CAN SEE FEEDS FROM ALL THE CAMERAS. I CAN LEAD YOU TO MY BROTHER. HE HAS THE ONE WHO IS KILLING EVERYONE, AND CAN CONFIRM WHO I AM.'

"I can't believe this is a game," said Dahria, shaking her head.

Tim typed, 'ARE THEY STILL AT THE MEDICAL CENTER?'

A few moments passed, and the text answered, 'YES, IT LOOKS LIKE THEY ARE GOING TO TIE HIM UP.'

"Let's get over there," Tim said.

Dahria had Alexa on her mind, but something kept her from asking. Maybe she feared Alexa was dead, or worse, and wanted to hold onto hope a little longer. Or maybe she didn't want to know. She just couldn't take hearing about it. Dahria hated herself for not being brave enough.

Arriving at the medical center, Jones turned the wheel on the door and opened it. Tim, skeptical, peered in first and saw nothing. He stepped in with Tommy and Jones right behind him. Dahria pulled up the rear and stayed close. After they entered they saw medical tables, one with a little blood, some bandages, and other first aid supplies on it. They scanned the room but found nothing. Before Tim could whisper for them to spread out, a soft sound fluttered from somewhere.

"Someone there?' Tim asked reluctantly.

"Tim?" It came from behind a medical table.

Tim moved around carefully to an angle where he could look behind it. It was Damon.

"Damn Tim, you scared the crap out of me." Damon was crouched in the corner attending to John, who was lying on the ground not moving. Tim rushed over and the others followed.

"Where the hell have you guys been? Is he dead?" Tim asked with a worried look, but was glad the two were here.

"No, he'll be fine, just knocked out," Damon reassured him.

"What happened? Where's Nick?" Asked Tommy.

Damon replied, "We heard noises after we turned the switches on. A call for help. We followed the sounds toward the hydro hall and found this guy named Jake who had a bloodied knife in his hand." He sighed and continued, "Theod was on the ground close to him...dead."

They listened without interruption.

"We entered the tunnel, surrounded him, then he dropped the knife and surrendered. It was too easy. He naturally tried to deny everything. He said it was a mistake that he killed Theod and that he'd been lied to, blah, blah, blah."

"Theod's dead?" Tommy blurted and looked at Dahria, who held her hands over her mouth. She had never really liked Theod, but she would never wish death on anyone.

Damon stared at him, confirming. He continued. "Nick didn't fall for any of it. Me, I checked out Theod and later noticed that this guy Jake also had knife wounds. I was wondering where they came from. He said there was someone else there, but when we looked down the tunnel, there wasn't anyone. I noticed that his wound needed treatment, so I convinced Nick and John to let me walk him to the medical center, here. I patched him up, and he was adamant about Kevin being alive and needing help right away."

Tommy looked at Jones and Dahria with hope.

Kevin's alive? Tommy thought. *We've got to get him.* He let Damon finish.

"Nick wasn't having it though still. He wanted to tie him up and get back to you guys. That's when this guy knocked out John. It stunned the two of us. I...I am sorry but I froze...he was so fast. He was able to disarm Nick, getting his knife back and then he ran out of here and Nick chased him."

"Shit," Tim had no time to waste, "Which way did he go?" he asked.

"East, probably back to where we found him, into the hydro hall East end," Damon said.

"There's much more we need to tell you Damon, but we don't have time now," Tim pushed out. "Are you okay staying here with John?" Tim eyed Damon who was scared, but he nodded. Then he looked at Tommy, "You guys stay here too, you should be safe."

Tommy interrupted, "No way, we have to stick together, and if there's a chance to save Kevin..."

"There's no time!" Tim howled. He got up, "Just stay here and help Damon and John. Get back to that terminal and find out any more useful information, like how to get out of this hole!"

Jones and Dahria nodded in agreement but Tommy was upset. "But..."

Tim yelled back as he left, "I've got a hunch this guy Jake might be a little trustworthy. From the sound of it, he could have killed all three of them, but didn't! Get John to that terminal!" In a moment, Tim was gone.

Tommy let him go, he had no choice. He couldn't leave Dahria behind and didn't want to split up Jones either. He couldn't leave Damon alone with an unconscious John, either. If anything went down, Damon would probably leave John high and dry. Tommy had to trust him and hope nothing bad would happen.

43

Phoenix looked at his wound. From his assessment, it was rather deep, but missed major damage. *Good,* he thought with pleasure. Then the pleasure turned to anger, *That mother fucker,* Jake. He played the scene over in his head. He analyzed his mistakes and what Jake's strengths and weaknesses were as he was performing first aid on himself. It was superb medical work. Phoenix was an expert on anatomy, which proved to be a must in his profession. Chances to become injured weighed with every confrontation, but were rare. Jake was a special case, a professional, but that didn't mean Phoenix was okay with it.

The needle penetrated the skin and his face winced with pain. No sound came out of his mouth, only a breath. Disciplined. The suture thread pulled through the tiny hole of flesh wetting it and sliding on the silky blood. Pulling the thread firm to close the wound with each pass, Phoenix admired his work. He loved the blood. Pain he could tolerate. About thirty more passes and he could tie it off. He scrutinized it with care, cleaned it, shot it with some topical clotting ointment, then bandaged it. Phoenix twisted around to test his freedom of movement and found that it was not too limited. The man in shadow would give it a little time to rest, and replenish his energy.

Lying down on his small bed he relaxed and scrutinized over the details of the confrontation some more. Phoenix had learned a great deal about his opponent. He was formidable, capable, and seemed to have a real desire to see him dead. That brought a smile to his face and pleasure to his heart. He would use this information to his advantage.

The bets will be big on us brother. Phoenix put his hands under his head as he stared at the ceiling. His room was small, but had everything he needed for his adventure, his game, his art. A secret place designed to be in a perfect location, virtually impossible for anyone to find. Even if someone stumbled onto it, it was locked. Phoenix wondered if Jake had one too. The company obviously didn't tell Jake everything. Now, he wondered about the possibility of the company being straight with him too. Assuming now that the answer was no, it didn't matter to him. He gets to play and kill everyone, in time.

When the game was over, rewards were plentiful, even though the only reward he needed was playing the game. This was the life, he had everything he desired, and the company loved him. Phoenix was still going to get to play his game, and now, there was going to be a great showdown. Maybe the company planned this too. He smiled.

I think I may save you for last. That would be such a glorious finish and victory. I will pluck the rest of them one at a time.

Some meditation and focus helped to turn off his thoughts, and he was fast asleep.

44

John woke up with a severe headache, but he was okay. Damon gave him some medication to ease the pain.

Tommy noticed Dahria's behavior being different. He feared she may go into shock or shut down. He spoke into her ear, "I won't let anything happen to you.".

She hugged him tighter in response. A tear trickled down her cheek. He smiled and brushed away her fallen tear with the back of his finger.

"I fear for Alexa," she finally got it out. "I wonder..."

"Hey, it's okay, we'll find her. Let's keep up hope. There's always hope."

She snuggled into him more. "I couldn't take it if anything happened to you," Dahria said. "Promise me, you won't do anything stupid." She gazed into his eyes. Dahria knew that if a situation occurred, there might not be anything he *could* do.

He said nothing.

"Promise me." In her mind she didn't want to risk him for anyone, even herself. "I'd rather have you alive than heroic and dead."

"I promise." He just talked about hope, but he hoped he could keep that promise. "Get some rest," he said.

As if in response to being tired but not knowing it, she yawned and nodded, moving her lips together as if she put on chapstick. A tear was salty in her mouth as her tongue slipped out and caught the taste. She gazed into his eyes for a moment longer, kissed him, and lied down next to him.

After a few moments of caressing her hair, Tommy got up and strolled over to converse with everyone else. John was lying on his back and had his forearm arm on his forehead.

"How are you doing John?" Tommy asked.

John peeked over to Tommy. "I'm all right, but I've been better," he said.

"Hey, this might not be the best time, but we've found something we think you need to hear." Tommy glanced at Jones, "Did you tell him?"

"Nope, waiting for you. Go ahead."

"We received a message," Tommy tried to think of the best way to convey the information. "This computer we were looking at, a message popped up on the screen as we were checking it out." He paused. John didn't seem to care. "It basically said that we're in danger and other things."

John still didn't move. "Where'd the information come from?"

"The sender claims he's your brother, Dean."

John let his arm fall off his face and he looked at Tommy intently. He lifted his head. "What? Dean?" He closed his eyes and strained. The memory must have bled through. "My brother?" He nodded as if to confirm the thought. "Dean? He's alive? Where is he?"

Jones added to the conversation before Tommy could. "He said he was in the company building on one of their terminals and could look at video feeds."

"Video feeds? What video feeds? Company? Whoa, whoa, whoa. What are you talking about?"

"We're in a game," said Jones. It was hard to believe, but everything seemed to fit together. "A killing game."

"A game? A killer? What? This is a fucking game?" John said with frustration, anger, and awe. He tried to think about the information and process it, but couldn't seem to come up with anything in his own mind.

"I know, pretty crazy messed up stuff," said Tommy. "But your brother knew things. He could tap into these video feeds somehow."

"Video feeds? So he can see us?"

"Yeah, I guess so, he described what we looked like," Tommy said.

"Geez, I've gotta get to him. Did he have any information about the world? Can we actually get outta here?" John asked as he tried to sit up. His face cringed in a little pain as he grabbed the bridge of his nose to squeeze and push on the top corners of his eye sockets.

"Hold on there man," Tommy urged, "We can't do anything more right now. You need rest." He looked at Jones.

"You expect me to rest now?" John said with excitement. "No, we can rest when we get to the terminal in the South center.

Tommy knew John was adamant. He shrugged and looked at Damon for advice.

"He'll be fine," Damon confirmed.

"What about Tim?" Jones asked. "We can't just leave him."

"I have to get to that terminal. If my brother's there, he can help us, I know it," John conveyed.

"Besides," Damon said. "You said Dean can see in here through video feeds. If we're at a terminal, he can tell us where everyone is. He should see Tim too."

Tommy and Jones looked at each other. Jones said, "It's what Tim wanted us to do."

He nodded.

John took a while to wobble the distance, but with Damon and Jones' help he made it with reasonable time. Being careful, Tommy headed up the front, Dahria right behind checking behind the group often. Damon, John, and Jones headed up the rear.

Arriving at the center, Tommy's eyes were swollen. It had been an insane day, not to mention an insane week. With so much information to process, it stresses the mind and fatigues the body. He needed rest soon, but who knows when that could happen.

At the terminal in the south operations, John logged in while everyone watched.

45

Alexa tried to move her appendages for several minutes. Struggling with each motion, her limbs felt like they weighed fifty times what they normally did. The struggle was excruciating, but she noticed each time was a little easier. More feeling was coming back into her body as time elapsed. She was lying on a padded bench inside a small office, naked. Her awareness was creeping back into her mind. She felt cold, and extremely dirty, especially down there from what must have been a violation. *Oh my God!* Alexa wanted to wash, needed to wash, but right now that luxury was impossible along with grief. Right now she needed to get out of here. She could move her head and used it to look around. A severe headache pounded, like her brain was too big for her cranium. Noticing no one around, she tried to move enough to roll over. Successful with the roll, she fell onto the cold ground on her stomach. Being nauseous, the least of her worries, she pulled her arms under her and tried to push up to get a leg underneath. Her arms vibrated with strain like a bodybuilder lifting too much weight. Hardened tears created crusty streaks down her round cheeks. New tears formed and mixed with the dry salt and hurt the corners of her eyes.

She was terrified the rapist might still be close. Alexa peered around. Nothing, but she had limited vision in this office. She pulled her leg up as quick as she could trying to get it underneath her body. Succeeding, her leg was now folded up with her knee under her breast, laying on it. It felt like a foreign object. Struggling, she pulled with all her strength to get the other one under. Lying on both her folded legs, she pushed with every ounce of energy she had. It was the hardest push up in her life. Her arms strained from the physical activity. Now kneeling like she was praying, Alexa sat upright. It was a tremendous effort.

Where is he? She wondered, glancing around. *I've got to get out of here!*

She clumsily lifted one leg up, planted her foot on the ground, and leaned forward on one hand. Her other hand gripped the bench for support. She pushed up with her leg while helping with both hands. The pain was immense. The other leg followed, and she stood up. Her mass felt huge as she completed the motion. She was wobbly, like an elderly woman with a walker, but she was standing. Her head throbbing like a pressure headache from the flu, but she didn't care, she had to get moving.

Naked and alone, shivering, she looked around for her clothes. They were there, oddly folded up next to the bench. The only article of clothing missing were her panties. That triggered her memory, and the sickness to her stomach overwhelmed her and she threw up the contents of it. The emergency of the situation was her weapon, and she used it to fight the pain.

She risked taking the time to put on her clothes, needing to feel less vulnerable. It also gave her better protection for her feet. It was a struggle and took time, but she managed with sheer force of will. She peered out from the office into the room through the doorless frame. She knew where she was. Her heart was beating hard with fear. She kept looking behind her, fearful of the man standing there like he had done before, but he wasn't there.

Where do I go, where..., she kept thinking. *What am I gonna do? I have to get outta here. Now!*

Alexa, now dressed, wondered about going to the living cell blocks, but that was way too far. She sighed, *one step at a time,* the conference hall was the next room.

The lights shined, but even though she could see well, she felt vulnerable and exposed. She eased her way through the hall into the tunnel heading toward the conference hall. Whining and crying was what she wanted to do, but her fight reflex kept her focused. Gritting her teeth, she wiped her wet tears in the outer corners of her eyes with the back of her wrist.

Somewhere inside came an inner strength to survive, courage somehow inoculated her veins. She didn't know how it got there, but it was there. The feeling almost turned to anger. She swallowed hard, focused, and kept moving, able to tame the beast.

46

Back at his office, Townsend viewed Alexa prod down the hall. He had seen her lying naked and struggling to dress. It didn't thrill him, but it wasn't the ugliest thing he had ever seen either. The games had its little bonuses occasionally.

Struggling with each step, Townsend observed her arrive at the location where Theod's corpse still decorated the floor. She was startled by him and seemed to panic. Alexa backed away in horror. She almost stumbled, but forced herself to step around him and went through the door.

"Where are you going girl?" He said to the screen. She was heading in the direction of the conference center. Watching her for a few more minutes, he assumed her destination would be the living cells. Townsend would let her reach them and get comfortable. She was still alone, just the way Phoenix liked it.

He opened a different video feed. Tommy, Jones, and John appeared, they were sitting at the terminal staring at it oddly. They looked intrigued by the computer. Damon was somewhere else moving around.

"Hmh," Townsend pondered out loud. "You would think they've never seen a terminal before." He shook his head thinking how dense their minds must be.

Shifting over to another feed, Jake was cruising down the tunnel looking like he was searching for someone. Townsend watched for a minute.

"Looking for someone to kill Jake? Go get'em." He wasn't interested in watching an actual kill so he turned to another feed, letting Jake do his business. Something odd showed. A giant face of a man was staring right at him on the screen. A wash of adrenaline flushed his system, Townsend tensed for a moment then laughed.

"Geez, asshole, what the hell?"

As he studied the man, Townsend frowned. The man was not from the game.

Looking right at Townsend, the man frowned also, then waved. He made other gestures to him through the screen.

"What the hell?" He couldn't hear this man but was able to read his lips. He asked, 'Can you see me?'

Putting a fork into an electrical outlet was a better feeling of shock. Townsend couldn't believe it. It was a two way feed.

47

"Kevin!" Jake yelled out. He was barreling down the tunnel. "Kevin! I'm trying to help you!" Jake knew this wasn't the best method to get his attention. Kevin was too smart to answer, but he had to try. "I realize now you were telling the truth!" Jake continued down the tunnel. Giving away his position to Phoenix was a big disadvantage, but it might also get Phoenix's attention off Kevin. And he knew Phoenix was probably taking time to patch his wounds up.

After searching every place down the tunnel, it ended in a T-junction, splitting into two sections, one heading north and one south. Large metal pipes decorated both sides of the tunnel. The pipes were hooked into a gigantic container that was responsible for this complex's resource of water. Jake also noticed several large metal pipes connected from this tank and went into the dirt and rock ceiling and disappeared. The tank had a few large pumps looking like they could send a tsunami onto a beach. He had observed the schematic of this place, but never stepped foot in here until now. Each one of these tunnels hooked up with other passageways that led to the north and south power centers. A maze of pathways. He had to take a chance and pick one. Jake could only hope he thought like Kevin.

He stood for a second and yelled down the tunnels. "Hey Kevin! I'm trying to help you! There is another guy coming for you!" He felt weird saying that, yet stopped and listened hard. Nothing came back in response. He tried one more time before moving, "Hey...!" Just as he started to say the next word, something hit him hard on the back of the head. Jake stumbled forward and his legs lost strength. The electro-chemical messages sent from his brain did not respond to his muscles. He stumbled.

"That's right mother fucker!" The voice resonated in the tunnel with intensity. Another blow aimed for Jake's head hit part head and part neck as he tried to catch his fall and parry the blow. Jake's consciousness faded. He made a terrible mistake and wasn't prepared for someone else to sneak up on him.

Fuck, Phoenix, he thought. *I'm done. I'm sorry.* He struggled but ran out of energy, gave up and went limp, unconscious.

"Yeah, you piece of shit, how does it feel?" Nick loomed over Jake. Nick was just about to kick Jake when he heard something coming from far down the tunnel. He turned toward it and raised his table leg getting ready to swing.

A figure appeared from behind a large pipe down in the north tunnel.

"Hold on! Wait! Don't swing " The figure held his hands up to signify that he had no weapon. "I'm Kevin."

"Damn dude! You scared the shit out of me!" Nick said. His face relaxed and his club hand fell. He glanced at Kevin's shoulder and saw blood. "I recognize you. Kevin? You said?" Nick squinted as he perused Kevin for injury. "Are you all right?"

"Yeah. The cut isn't that bad. Got lucky." Kevin looked down at Jake. "Jesus, did you kill him?"

"I don't know, but he deserves it. He killed Theod."

"I know," Kevin said with sadness and sympathy, "I saw it happen." Kevin didn't know what to think. Lots of emotions were swirling around his head; Upset and wanting vindication for Theod, happy he found someone else alive, angry about this place. He wasn't sure about anything except one thing, Kevin wanted answers.

"You saw it?" His eyes opened wide. "Mother fucker!" Nick kicked Jake again in the side..

Kevin couldn't help but stop him. "No! Hold on! Stop!" He told Nick and grabbed his arm. "Let's think this through. He's out cold already, he can't hurt us. We may be able to use him. He knows some things about this complex that might be useful." He looked into Nick's eyes, pleading.

Nick, who wanted to beat this man into oblivion, paused. "Damn it!" Even trudging through his anger, he could penetrate good sense. "All right, let's get him tied up then, fast."

Kevin nodded.

"You go get some rope or duct tape or whatever you can find. I'll stay and watch him, but if he moves…" Nick gripped his club weapon and shook it a little.

Kevin understood, "I'll be back as quick as I can, don't do anything."

Kevin didn't have to go too far and found some tape.

They taped him up and dragged him to an office close by. "Where is everyone else? Are you with anyone else?" Kevin asked.

"Back at the medical center. We caught this guy right where Theod was. John and Damon were with me." He explained to Kevin about turning the power back on with Tim, Tommy, Dahria, and Jones and how they came to meet this guy, the killer named Jake.

Kevin's elation of hearing that more people were alive gave him hope. "I'm glad there are survivors." He didn't tell Nick about *his* confrontation with Jake yet.

"What do you think we should do with him?" Nick asked.

"I don't know yet. I think that's something for everyone to decide. Right now, I think we should find the others. Now that we can move with freedom, it shouldn't be bad."

A moan expelled from Jake. He was sitting in a chair in the office, taped to it. The chair was in turn taped to the heavy desk, his arms bound behind him, and his legs taped to the chair by the ankles. Jake's head moved and lifted. His eyes blinked many times and his lids opened slowly. His headache was enormous. Pain showed in his furrowed brow, and his vision took time to clear. Jake tried to move his hand to his head but it wouldn't budge. He observed two men staring at him. One of them had a smirk, the other was...Kevin. He rolled his eyes into his head. His body language grunting 'oh shit.'

48

The relief was exhilarating. John, Tommy, and Jones logged onto the terminal to assess the situation with Dean. Tim was found to be okay, wandering the halls searching for Nick and Kevin. He conveyed that two men taped the killer to a chair and held him there. From his description, they were identified as Kevin and Nick.

Tommy was elated that the killer seemed human and not a perfect machine. Maybe he could protect Dahria after all, especially now that he was caught. *Not such a badass now*, he thought.

Dean wrote that he would continue to hunt for useful information and would be in touch later at a specific time. Soon after, John, under the advice of Damon, had to sleep to recover from the head trauma.

Damon was catching some rest along with Dahria.

After a short while, Dahria woke up. Tommy and Jones informed her about the situation. She was elated. "Oh, thank God!" she said out loud for everyone to hear. She looked like a ton of bricks was just lifted off of her and she grew three feet. She exhaled a deep breath. Looking at the ceiling and closing her eyes, she felt a sense of joy, like a forgotten golden sun shining on her face. Dahria hugged both Tommy and Jones. The boys accepted, human contact was refreshing.

"Hoo!" Jones added. "Son of a bitch! I can't believe it. That was some crazy shit!" His eyes had slight tears in them.

"Hell yeah, it's over." Tommy shook his head.

"I can't believe I can be this happy in this sick place!" Jones burst out.

"I know, with one bad thing after another, this is the best thing that's happened in such a long time," Tommy said.

Tommy looked at Dahria and gave her a quick kiss on the cheek. He could see that something was bothering her, he knew it was Alexa.

"Don't worry, we'll find her," Tommy said.

"I know we will…but," Her eyes looked down.

"Let's not lose hope, come one."

"Hey," Jones said interrupting, "If we're going to look for Alexa, let's start in the cafeteria! We have freedom now, are you guys as hungry as I am? Let's go!"

"I don't know about that. What about John?" Dahria asked.

Jones looked at John still sleeping. "We'll be back before he wakes up. Besides, Damon'll be with him."

Damon looked up at them, his hand showed a motion similar to swatting a fly. "You guys go ahead."

"We'll bring you back something," Dahria said.

---#---

The three walked along the halls and tunnels toward the cafeteria. They talked and had fun with each other, trying to regain the better times they had before the nightmare started. Jones and Dahria, happy just to forget things for a while, walked and conversed with each other, but Tommy was already thinking about the dead. He couldn't help it. He tried to get it out of his mind because he knew nothing could be done about it yet, anyway. Soon, they could. That gave him some comfort even though he dreaded the actual experience.

They arrived at the cafeteria.

Unfortunately, there was no Alexa.

"Damn," Dahria said.

"Let's eat, then we can go look further," Tommy said.

She nodded.

"Oh my gosh," Dahria moaned, "This is so good!" She was digging into her food and chewed heartily. Appearance didn't matter as she scarfed it down like she hadn't eaten in weeks. She knew her look was goofy, but she just smiled and giggled at them as an overstuffed piece of food fell from her mouth. She picked it up and shoved it back in. Her lips closed around her finger and she pulled it out making a kissing popping sound. The action looked like she was eating a gourmet restaurant dish. Tommy and Jones exchanged curious faces like they have never seen this before from Dahria. They both laughed and continued stuffing their faces.

A healthy belch erupted from Tommy's gut. "More," Tommy grinned. He got up, sauntered into the kitchen to increase his supply of food. Jones looked at Dahria for a moment, smile fading.

"So how're you doing, Ria?"

Jones was a mediator, the go-to when someone was upset and needed an ear or a shoulder.

"Definitely happier now," she nodded. "I just feel bad for everyone who didn't make it." Her eyes shot downcast. "And Alexa…"

"Hey, it's not your fault, And we don't know if she's…" Jones put his hand on hers.

He changed the mood. "Don't worry, you've got your love muffin in the kitchen." He batted his eyelashes while she grew a huge grin and giggled. His facial expressions were difficult to ignore. Jones was his usual self, but in the back of her mind there was a shadow of tragedy.

"Shut up," she said without scorn.

He laughed and got up. "Fine, I need a new drink, anyway. I'm going to join my *other* friend." The fake frustration was funny. He left to get fresh juice from one of the large refrigerators.

As he left, Dahria kept eating her food. She took a slurp of her drink and looked around. No worries at the moment, but she didn't like being alone. It was quiet except for a voice coming from somewhere.

"Dahria!"

Her ears perked up and her head lifted sharply. She stopped eating in the middle of her bite and froze like a statue listening. Could it be?

Was that...Alexa?

The voice came again, "I'm over here!"

Dahria looked behind her and stood up with excitement hearing Alexa's voice.

"Alexa? Where are you?"

"I'm over here!" The sound came from the hall.

"Tommy! Jones! It's Alexa! She's alive!" She called back to the boys.

Dahria ran to see her friend.

49

From a secluded spot, Phoenix watched them eat. The young teenagers looked happy. His heart beat faster and a small wash of endorphins flowed through his body when he saw her, Dahria.

Yeah, that's her, he smiled. He felt an erection coming on as he looked at her, his inner lust activating. He studied the contours of her face. The magnifier glasses made the details easy to discern and appreciate.

They were at the table having a good time eating, talking, and laughing. It almost made him jealous, but his soul was invisible. Instead, anger inflamed him as he watched them having such a good time when they should be upset. The man in shadow wanted fear to be the first thing on their mind. Phoenix wanted people talking about him, fearing him, controlling their thoughts. It was about power. He was going to love getting it back, and get it back for good. Helplessness was an excellent tool and struck deep into hearts and had lasting effects.

Phoenix noticed the obvious boyfriend get up and go into the pantry area, disappearing into the next room. The other guy talked to her and they laughed and joked. She hit him in the arm gently. After a few moments of playful banter, the darker colored kid laughed, stood up, and disappeared into the next room also.

He giggled in his mind with elation. *This just couldn't get easier.* He took his sound thrower and aimed it at a wall behind Dahria. His pre-recordings set to play, he fired them.

"Dahria!" The voice quality was amazing. He played the next lines, and she was visibly excited. Appearing like she couldn't contain herself she ran right toward him. Phoenix laughed a little out loud. He tried not to, but this was just too funny. She came running blindly and he stepped out. She ran right into his arms! It was almost like something meant for them to be together.

Phoenix had one arm around her waist, hand on the small of her back, the other hand straight up to cover her mouth. It was not the proper way to keep someone from yelling, but he couldn't help the desire to feel her pressed against him, even for a second.

"Hi there, sexy thing."

She screamed. It was muffled from his hand, but some sound got through. No big deal.

Phoenix turned her around quickly, and she struggled. She screamed again, and he made sure the knife was out fast.

Right on her throat, she could feel it. Cold. Dahria stopped struggling and screaming, the painful dig of the point of the blade pushing into her throat.

"Shhh," he said into her ear. Her head was right next to his, her back against his stomach and he forced her posture to lean back, making her off balance. He was in full control. His hot breath was uncomfortable in her ear. Her struggling was replaced by trembling. His eyes were on the tunnel ahead of her, waiting. They came running as expected, as planned.

"Hello boys," Phoenix hissed. It was like a serpent hiding in a desert plant. He was calm.

Jones continued to run forward, but Tommy was in front and put his arm out to hold Jones back. He noticed the knife at Dahria's throat. Tommy looked at him holding his helpless girlfriend, then at his eyes. They were sinister, and serious.

Dread enveloped Tommy and a sickening feeling in his stomach stirred. *How'd he escape? Nick and Tim must be dead. Son of a bitch!* Uncanny rage built in his heart, but this killer had bars around him. And Phoenix held the key. Tommy told her he would protect her. He told her he would not let anything happen to her. It was a struggle to keep it bottled up inside.

Neither one of the boys spoke, but Tommy raised his hands to signify that he wouldn't try anything. Tommy glanced at Jones, but he looked more petrified than Tommy was.

Phoenix eyed him and communicated with his evil smile. Tommy saw the intent. The man wanted him to see how vulnerable everyone was. How vulnerable *she* was. He had his girl, and he wanted Tommy to feel helpless. It was the most unpleasant sensation he'd ever felt. Even worse, he feared this was just the beginning.

"You're smarter than you look. Tommy is it?" Phoenix asked.

Tommy said nothing.

The killer nodded, taking that as confirmation.

"I see. I'll take that as a yes. Let's see how much she means to you, shall we?" Phoenix's hand slid from her waist to her breast and grabbed a handful. He held the knife across her neck to maintain control.

Dahria felt the violating grab and sank down and whined. Squeezing her eyes together, she sobbed and tears leaked out.

Tommy's anger was almost beyond control, but he was also frozen from shock. If he did something she would be dead before he could get to her, and the grab was a small price to pay versus her death. He couldn't bear the thought of the future.

"Leave her alone," Tommy knew it wouldn't help.

Phoenix tested Tommy with the grab. *Good, he has some control, this will be entertaining.*

"Aw, don't worry, kid, I'll make sure and take real good care of her. I'm a wonderful date."

"What'd you do with Nick and Kevin?" Tommy asked.

The killer ignored his question and ordered, "You," pointing at Jones with his eyes, "stay here, and you," glaring at Tommy, "slowly walk in front of us." Speaking to Jones again he said, "If I catch you following us, your friend Tommy boy here will be gutted, and she will suffer even worse."

Jones turned pale, which was quite a feat considering his darker color complexion. He looked at Tommy unsure. His mouth opened and jaw dropped, stunned.

Tommy looked back at him and gave a sad nod almost imperceptible. Tommy darted his eyes trying to convey a 'go get help' signal.

Jones caught it and knew better than to nod. All he could do was stare back. Jone's jaw clenched.

"Let's go lover-boy," Phoenix said.

Tommy kept his hands up as he passed them and walked in front.

"Hold on, Dahria." He said as he walked.

"Awe, how cute. Let's see how strong your relationship is. You don't mind if I cut in for a quick dance, do you?"

Tommy's only answer, "Where am I going?" His voice had obvious disgust in it, but it was almost lifeless. He was trying to think of some way to help Dahria. Tommy collected as much information as he could.

"Living quarters of course, E-Block West."

As soon as Tommy was in front and a few paces away, Phoenix reached into her shirt, scrambled under her bra and pinched her nipple. "Giddy up girl!" He said laughing as she involuntarily jolted and released a gasp in disgusted shock. He moved his hand back down to her waist and held her tight. Tommy looked back curious on what he had done. It was excruciating not being able to see anything.

The evil man motioned with his head, "keep looking forward, dude, I'm just grabbing the reins trying to tame this wild beast."

Tommy struggled but obeyed. He walked all the way through the storage room hall and came upon the concrete stairs. They led down to the living cell blocks. He couldn't see behind him, he was helpless. The feeling was immense and terrible, like being tied up and whipped over and over again. Tommy was bouncing thoughts of the situation around in his mind; Run, fight, hide, rush. Every scenario risked Dahria getting hurt or killed. He had to get that knife off of her neck, but how? Tommy remembered she had a small knife, but in this case it would prove useless, unless the right situation presented itself. He thought about some kind of signal or marker he could leave somewhere but the killer was watching him, and Tommy couldn't see anything except what was right before him. He prepared himself for what might come, sexual assault and murder. *No, no, no. He can't do that. I won't let him do that.* For now he would have to obey, like a dog with its master.

"So, have you two done the nasty?" The killer asked in a surprisingly laid back conversation, like a party with a group of friends. "Oh my gosh, I'm sorry. That was so stupid of me. Of course you have. You're young, but not *that* young. Bet she loves the hot stuff, eh'buddy?"

Neither one answered. The only sound was coming from their footsteps and Dahria's sporadic sobbing.

"Dude, aren't you her boyfriend? Aren't you supposed to comfort her? Can't you see she's upset? Tell'er your sorry, tell'er she's gonna be okay." He knew the chords to play, and Phoenix strummed the strings hard enough that they broke in Tommy's heart.

Tommy was stone faced. He was clenching his teeth down hard enough that he could hear the muscles in his ears, but he kept moving. He had to.

Phoenix laughed as Tommy didn't answer, so he switched his attention to her. "And what about you my love? Do you love this guy? Is he your play toy? Do you have room inside for me too? Your heart, I meant your heart. I hope you didn't think…ew, that's disgusting. You don't think this is about sex do you? Oh my gosh. I'd be horrified."

Tommy couldn't take much more of this.

Dahria only answered with extra tears sliding down her face. She tried to collapse, but his grip was strong, and he urged her forward with his hips. Dahria felt his erection pushing her forward. She was so nauseated by the touch that she moved forward to get away from him. That was exactly what he wanted.

"That's enough," Tommy stopped and risked a glance back.

Phoenix stopped and Tommy could see his smile fading. "You just mind your fucking manners," he said with undoubted seriousness. "I'll kill you in a heartbeat and *still* have fun with her."

The killer didn't want to ruin the scene by Tommy mustering up the guts to do something just yet, so he stopped taunting. The entertainment would be flustered, not good.

"Move!" The killer said with force, his playful banter gone.

Tommy didn't move for a second, then he heard a gasp from Dahria. The point of his blade poking harder into her throat. Tommy was reluctant, but he did as he was told. He turned around and kept walking, coming to the first living cell block.

"Right here, go in," Phoenix ordered.

Tommy opened the door and stepped in.

"Walk straight ahead all the way to the wall and face it, keep in sight, don't turn a corner."

Tommy was struggling with helplessness. Sweat accumulated on his body. He knew the horrible assault or murder was closing in. The dreadful conclusion was running them down, like being tied to a train track and the engine almost upon them. He was in a closed room now, nowhere for them to go. He wondered if he should have tried to run for it and get Dahria later or tried to rush and fight him. However, he developed that both scenarios would only end badly. This was horrific to the point of extreme pain in Tommy's head.

"All right my man, let's talk. Turn around," Phoenix said, getting down to business.

Tommy observed him holding Dahria, the blade still shining on her neck. Wet tear lines on her face, like streams. Her eyes squinted, pain from the blade on her neck.

"Have a seat."

Tommy did so without saying a word. He looked at Dahria. She looked as worn out as an old pair of shoes, the previous energy depleted. She couldn't put up a fight even if she wanted to. He looked into the killer's eyes. Phoenix was a solid man, strong, trained, Tommy was a mere teen, a kid. He was smart enough to know he didn't have a chance with an aware trained opponent. The last thing in the world Tommy thought he would do was obey, but that was his only choice.

"Wow, you're doing great kid, I must say," Phoenix said with approval. "I hope you find this next part as pleasurable as I do, but before we get down to business, let me assure you that I am very good at what I do. Stay in that chair, or the last thing you'll see will be her life spill out in the color of red."

Where's Jones? Please let him get help. Tommy was desperate.

50

Blood dripped down the open gash at Jake's zygoma facial area. The punch hurt and he winced in pain. Jake looked at Nick with anger, but understood where this was coming from. He couldn't blame him, but needed to release the information. His mouth was taped so the only sound that escaped was a muffled bunch of humming.

God damn it! Jake managed to think through a pounding headache. He was too focused on finding Kevin to be fully aware of his surroundings.

"That's for John!" Nick said as he punched Jake one more time, hard. "And *that* is for everyone else you killed in here. Just wait for me to get started on Theod."

Jake struggled against the tape, but couldn't gain any leeway. He had to take it. Jake was thinking of how ironic the situation became. He turned sides against the company and was now trying to help this guy as he was beating the shit out of him. However, Jake *was* a killer here, and he killed. Those two facts pounded in his head harder than the punches.

I deserve this, he looked at Nick with an invitation. *Go ahead asshole, punch again.*

Kevin observed, but was afraid of restraining Nick. He looked like he could turn on Kevin with rage. Kevin knew

Nick's bad temperament and the situation was going to happen if Kevin wanted it to or not.

Nick took out Jake's knife and held it to show him. He had fury in his eyes.

"Nick, hold on." Kevin had to do something. He couldn't let him just kill someone even if they deserve it. Kevin had questions and everyone needed answers. This was not Nick's decision.

Nick stopped and looked at Kevin as if he were a traitor. A look of 'how dare you stop me,' was written all over his face.

Kevin continued nervously before Nick could correlate anything, "Now just hear me out for a second. We don't have the right to decide what happens to him. I can't let you do this. We *need* him."

Jake looked at Kevin with distraught eyes. He was weak and looked apologetic.

Nick lowered his bloodied fist and then wiped it on Jake's shirt without being gentle.

"It won't change anything. This guy is a cold-blooded killer." Nick looked at Jake. "He deserves to die."

"Maybe he does, but not *yet*."

After a moment of staring at the pathetic Jake, he scoffed, but backed away and let Kevin proceed.

Kevin walked closer and looked into Jakes eyes. He saw the restraints, and they seemed to be holding just fine. Jake was breathing heavily through his nose. Kevin couldn't help having mixed feelings about him. He was disgusted on one side, but felt pity on the other. Kevin saw a helpless man. He wouldn't partake in hurting him. Kevin peeled off the tape over Jake's mouth.

"I'm sorry Kevin," he said. "I really am. I...I've been lied to." He was talking slowly, but had a genuine conviction.

Kevin discerned Jake seemed regretful, but he still didn't trust him. He witnessed a brutal murder, and he would never forget that. Kevin glanced at Nick. He was sitting on the ground with his back on the wall not interested in the conversation and playing with the knife.

"So, is your name really Jake?" Kevin asked questions, opening an easy dialogue.

He sighed and pursed his lips together and then nodded, "Yeah." His soft voice was drained of energy.

"So what's going on? You were looking for me...to kill me?"

Jake shook his head. "No, I was coming to help you. I know how that sounds, believe me, but the fact remains. You're in danger...still."

"What do you mean?"

Jake's head lolled a little and then he mustered up the energy to talk. "There's another killer. A sick, perverted, cold, remorseless killer. He thrives on the hurt and loves to torture people. He was coming right for you."

Kevin was skeptical, but it still gave him chills and he glanced in both directions of the tunnel checking them.

Nothing.

Jake observed him and said, "I know, this looks bad, but the guy must have gone somewhere to take care of his wound."

"His wound?"

"We fought. He's as trained as I am, but crazy. I was able to get in a stab, but he got me in the gut."

"Yeah, *you* got *me* too," Kevin added.

Jake rolled his eyes and sighed. "I know Kevin, but you've got to believe me. You're all in trouble, and if I am the only highly trained man here besides that killer...and I'm all tied up...we're *all* sitting ducks." Jake let that sink in. He knew Kevin was smart, but didn't know if he could persuade him, much less the others. Jake knew of certain information about this place, but realized he had to keep some of it confidential. Otherwise, he feared the company might get involved and just stop the game. That meant an extermination. Jake was becoming a liability now, but he thought the company might have planned for this scenario, anyway. What did matter was

Jake and the rest of the people would still be hunted by
Phoenix. It only upped the stakes of the game, and Jake knew
it. He could only regurgitate information on an as needed
basis. Right now he was alluding to saving these people and
killing Phoenix.

"I don't know how I can trust you," Kevin admitted.
"You say all this, but the second we turn our backs…"

"There's more," he cut him off. Kevin glared at him,
"you're in a game, Kevin."

Kevin stared at him for a long time processing the
information. He frowned, confused.

"I know why you can't remember the past very well. I
know what they told you about why you're down here. The
earth was at war. Countries were attacked, the atmosphere
was destroyed, and radiation levels grew to an uninhabitable
degree." Jake could see the awareness on Kevin's face like it
all started to make sense.

"Holy…" Kevin was lost in his own mind. A few lost
memories appeared. Images and information started to
become more clear.

"Enough of this shit!" Nick's anger was fierce, and he
rushed over with the knife. It was obvious he was listening
from afar. "He is filling your head with garbage!"

Kevin wasn't so sure, but he knew enough to stop Nick.
Jake was too important. "No, Nick, stop!" Kevin stepped in
front of Nick and held his hands up. "You can't do this."

Nick had rage in his eyes, "Get outta my way!"

Kevin didn't move. "Are you gonna kill me too?"

"I can't believe you're sticking up for this killer, traitor!"
Nick was infuriated and added, "You're just as bad as he is,
you piece of shit!" Without a warning Nick pushed Kevin
into the office hard.

Kevin grabbed his shoulder as he hit the rear wall in pain.
"Arghh!" He yelled.

Nick quickly closed the door and pulled up a chair and
jimmied it under the handle to lock them in.

"Wait! Nick!" Kevin screamed. "You can't just leave us in here!" He tried to push on the door but it wouldn't budge.

"I think you two are made for each other! I'm gonna find the others and then we'll decide what to do with both of you!" Nick stormed off.

Kevin watched him leave then glanced around the small office.

There were walls with glass on the upper portions in the front, and only one solid door, opening outward.

"Don't worry man, this is in no way permanent," Jake eased. "The glass might be very hard to break, but..." his eyes moved up and viewed the ceiling.

As a response, Kevin followed his gaze up. He smiled. "Of course," he said, feeling better about the situation. "That should be pretty easy."

Kevin stared at Jake with skepticism and thought longer.

After a few moments, he made up his mind and unraveled the tape. He was nervous, but it seemed like the only way.

As Kevin unraveled his legs, Jake grabbed his own wrists and ankles and rubbed them. He grabbed Kevin's shoulder and looked directly into his eyes. "Thanks. I'll make sure you won't regret it."

Kevin felt some relief. Jake was free and didn't attack him. He nodded. Trust would have to be earned, but the action was at least a good start.

"All right, come on. We've gotta get out of here," Jake said.

"You're pretty beat up, are you going to be okay?"

"Yeah, it hurts, but I'll be fine. Pains just in the head," Jake said, not meaning for it to be an attempt at humor.

Jake looked up, then around the office. There wasn't much furniture except a desk and a couple chairs. Stacking them on top of each other on the desk, Jake could reach the ceiling. With a grunt of pain, he lifted himself up with Kevins help then helped Kevin.

On the rafters it was a tight area, but they only needed to cross the wall and then they could drop down.

In the hall Jake said, "I need to get to the medical center. Do you know where your people are?" asked Jake.

Kevin shook his head truthfully, "No, I was with Townsend and Theo…" He stopped.

"I'm sorry," Jake said. He changed the subject, "Townsend did you say?"

"Yeah, do you know him?" Kevin asked, then paused, thinking.

Jake stared.

"I suppose you do, guess he's working with you." Kevin realized the bastard must've left him alone with Jake on purpose, to be hunted and killed.

"I'm sorry again," Jake responded. "This place is more than just a maze of tunnels."

Kevin asked a hard question, "Is anyone else in on this game? Who's responsible for this?"

"My mind was cloudy at first, but I've had time to sort through information, and a lot came back. I think I may have been…worked on too. Trust me when I say this Kevin, right now you're better off *not* knowing."

"So there *is* someone else in on it." He couldn't imagine who it might be.

Jake sighed. He owed it to Kevin, but what could he say, what was safe?

"There is one that I know of. One who is a *real* threat," Jake said. "He is a hunter, a killer. Skilled in the human anatomy and tactics, hired by the company to make revenue for them. His name's Phoenix."

"How do you know that?"

He looked at him with knowledge as Jake remembered, "cause even before I fought him…I met him."

51

Jones was conflicted. He couldn't follow them, what the heck could he do? He couldn't fight the man, he had too much advantage. Jones needed to get help.

Watching in horror, the three disappeared down the dim hall heading toward storage room A. Beyond that were the stairs to the living cell blocks. The south operations hall was the last spot Jones remembered Damon and John were. "Shit!" he yelled. South operations was far. Jones turned around and ran. Through the halls, centers, darting around obstacles, Jones bolted into the south hall.

"Damon! John! Where are you guys?"

"Holy sh…!" Damon jumped in surprise from his previous uneventful situation. "Damn, kid!"

"Damon! Tommy and Dahria are in trouble! Hurry!"

John opened his eyes and sat up with an effort. He was feeling better, but still had a dull pain in his head.

"Slow down, kid. Where are they?" asked John.

"Over in the north end of the cafeteria! This guy took'em. Kidnapped. The killer! They went down the hall to the living cells!" His voice was frantic.

John was taken aback. "I thought Kevin and Nick taped him up?"

"He must have escaped!" Jones concluded.

"Shit!" Damon said, his eyes grew worried.

"Damn! What happened to Nick and Kevin?" John gave them a moment of thought before he turned his attention to the immediate problem. "Okay, let's stay calm," John said. "Is there anything else?" He was trying to approach this situation with care. More information meant a better chance of helping. He wondered if he had time to check the terminal for Dean's help.

"Let's get on a terminal and see if…"

"He's got a knife to her throat! I don't know what he's gonna do! Come on!"

John looked at Damon. He had a distressed look written on his face. John thought about his brother, but time was precious, he had to help the two kids. His headache throbbed, but he focused.

"Dammit!" Damon cursed. He didn't like the situation one bit.

"All right," John continued. "Let's find something we can use. Damon." John stared at him for help. "Hurry!"

Damon thought for a few seconds and it made Jones infuriated.

"We can't wait around all day, dude!" Jones spat.

Damon turned toward him and said, "You're not helping! I am stressed enough!" He fumbled around through drawers and cabinets. Nothing but a couple of ceramic mugs. He sighed.

"Perhaps I can help." A voice offered. It echoed from one of the four entrances in the room. It was a commanding solid voice, Townsend.

A GAME OF RED

52

Tommy's heart beat fast. Phoenix closed the door behind him with his foot. He had control of her the entire time and his eyes fixated and focused on Tommy. He brought out zip ties and laid them down on the table.

"Grab the handles, sweet thing" he ordered.

Dahria looked at the handles and zip ties on the table.

Once she's cuffed, it's all over! Seeing his only chance, Tommy rushed him! He was lightning fast being so young, but Phoenix was too many steps away.

Phoenix was ready for the charge like he was expecting it. He was unbelievably fast and kicked Dahria behind the knee to fold her legs. She fell. The hilt of her small knife exposed as her pant leg crumpled up. Phoenix handled Tommy with ease, using Tommy's own momentum to sidestep him. In turn, he gave Tommy an extra push and accelerated him.

Ramming into the wall, stunned him.

Phoenix strolled over to Tommy with his knife before he could recover.

"No!" Dahria yelled fearful of his death. The knife found its way into her hand, she held it tight.

Phoenix didn't even acknowledge her. "Nice spirit kid!" He had Tommy's arm bent up behind his back. His knife at Tommys neck, he said "but let's not ruin my game just yet."

He gave Tommy a hard punch in the kidney and threw him back toward the chair.

Tommy stumbled then fell and rolled onto his knees. It hurt.

Phoenix shifted his attention back on Dahria, who was still on the ground. She lunged at him with her small knife. Dahria was trying for an abdomen or groin stab, but she was no trained specialist. It was clumsy.

"Wow," he said surprised, deflecting and disarming her in one smooth motion. "I'm impressed."

Phoenix grabbed her with lightning speed again, stood her up, and pushed her face on the table. She let out a painful sound as he slammed her into the wood. His weight bore down on her. While Phoenix had both of them stunned, he cuffed her hands to the handles that were screwed to the table.

Dahria was shaking. Her top half was resting on the table, but her legs stood on the floor. Her chance of escape, gone.

Phoenix ripped her pants and dropped her panties. "Wow!" He said gazing at her private area, then walked over to Tommy.

She tried to get up but the zip ties held her bent over the table. Tommy was on the floor fumbling to get up.

"What do you think of that?" Phoenix said.

"Fuck you!" Tommy returned.

"Oh really?" he asked in astonishment. "I intend to. Well, *her* I mean." He scoffed. "Don't make me kill you first. Think about it, then what? She lives without you. Wouldn't you rather be back together? People screw all the time, don't worry about it." Phoenix man-handled Tommy back into the chair.

"You're going to kill us anyway," Tommy countered. "I know what you are, and I know what's happening. Don't do it."

He was a killer, and a rapist. And it was a place of torture. The reality of life could be precarious.

Phoenix walked over to her naked rear end. Then, he stopped and listened.

Every second was like torture for Tommy, watching the guy listen to what seemed like silence. He observed the man in shadow turn his head slightly, silent. He then turned around and looked hard at Tommy. His face was angry. Tommy could see his jaw bruxing. "I'll see you *both* again." The voice wreaked of rancid hatred.

Without warning, Phoenix exited the living cell.

53

Alexa's strength crept into her limbs one small particle at a time. Her muscle movement came back and the fine motor skills faded into control. Her mind processed thoughts as the fog rolled away. Amazed that she made it so far unscathed, she grabbed some food and water from the cafeteria. She knew the place well. Noticing there was food on a table near the entrance to the kitchen, it was messy. *Someone was here just a little while ago.* While it caught her attention as peculiar, it wasn't of grave importance right now. She felt like she just finished swimming in a sewer. Alexa was desperate to get clean. Her memory of what happened was like a nightmare, however foggy. Alexa was helpless against it, used like a piece of meat. She surprised herself by feeling angry instead of embarrassed. Alexa wanted to capture this man, make him pay, make sure he didn't do this to anyone else. A little ball of fire grew in the pit of her stomach. Every thought seemed to spit lighter fluid on it, making the fire immense and hot.

She started walking and as she rounded the hall just before the stairs to the living cells, she had an immediate sinking feeling. A dark hand coldly touched her heart. She froze, listening. It was like a shadow of a spirit moved through her body, leaving it frozen to the bone. Chills electrified her and she shook.

After a few moments, the sensation passed and she came upon her living cell. She peered into the small slit in the steel door. Unable to see inside due to the dark, she listened. Her breath was the only sound, so she held it.

No sound.

She opened the door being as quiet as she could. The door itself was clunky so the word 'quiet' was not in the door's vocabulary. Not overly loud, it grinded open from metal on metal contact. She glanced in both directions of the cell hallway.

Empty. She stepped in quietly. A motion activated light flicked a few times and then stayed on. It shined in the room, enough to see everything in a dim light, except the washroom. She hit the main light and checked the washroom before closing the door. Clear. Closing the door she put the bar over the latch to lock it. The locks were clumsy, but if anyone tampered with it, it was loud like an alarm and would alert her if anyone messed with it.

She took her time in the washroom. Alexa stared at herself in the scratched and damaged mirror. Her eyes moved towards the glistening necklace still around her neck. She broke down and sobbed, losing control. The intensity of the situation pounded in her head.

Putting her hand over her mouth, the emotions leaked out like a broken rubber seal on a pressurized oil cylinder. Alexa grabbed the necklace and wanted to rip it off and throw it away, yet something made her stop the action. She relaxed her grip and gazed at herself in the mirror again. This time her face showed more courage. A determination. She stared at the necklace. It sparkled and was elegant. It was a memento, a reminder of control. Part of her now, Alexa would keep it as a symbol, a stand against herself, a show of bravery against fear.

After a few minutes she washed vigorously. While it felt refreshing, there seemed to be filth that would not wash off, like metal with caked-on grime that hardened over years. The wound would eventually heal, but the scar would last forever.

Alexa finished and got dressed into some new clothes. She brushed her hair and stared at herself for another long moment. Tears rolled down, and her image revealed a broken woman. This enraged her even more.

I will not be like this! She was angry, determined. *I will not let him do this!*

"I'm better than this!" she told the mirror image, wanting to hear herself. Her thoughts of the events fueled her anger. She made her tears stop flowing. Wiping them away and breathing in deeply, she exhaled with a new look on her face, fortitude, courage. Her face turned to stone. Her eyes turned almost evil.

"I'm going to get you," she said. The calm and devious manner made her feel powerful, "And when I do, I'll make you play *my* game." She looked deep into her own eyes. The smile erased from existence, she didn't know this person she was now looking at. She knew she would never be the same again. It scared and excited her at the same time.

54

Dean was looking at the image of the man looking back at him shocked. After waving and asking him if he could see him, the man's face contorted into anger like he was caught doing something wrong. The image blurred for a moment, fuzzed, and became black. Dean was taken aback.

"Why the hell'd you do that?" He wondered. Then Dean thought it possible this guy might be in on it somehow. That was the only obvious conclusion. Tucking that into his mind, he noticed his eyes were dry. Every time he blinked it felt like pebbles were rolling around in them. He had been looking at screens for over fourteen hours. Dean was able to find many useful details about what was happening, but he needed to dig further into other files. Dean also needed further access, but that wasn't easy.

He needed a little rest, allowing only fifteen minutes before he got back to work.

Afterwards, he targeted an employee and followed her. She was wearing formal clothes and did not have an id. That meant she should have access to the documents he needed. Dean was an expert at being invisible. He watched and studied. Following her to an office, obviously hers, with a computer terminal. He watched.

Sometime later, she left. Making sure not to draw attention, Dean pretended his work continued in her office. To an outside wondering eye, if any were around, it looked normal. Dean tried to keep everything as discreet as possible. He took out a Nano splicer and placed it close to the screen, but in an inconspicuous spot, hoping no one would see it. A few moments later he left the office.

He went to his previous secluded terminal, got his pistol pieces out, ditched the cane, and assembled the Sig Sauer. He tucked it into his back waistband concealing it.

Logging onto the terminal he viewed his Nano-splicer in the woman's office. As of right now, it was clear. He had to keep watch until she logged back on.

55

"You're alive?" Damon looked at Townsend shocked. "Where have you been?"

"I've been coming up with a plan."

Jones was shaking with urgency. "Come on! We've got to help Tommy and Ria!"

Townsend turned toward Jones with a concerned face. It was hard to read with the rough texture and few scars, but Jones could see it. "Tell me everything. Where are they now?"

"I'm not sure exactly where they're going, but they were headed toward the living cells."

"Do you know which side, east or west?" Townsend asked.

Jones shook his head, he couldn't answer that. "He said if I followed them, he'd kill them."

"Okay, nice work getting here," Townsend said.

"Let's get back there and help," John said.

"Not yet," Townsend contradicted, gaining questioning looks on their faces. Jones was flabbergasted, but before anyone could protest, he said, "I've found something that may help us. Since you don't know the exact location of where they're heading, I think I can pinpoint it. That'll get us there faster."

Questioning faces turned into confusion.

Wasting no time he jerked his head in one direction, "This way."

Townsend led them through tunnels in the general direction of the command center. Once there, Townsend picked one of the few small offices. Townsend entered first. It was a small room with a door sealing it. Inside, there was a desk, a terminal, a few chairs, cabinets, sink, and a small couch. It looked like a tiny apartment for one person. John and Damon looked around amazed at the luxuries.

"Wow," said John with envy.

"Geez," replied Damon, upset he didn't have a room like this.

Never seen the office before, John grew a larger respect concerning how big this complex really was. He understood why. It made the game better.

Townsend stood at the terminal while Damon eyed the couch. Jones was up on Townsend's side eager for him to move faster. After the terminal flashed on, Townsend opened video feeds. They displayed halls and tunnels. Empty.

"What the?" Jones asked.

Damons attention was ripped from the couch to the screen. Jones and John looked at each other.

"Holy shit," John said, "We can see everywhere."

Townsend opened several more feeds. "Here. Look." He pointed and moved out of the way.

Jones, Damon, and John moved closer to the screen to get a better look. They saw many tunnels, centers, and other areas.

"Ugh," Jones said and winced as he saw many deceased people lying around.

John asked Townsend. "How long have you known about these cam…!"

Slam!

Bump, bump, bump. The sounds echoed so loud all three of them jumped.

Jones and Damon looked back like someone punched them in the jaw. John was quicker and ran towards the door as he realized what was happening.

"That son of a bitch!" John yelled. Before he could reach the door, the wheel spun to its end. John grabbed it and tried to turn it the opposite way. By that time, Jones recovered from the intense images and ran toward the door to help John. They both grunted, but it didn't budge. It felt like it was welded together.

"God damn it!" John added. He sank his head and ground his teeth. "Townsend! You son of a bitch!"

Jones didn't know what to say. He couldn't believe what was happening. "What the hell's going on? Townsend?" He looked at John.

John said to himself, "I can't believe I fell for it. Fuck."

"You've got to be shit'n me!" Jones said. He glanced over at Damon. "Is *he* the killer?"

Damon stood back up, regret in his eyes. He took his hand and combed his brown hair with his hand. He sighed and nodded, "He's been watching us this whole time."

Jones' eyes grew wide for a moment then turned to anger fast. "No!" he yelled as he kicked the door several times. "Ahh!" Jones slammed into the door with all his weight. The door replied with apathy.

"Calm down kid," John said with an understanding tone. "That won't do any good."

Jones was smart enough to know John was right. He looked at him with worried yet hungry eyes. "What're we going to do? My friends are..." he choked. The thought of what happened to them ate at him.

"I know," John replied. "I'm sorry kid." He didn't have an answer yet.

"John. Did he kill them?" Jones just didn't have it in him to go back to the terminal and look.

John went over the screen, but it had already timed out and was black. "I'm sorry kid."

"We have to figure out a way to get out of here." Damon said, but no one was listening anymore.

Tommy, Dahria. Jones closed his eyes. He blinked away two frustrated tears that formed. He locked Townsend away in the back of his head. The respect and high pedestal disappeared, hidden behind anger. A new thought appeared, *If Townsend's in on it, who else is?* He looked at John and then Damon. How could he trust anyone anymore?

56

Tommy hugged Dahria. She was sobbing, her head buried in his shoulder. He was able to struggle out of the binds. Neither of them spoke, but both of them thought about what *almost* just happened.

"I'm so sorry baby" Tommy whispered in her ear. He caressed her hair and held her. Tommy couldn't help but think of his deteriorated security of how Dahria might feel in his arms now.

"He almost, he almost..." She was choked up.

He pulled her head up, imagining the emotions of embarrassment, and whatever more, but they had to get moving.

"I know. I know babe, but look at me. I'm sorry, but let's remember that nothing happened...you're okay. We got lucky." he said. His thumb wiped away a gathering tear under her eye. His touch helped her gaze connect into his.

Dahria nodded her head. Emotions leaked out. "I felt so helpless."

"Me too, me too. I just hope you can feel safe again." Without wasting too much time, Tommy urged, "Honey, we've gotta get out of here. It might not be over, he knows where we are."

"What do you think happened?"

"I don't know. It looked like he heard something, but who cares. Just glad he left when he did. We've got to find the others and do what it takes to hunt this guy down, together with everyone," Tommy said, trying to show strength, but a tear gained enough weight to slide down his cheek. Turning his head, he wiped it away fast. She didn't see it.

57

What was that? Alexa listened, pulling herself away from the mirror, her heart rate increased. The sound seemed real. Was it? She listened to verify the sound again Nothing. She forced her breathing to slow down and her heart rate followed suit.

Searching around the room to find anything she could use, she spotted something. Her smile, evil on her face, found the object and took it. She turned a chair on its side and kicked the leg down as hard as she could. The leg snapped. Irregular splintered wood and a jagged edge appeared to be a good stabbing weapon. It was obvious she needed help, and the others would need hers. She refused to be helpless ever again. Alexa would protect herself, to the death.

She gathered her wits and opened the door of the living cell. Alexa's face froze as she noticed another living cell down the hall open at the same time.

Oh shit! That's the sound I heard! Alexa was rethinking how brave she thought she was. She used the memories to give her strength, but it also gave her fear. Gritting her teeth, she continued to watch a figure emerge. The person was careful, peering into the hallway and the face turned toward her for a second.

Alexa's heart stopped.

A rush of relief washed through her body as she recognized Tommy. He was far down the hall, but his distinct features were unmistakable. She noticed another figure peek out right after.

In her flushed excitement, Alexa forgot about being careful and opened the door to call down the hall. "Dahria! Tommy!"

Dahria screamed!

"Dahria, I'm over here!" Alexa stepped out through the door.

Recalling the phrases from the rapist's trap, Dahria bolted down the hallway in the opposite direction!

Tommy, confused, chased her.

Alexa was *beyond* confused. *What the hell?* "Hey! Where are you guys going? It's me, Alexa!" She ran after them. "Wait!"

Tommy didn't know what was happening. Dahria was running full speed away. "Dahria, wait, what's wrong?"

"It's him! He said that before!"

"What?" Tommy asked.

"Just come on Tommy!" She was crazed in her determination.

She didn't wait for him. He continued to run after her.

---#---

His laugh was loud. "Oh my God. This is too fucking funny!" Slobber along with a few wet pieces of food exited his mouth and fell on his shirt. He flicked it off with his fingers.

Another bunch of chuckles saturated the speakers.

"Can you believe it?" One player asked in awe.

"Damn, that dude knows how to play a game!"

The players were watching the humorous fleeing of Tommy and Dahria running from their own friend Alexa on their screens. They placed more bets on how long it would take them to realize it was Alexa. After a short time they watched the hilarious scenario play out. It was a great time, and the champion of the bet accepted his winnings graciously.

"That's right, fuckers," he said.

58

Nick was furious. *Fucking idiots.* He left Kevin and Jake locked in the office and was heading back to the medical center. His feelings against Jake were immense, and he thought Kevin had now turned against them. Nick needed to bring these two to justice. Kill them. He squeezed his knife tight. His mind was swimming with thoughts that were jumbled together. He couldn't think clearly anymore and he became lightheaded. After going through the medical center, he was pissed that no one was there. The next place he thought to check was the living cells. It took a handful of minutes to reach it.

"Yo! Damon! John!"

No answer. *Urgh! Where is everyone?*

The walls were closing in like he just realized he was alone. His breathing quickened, and he backed up into the wall and slid down it into a crouching position. He brought his hands up to his face and pressed his palms against his eyes trying to make them clear. The tunnel seemed to grow darker. Panic crept into him as his thoughts turned as dark as the tunnel seemed. His heart beat faster.

"Okay, okay," he said to himself in gasps. "Take it easy, take it easy. You'll figure this out." Nick closed his eyes and rested his head back against the wall. Feeling like he was on a roller coaster ride, he calmed his breathing and slowed his heart rate down. Letting his legs slide out into a full sitting position, he continued to breathe deeply. Shaking his head, he glanced around again. Still light-headed, the walls faded back to normal. A small sense of relief presented itself.

Sitting a few minutes longer to release pressure on some nerves, he struggled to get back up and continued to the first door of the living cells. He opened the door with a grinding metal sound.

"God damn it!" he cursed out loud, banging on the door. Nick felt a cold prickle on his back, like an open window on a house in the winter. It gave him chills, and he turned around with his knife erect and realized he was not alone.

"Hi there," a soothing voice came from a shadow off in the corner.

Nick squinted, having trouble seeing any definition in the figure. The man stood in the dark, enjoying the moment.

Calm.

Nick didn't know what to think, but one impossible thought entered his mind, *Jake?*

"It's all right man. You don't know me, I've been hiding from this maniac who's been killing people. You sure did make a lot of noise. *Anyone* could hear you coming." the man said. "Say, that's a nice knife."

Not Jake. "Who are you?" Nick asked.

"I'm Phoenix…and you interrupted my…meditation."

59

A little boy looked out the bay window watching the wet rain falling on the scenery. A beautiful sight, an extravagant house, but the boy liked the rain.

His parents named him Phoenix. He watched the trees sway back and forth from the breath of the wind. The clouds, gray and dark, covered the sky to hide all blue. He wondered if a tree might break, or the turbulence might overwhelm a flying bird to crash into an obstacle. He wanted *something* to happen. Anything for entertainment. Something to swerve the normal expected events of everyday life.

He observed the water streak down the window and studied them like a scientist, curious. Pondering thoughts of reality, life, and purpose, he came to the conclusion that in the grand scheme of things, not much mattered.

One day I will pass on and die. So what? We all die? Even renowned people are long forgotten compared to space-time. People are only contributing to life for a hundred years or so. Legacies might span generations longer, but it's not likely to last much beyond that. A million years? The universe blinks in a million years, insignificant time for time itself. There is no memory of existence when there is no-one to remember.

So, if every living thing dies, what am I going to do to live?

He had a special gift, a wondrous mind. Schooling wasn't tough for him, but social acceptance was a different story. It was hard to relate. An outcast, he kept to himself, but that was the way he liked it. He didn't feel a need to be accepted, or praised. Phoenix praised himself.

The front door opened. Phoenix turned his head with intrigue. His mom walked in with her usual expensive clothes and high heels making loud clicking noises on the tile floor. Her umbrella dripped with rain water as she folded it up.

"Hi mom," he said, being polite. Phoenix walked up to give her the usual hug. He loved it and buried his face in her expensive breasts. She hugged back curling her arms around him.

"And how is my munchkin today?" She asked.

"Mom, stop with the munchkin thing, I'm eleven," he pulled his head out and looked at her with a frown.

"Okay, okay, fine," she replied laughing letting him go. "What'cha doing today?"

"Just watching the rain from the window. I love it."

"I know you do. I hate the rain," she had a sense of frustration, "It just complicates everything. Makes everything wet."

Phoenix just smiled.

"All right Nix, I've got to go change. Be back in a little bit" She gave a loving rub to his light and fluffy hair as she left.

When she went up the stairs, Phoenix went to his technology. He switched on the device and observed his mom walk into her bedroom upstairs. She took off her clothes. His eyes watched carefully and he could feel a small tingling feeling in his chest. She undid her bra and the tingling feeling went into his groin. Mesmerized by her shape and movement, her breasts moved and bounced with elegance. Phoenix focused on the darker red center medallions. The sensations vibrated more.

The female body fascinated him. And his mother bought her body. Someone sculpted this, it was science, art.

A few years passed and on one sparkling day, Phoenix noticed a girl walking toward him at Randscend Park on an early Sunday afternoon. He had been watching her pattern for some time. On a particular day she went for a walk with her dog, alone. Sometimes she had her older brother with her. He was large and muscular. Perhaps eighteen, he looked like a flag-ball player. It was the perfect time, her brother was not around. A beautiful day, sun shining, a cool breeze flipped his hair around. Lots of people were coming and going, completing their own agendas. Most of them were either watching their kids play, or passing by.

Phoenix thought the girl was beautiful, and she was around his age, perhaps a year or two younger. Phoenix walked over to her with confidence and looked into her eyes to make sure she knew he was giving her attention. Phoenix smiled, she returned it being polite. As she came closer, he drifted his attention to the dog.

"You have a beautiful dog," he said with benevolence. "What kind is it?"

She laughed and replied, "Thanks. She's a terrier."

"Can I pet her?"

"Sure."

"Hey there girl," he let the dog sniff his hands for a moment before showing his love. Of course, he didn't love the dog at all, but that wasn't the point...*she* did. He knew how to use her passion. After a short time, he learned her name was Stephanie.

It seemed to Phoenix that they had a lot in common, she was a nice girl which was interesting to him. Something unexpected happened that Phoenix was unprepared for. He made a genuine connection, and he liked it.

---#---

The next several months were more challenging than Phoenix thought. At first, he had real feelings for her. These confused him, but he quickly learned it was too much work to get what he wanted. He wanted to touch her, have sex with her, just like in the videos he'd watched and studied, but Stephanie wasn't into that. He learned that patience went a long way with her as they kissed and hugged. Phoenix knew she liked him, but she was reluctant to go any further. She allowed him to touch her with clothes on, but he wanted more. He *had* to have more.

Late one night, the surprise came when they were laying out in a deserted shack one night sneaking around without their parents permission. Passion seemed to be more intense than usual that time. Phoenix's hands were inside her shirt feeling the silky skin on her back. He loved it, but he wanted more. His heart beat uncontrollably, his mind hard to control. He wanted her breasts. Her *bare* breasts. Phoenix had to do it. As his hands were moving along her back, he moved over the bra strap. It took him less than a second to undo it with one hand, the practice on his mother's bras paying off. The straps shot to both sides of her back. Phoenix was prepared for resistance. It surprised him she let out a soft moan to let him know she liked it. His heart beat faster as she offered her mound. He couldn't believe it. His mind was flashing with green lights, go, go go! Her breasts were amazing. He caressed the soft yet firm round contour and found the hard center. She moaned and kissed him harder. His erection was full force, almost bursting with excitement. That was his moment, his freedom for passion! A ticket to manhood! Phoenix was walking among the clouds from the release of endorphins.

"What the fuck!" A bright flashlight shined on them.

Stephanie was shocked and embarrassed, pulling away from him, but Phoenix had other emotions. He was beyond angry from the interruption. It was impossible to make out who it was with the light shining on their faces, so Phoenix lifted his hand to shadow his eyes.

"What the hell do you two think you're doing!"

Stephanie recognized the voice. "Roy?" She asked to verify.

"Get up Sis! Go home!" He came over and yanked her up by the arm. That was when Phoenix realized that Roy was not alone. Two more boys were there. Phoenix could see their shadows. They were giggling.

"Ouch, Roy! You're hurting me!" Stephanie shouted.

"Just shut up and go home!" Roy wasn't smiling. "I'm going to have a whirlwind with this moron!"

Phoenix, beyond pissed, was not smiling either.

"What? No, don't hurt him, it's not his fault!" she knew what would happen, she knew her brother. Stephanie struggled in Roy's grasp but he was too big and strong.

Roy swung her with force into one of the other boys, "Hold her!"

One of Roy's friends grabbed her in a bear hug doing as he was told.

Phoenix had evil in his eyes. These guys stopped him from his passion, his goal, his game. He stared. It was ominous.

"Look at him," one of them said, "It's like he's meditating."

They laughed.

Fighting with all he had, the ass kicking was brutal and Phoenix was on the bloodied and battered end.

You motherfucker, he thought. The occurrence prompted Phoenix with an obvious new goal. He would make sure that would never happen again. Breathing heavily, his anger made the pain a little better. He could taste blood in his mouth, it was like pure fuel for him. Phoenix struggled to get up, but could not stand straight. He grabbed his ribs with his hand and stumbled the distance home.

---#---

Eight months later, Phoenix acquired skills in physical combat, knife skills which turned out to be assassination skills, and firearm skills. Access to media was easy for anyone, but only practice and dedication made the difference for professionals.

At this point, he was confident he could attack someone in surprise, or even defend himself in most common situations.

It was time. He secretly kept in touch with Stephanie, but wasn't ready until now to get back with her.

He looked into the mirror at himself. "All right, Mr. Roy," he smiled to himself, "Let's see how you do *this* time.

He made the connection.

"I can't wait to see you, Nix!" She said with excitement. Her round face on the screen was inviting. Some of her hair was in front of one eye, making her more attractive, like a hidden treasure locked in a chest that he had to open.

"Me too." The reply vibrated out the speaker from the device.

They got together, and the experience was invigorating! There were no interruptions this time. They lay together for some time after, enjoying each other's company.

I did it, He was happy. *That was amazing. I'm a man now! Time for round two!*

She was pleasantly surprised.

---#---

A short time passed, and the relationship was announced to both parents. Phoenix was going on seventeen and didn't want to hide it anymore.

Roy fumed and took it personally. Stephanie's parents were extremely against it.

227

"He's kinda strange," her mother said to her when they were alone.

She looked at her mother with wide eyes. "He's not strange! He's very smart, mom. It just takes time to get to know him. He's nice to me and I love him!"

She looked at Stephanie with sympathy but concern, "What? You don't even know what love is! Something's off Stephanie. I don't want you to see him!"

She was keeping the truth from her family. If they knew they were being intimate for many months, her family would ignite TNT.

"You're being so unfair!" She twirled her body around and paraded out of the room.

"Stephanie!" her mom called out.

No response.

Her mother sighed but decided to let it go for now. She would need the help of her husband.

The next several months Phoenix kept up with the relationship, going past Stephanie's parents' refusal. However, things started to change. Phoenix wanted more. He wanted her down on her knees, from behind, and other positions that were strange and aggressive to her. Their relationship became strained.

"Come on babe," Phoenix prodded, "Let's just try it."

"No," she said firmly. There was no need in her mind. It was just fine the way it was.

Phoenix became frustrated and angry and turned to leave.

Stephanie was tearing up. She didn't want him to leave, she loved him, but she hadn't seen this side of him before. He was changing. She wanted it to work out, so she grabbed his arm.

"No, wait! Nix! Don't go!"

Phoenix pulled his arm away out of her grasp. She held on too hard and scratched him as he freed his arm.

"Ouch, Steph!" His arm flailed and hit her cheek. The slap was harder than Phoenix wanted, but he didn't look shocked at all. Stephanie did.

"So!" A voice boomed.

Stephanie already didn't understand what happened, but the loud voice startled her.

Phoenix turned his head like a robot, not at all worried about what was coming through the door.

It was Roy...and some of his friends. "You think you can beat up girls do ya?" He came in. Two of his friends followed him, smirks on their faces. It looked like Roy got bigger.

Phoenix stood there like a two-ton statue. He looked immovable, and unafraid. He said nothing.

"No Roy! He didn't mean it! I scratched him, don't Roy!" Stephanie pleaded.

Roy paid no attention.

Phoenix's eyes never left Roy, "don't worry Stephanie, it'll be okay...for me." Phoenix's voice sounded nothing like Stephanie had ever heard. It scared her.

She put her hands up to hold Roy back, but he was large and muscular and brushed her aside. Stephanie wasn't so easily discouraged and came at him again as Roy moved closer toward Phoenix, who didn't budge. Roy's two friends moved to each side of Phoenix surrounding him.

Stephanie was an obstacle to Roy getting to Phoenix. He gripped her arms, looked her in the eyes and said, "What is the matter with you? Can't you see he's a psycho? Now get out of the way and this time he's not gettin' off so easy." He threw her aside and she fell.

"So, apparently you like man-handling girls too, big boy Roy" Phoenix said with an eerie calm voice.

Roy came at Phoenix, full forward. He threw a solid heavy punch when he was within range. His size made him slower than one without the massive inertia.

Phoenix dodged the right hand with just a side step and watched Roy's fist slide by his face. As Roy was finishing the throw, Phoenix planted a solid strike into his kidney. As his punch landed, one of Roy's friends came at him from behind. An elbow to the midsection sent him to the ground.

The other friend ran to Phoenix, threw a punch that missed, and Phoenix was able to grab his arm and twist.

It snapped.

"Ow!" The unlucky friend screamed in pain.

Roy recovered much quicker than Phoenix anticipated, and was on him. Roy kicked him. There was nowhere to go, and the blow hit his side. There was power in it and pain radiated from the injured zone. Phoenix felt queasy, and it forced him to let out a guttural sound.

"Stop it!" Stephane yelled. She was on her feet again and jumped on Roy's back trying to get him off Phoenix.

That gave Phoenix time to reset. His side hurt from a possible broken rib and he had to keep it curled in.

Fuck this. Play times over. Time to turn it up, he thought. His hand disappeared behind him.

"Get off!" Roy shouted at her sister with rage. He sounded different. Fury, an unstoppable hulk wanting death. Roy spun around fast trying to throw her off.

He succeeded.

She flew off him and stumbled right into Phoenix. Both his arms came out in front of him to catch her. One hand palm open to help, the other gripped tight on the instrument he was trained to hold with memory. She rushed into him.

She released a terrible sound. Quick breaths were emitted like she was drowning in ice cold water. He looked into her eyes. Her face was shocked, her mouth open, eyes wide, disbelieving what just happened, she was numb.

Phoenix tried to hold her with his one hand. He looked down at his other hand. The knife handle was there, the blade disappeared into her body.

That wasn't supposed to happen to *her.*

Roy stared at them in shock. The sound his sister made was unmistakable. Her weight became too great for Phoenix as she lost the strength to stand. She fell hard to the ground, revealing the knife still in Phoenix's hand.

He watched her fall, then lifted his head and stared at Roy. Anger fixated on his face. Those eyes, they held death.

Death for Roy. A half smile carved into his face. Phoenix would enjoy this next scenario. It unfolded just as Phoenix knew it would.

Roy had never seen evil until that moment. The reaper came.

Only one person made it out of there alive. Phoenix rose from the ashes and flew.

60

After hearing some noise, Tim stumbled into Kevin and the man named Jake.

They exchanged information about Nick locking them in and leaving in a huff. The next set of information was intense, but Tim thought it made perfect sense. The company, the games, the killings. Jake being an avenger. The other killer, Phoenix, all fit together. However, Tim had reservations about Jake, he was hiding something, but he had to trust Kevin for now. Tim realized that Jake could have killed Kevin anytime he wanted. Unless this was part of Jake's plan. He would remain skeptical and aware.

Kevin learned about the computer terminals and a man named Dean who was communicating with them. He had a brother here, John. Dean was helping all of them. At least, that's what they believed.

"My God. John? All this time? The earth's not winterized," Kevin's voice had sadness, frustration, and bewilderment.

After some time passed, Kevin side-stepped the solemn moment and asked, "If the earth's surface is safe, can Dean figure out how to open the iron door?"

"I'm not sure," Tim replied. "I don't think so yet, but he's looking."

"Damn," he was imagining the concept of being able to leave this place.

"Yeah, but we must be careful about Phoenix. He's still hunting everyone," Jake said.

"Can you...?" Kevin asked.

Tim looked at Jake with hope. He noticed all the bruises and dried blood, but it didn't appear to be too bad.

"Take him?" responded Jake. "I should, yes. He is good, but not *that* good. I gave him a sting. Besides, we outnumber him. It's just a matter of time to find him."

"I wonder if Dean can help find him. He seems to be able to tap into video feeds," Kevin was on it.

"Let's go find out," Tim suggested.

Nodding heads showed agreement.

As they walked the silent tunnels, the only sounds were their shoes impacting and grinding the dirt on the ground. One man sniffed, another cleared his throat. The lights were on, but the tunnels still cast plenty of shadows. Coming up to the command center, they passed many empty tables and chairs. It looked abandoned, eerie. Continuing to the cafeteria, the group turned south to enter the tunnel to the medical center where Tim thought everyone should be.

Jake saw him first. He stopped and looked up at an angle. Kevin bumped right into Jake's back like he was a solid wall. After the confusion of why he stopped, Kevin saw Jake's face aiming up and followed his gaze.

There was Nick. Kevin backed up as if a lion was about to jump on him.

"Shit," Tim let out.

Nick was tied to a large concrete column. It was a grotesque scene that showed obvious signs of torture and pain. Blood dripped out of his mouth and eyes, which were almost entirely white with the pupils behind the lazy looking eyelids. Trails of blood had leaked out of his pectoral arteries on each armpit and had run down his arms. It still looked wet. A pool of blood was on the ground.

"Jesus Christ." Tim was disgusted.

Kevin's throat was dry. A sour and bitter taste bubbled into his mouth from his agitated stomach. He gagged and he threw up a little. Spitting out the foul contents, he had to look away.

Jake had nothing to say. He walked closer and noticed something written in blood on the wall next to Nick. It read "I love this game."

"Son of a bitch," Jake shook his head.

61

Dean studied the video screen. It took two hours, and the woman walked into her office. Dean sat up. The woman sat down, glared at the screen, and it blipped on.

Perfect, Dean thought, smiling. He watched his screen flicker as the data from the nano splicer sent the information to his computer. It was a perfect mimic.

"Yes!" he said with excitement. His patience and experience paid off. He looked at the icons. Navigating around lots of files, he found schematics. It was a map, a blueprint, but of what? This building? The company?

Dean scrolled around to find an identifying mark on the bottom or a legend. There it was.

'SITE: 41A-NM.'

Dean rummaged through multiple files to find some kind of reference for the site.

Hours flew by. Dean looked through hundreds of files. Dean located an important file which showed one manifest with names. He was able to link it to one site schematic. 'SITE: 3A-GD.' His heart beat faster. He knew this was the complex John and these people might be trapped in. He studied the map.

Yes, he thought. *That must be it!*

It was a large complex. A myriad of tunnels and halls connected stations, rooms, and storage centers. In the center was labeled a command center, which lots of other tunnels were connected to. There was a lot of information, but after scanning over the documents Dean found an interesting feature...an exit.

---#---

From somewhere else, a cubicle operator in the company watched one of his screens with apathy. Eight other screens had different feeds on each of them. Many of them displayed empty halls, corridors, and rooms, but some had figures on them.

One screen, three men were standing looking at someone tied to a concrete column above the floor. The bleeding man was deceased. The cubicle operator who was monitoring the screen paid no attention from being desensitized to the common sight.

A different screen, the cubicle operator was watching a man sitting at a terminal. The man was surfing around different files and studying them. It happened to be Dean, but the cubicle operator didn't care. He was just following orders.

"That's it, yeah," Dennison pointed to the file on the cubicle operator's screen. "Make sure he gets that one."

"Yes sir," said the cubicle operator. He moved the file over to make sure Dean had access to it.

After a few more minutes, the two observed Dean fiddle around with the plans, they watched him zone in on the target area. It was the exit of the complex.

"Perfect. This is going to be hilarious!" Dennison said, laughing. "The crowds are going to just love it!"

---#---

Dean was excited. He stumbled onto a schematic for operating procedures of the escape exit door. It took an hour, but it was worth it. He now had the key to his brother's survival and the rest of these people.

Making sure he understood the operating procedures for the door, Dean opened the video feeds, but unfortunately no one was there to receive them. "Hmm, where did you guys go?"

After a few moments he spotted the kids. There was an obvious danger they were concerned with as they were checking around every corner. Dean studied the schematics and tried to figure out where they were going. He scanned ahead and found video feeds showing what they were heading into. They appeared to be clear of any obstruction. Dean scrambled for terminal locations in the kids line of movement. If he could get a message flashing across a screen with them walking by, it may get their attention.

62

Dahria was hugging Alexa, crying and laughing at the same time.

"I was so afraid you were dead," Dahria said.

"I'm so glad you're alive too."

After running like crazy after Dahria, it had taken a few seconds for Tommy's curiosity to build up, allowing himself to look back and observe Alexa running after them. It took a few more seconds to convince Dahria to stop. Once the confusion was over, Dahria and Alexa had a tearful yet joyful reunion.

After only a few moments, Tommy pushed, "I hate to say it girls, but...let's get going." They understood. The killer could be anywhere.

Tommy led the way to the cafeteria. Dahria and Alexa trailed behind him. Tommy was on edge, ready for anything that might confront them. His mind felt like it was working overtime and swelled in his head. He noticed the girls seemed to be doing okay, but they had no time for conversation. Their goal was to find others.

As Tommy came to the cafeteria hall from the tunnel, his amygdala worked hard giving him fear. He crept close to the wall and peered around. He scanned the tables, chairs, food racks, counters, and even got down on one knee to check underneath furniture as best he could. With plenty of spots someone could hide, Tommy wanted to get through here as quickly as possible. He thought of Jones but realized the chances were beyond slim that he would have stayed here. He hoped Jones was okay.

Tommy motioned to the girls behind him to follow, and they crept through the cafeteria. As Tommy hurried, he was glancing and scanning the room like a robot. His eyes crossed a computer terminal. Tommy caught something that flashed on the screen. The movement made his eyes glance back for a second. He could only read some of it.

'HEY KIDS.' The visible words flashed.

Tommy squinted and wondered if it meant anything. He was on the edge. *Should I stop? Keep going? Damn.* He remembered Dean and decided it might be worth a quick look. Glancing at the girls behind him Tommy whispered, "Follow me."

Dahria's brow furrowed in confusion and in a soft voice asked, "Tommy. What are you doing? Let's go." She urged him with her arms to move forward, but Tommy had already turned and walked over to the terminal.

As he sauntered over, he read the screen. 'HEY KIDS. IT'S DEAN. I FOUND IT! I FOUND THE WAY OUT!'

Tommy put his fingers on the keyboard and typed, 'WHO ELSE WERE WE WITH?' Without looking back, he told both girls, "Keep watch."

'THE DARKER FELLA, AND TIM,' came the response.

The confirmation enlightened him. Tommy glanced at both girls, they were watching both directions.

'GOOD. THAT WAS JONES YOU MENTIONED. DO YOU KNOW WHERE HE IS?'

'I CAN SEE THE THREE OF YOU. I FOUND A FEW OTHERS, TIM WAS ONE, BUT, I WILL LOOK...NO, NOT JONES.' The text flashed on the screen.

Tommy felt the need to move. 'I'M TOMMY. WE ARE IN SERIOUS NEED TO GET OUT OF HERE AND

FIND OTHERS. WHERE IS TIM?' Tommy was typing as fast as he could. He didn't want to stay here any longer than necessary.

'DON'T WORRY, NO ONE IS AROUND YOUR AREA YET. I'VE BEEN STUDYING PLANS FOR YOUR COMPLEX. THERE IS AN EXIT DOOR AND I HAVE FOUND THE PROCESS FOR OPENING IT.'

"Oh my God," Dahria said with hope, catching the screen for a second.

"What?" Alexa glanced at them for a moment. After reading the screen, she smiled at Dahria who returned it.

Tommy held his rejoice until they were gone and the killer behind them. Tommy thought and typed.

'WOW. OK THAT'S GREAT.'

'TIM IS RIGHT OUTSIDE THE MEDICAL CENTER. YOU SHOULD BE CLEAR. "WHEN YOU MEET HIM, WE CAN CHAT FURTHER.'

'DONE.'

"We still need to be careful," Tommy told the two girls.

"Of course," Alexa was agitated. "Let's get going. The sooner we get out of here the better. If this piece of shit tries anything, we go all in."

Dahria had never heard Alexa talk like that before, she was usually the happy and bubbly type. At that instant Dahria knew a part of Alexa changed. She wondered what happened.

Alexa stared at them both. Serious eyes made Dahria nervous. Tommy understood Alexa's frustration and anger, but returned a look of amazement at the strength.

"Alright then," Tommy conceded.

The group headed to the medical center. As they came up from the tunnel, they heard soft voices and Tommy stopped. The girls followed suit. His breath halted to listen. He heard more than one voice. Slowly, Tommy snuck up to the opening and looked in. There were large concrete support columns on the four sides of the center. Tommy slid around and saw three men. He relaxed as he saw Kevin, Tim, and some other guy.

"It's okay," Tommy told Dahria and Alexa. "It's Tim and Kevin...and someone else."

The girls looked relieved.

Tommy noticed they were looking at something up off the floor, grim faces didn't sit well in his stomach. They headed toward them.

63

Phoenix was in his secret chamber. After painting a beautiful art piece with Nick, he washed all the art media off himself like erasing a canvas. He was anxious to get back to finishing his previous situation with Dahria, but he decided to rest for a few moments. Playing with his dark blonde hair by curling it around his finger, he pulled on it a little, and let it unwind. Slowing down his breath, he rested.

As he stared at the ceiling, a few memories popped into his head. Phoenix didn't mind it. Most of the time it helped him relax as the memories were soothing. One time in particular stood out.

---#---

There she was. Stephanie. Phoenix stood heavy on two feet. He felt somewhat close to her even though there was about six feet of earth separating them. Somewhere under the ground her body replenished the energy in which it once came from. Her tombstone stood with faith. Many other stone faces were staring at Phoenix, but he only gazed at hers. He didn't know why he visited the place from time to time, but Phoenix knew he liked the memory. It confused, yet intrigued him. He wasn't sure if it was the memory of her, or if she led him to his first combat kill, Roy, or his first sexual experience. Probably both. Phoenix didn't enjoy what happened to her, but the vigor of killing Roy proved immense. It was a strange sort of balance. There would always be other girls.

She was beautiful. So was he. His bone structure was straight, and he had a relentless desire to stay fit and healthy. A touch over average height at a little over six foot, strong bones, slim but muscular. His eyes, a deep green with hints of blue, like a cold hurricane coming through the sails of a boat. His eyes held incredible beauty, but underneath held devastating destruction and evil.

It was a comfortably warm day and the cool breeze felt amazing. Phoenix looked down at the grave and thought of her. She was gone, and it was time to move on. It was time to scratch the itch.

Along with the leaves rustling on the grass creating gentle high-pitched sounds, there was a rattlesnake type snippet sound coming from far away. It pulled Phoenix out of his thoughts. He lifted his head in no hurry to see what was going on. Nothing but the trees swaying from the wind being redirected by the wood. Turning his head he saw someone. Her hair pulled back tight. Her face, like a porcelain doll, looked silken. She was concentrating on pedaling her bike with long toned legs moving rhythmically. She had an athletic yet curvy body as the proper tightly fitting outfit showed.

Phoenix would have thought it impossible for anyone to miss her in a crowd. Here, Phoenix had no trouble spotting her, she was alone. Phoenix admired her commitment and courage to promote a healthy lifestyle. Blood pooled in his groin making his member erect. It was an immediate and powerful attraction. He smiled to himself and had no choice but to follow her, enslaved.

A stroke of luck rang down from the heavens that day for whatever reason, her bike was fast enough.

64

Tommy was shocked when he learned that there had been *two* killers all along. He had seen what happened to Nick, the grotesque image pounded into his head. It was terrible to think about, flickering like a slideshow over and over. A life changing day, it was too much to process, too much to absorb. Tommy feared, if he survived, it would re-enter his life later as post-traumatic stress. Tommy just hoped it wouldn't overtake it. He thought about Dahria, almost raped right in front of him. Another thought…Jones. He feared the worst. It was obvious Jones didn't make it for help and the complex had an uncanny evil that followed it. He let an uncontrolled tear slide down his face.

"Hey." A gentle shake woke him up from his thoughts.

Tommy blinked and looked up to see Kevin.

"Are you all right? I mean," Kevin eyed him, "Stay with us okay?". He could tell there was something behind Tommy's eyes, but didn't want to push him.

A frown of confusion drifted away as Tommy cleared his head. He focused. "Hey Kevin, we were able to communicate with Dean. He knows how to get out of here."

"What?" Kevin knew about Dean from Tim, but couldn't understand that last part.

Tommy elaborated, "He apparently found out how to operate the iron door." In all his thoughts, he forgot about that. It excited him.

Kevin's facial features relaxed into awareness. "Holy…"

"All we need is a terminal."

They were in the south operations hall. A terminal was located down by the iron door.

Kevin walked over to Tim and Jake and filled them in. In a few minutes Jake led the way back to Tommy.

"I know you don't know me from anything. But I need you to trust me. I'm here to help." Jake said.

Tommy glanced at Tim and Kevin, who said nothing, but their stares conveyed a positive vibe.

Alexa strained against the tendons and muscles that flowed with fatigue. A few joints popped to relieve the nitrogen gas bubbles between the ligaments. Dahria, wobbled with a little dizziness. They needed rest from everything that had happened, but didn't have time.

The group traveled to the terminal located close to the iron door. The girls laid next to each other happy to get some rest while the others headed to the terminal. Tommy was exhausted but pushed on.

Tim was the one who logged into the terminal. It was clear that Dean was already watching. The text popped up immediately.

'TIM, HI. I'VE BEEN WAITING FOR YOU. GLAD YOU ARE ALL OK.'

'TOMMY TELLS ME YOU HAVE A PROCEDURE FOR A WAY OUT?' Tim typed.

'YES.'

Tim typed. 'HOW?'

As Dean responded, Jake thought about his mission to end Phoenix. He wanted him out of his position of fire, torture, and killing. Beyond that, Jake wanted to end the games, but knew that was a tall order. Phoenix was right in front of him, and that took priority. Jake also wanted to free these innocent people. At least if he could do that, he might feel at least some redemption in spirit, a little sense of self-worth out of it all. He didn't know if anyone could forgive him, but maybe he could forgive himself. Jake knew he could live with that. Shaking his head he focused his mind back to Dean.

'...THEN PUSH THE PRESSURE REGULATOR. ONCE THE LIGHT IS GREEN YOU SHOULD BE ABLE TO UNLOCK THE STABILIZERS. THE DOOR SHOULD OPEN.'

"That doesn't sound too hard," Tim concluded. "M'kay."

Tommy figured Jones suffered the same fate as Nick, but had to ask, "Has he found Jones or the others?"

Tim was dumbfounded that he didn't think of that. There was just too much happening so fast. 'DEAN, WHERE ARE THE OTHERS? CAN YOU SEE THEM? ARE THEY OK?'

After a few moments, the screen read, 'I SEE THEM, THEY AR...'

The sentence didn't finish. They stared at it.

Nothing.

"No," Tommy said. "No! Come on!" He said, banging his fist on the table.

They stared and waited still.

Nothing.

"Maybe the connection was lost," Tim's eyebrows raised.

'DEAN?' Tim wrote and then stared longer at the screen.

Nothing.

Tommy pulled his hair with his hands. He was desperate and mumbled an obscenity under his breath.

After several long seconds a message popped on the screen. 'ARE YOU ALL HAVING FUN YET?' The text burned into their eyes and no one said a word. Faces grew serious as they looked at each other. Jake pursed his lips together.

65

Dean continued typing the sentence when the screen went blank. He frowned. Out of reflex, he tapped two keys to wake the screen back up. It worked. The screen came back on, but it was a video feed. Dean was almost relieved...until he observed the strange image. It tickled his mind as he observed a figure sitting at a terminal peering at a screen. The shot was from behind. Dean tilted his head in confusion and the figure on the screen followed his exact movement.

Oh shit, Dean's body tingled as he gained the knowledge that it was himself.

A second later, a window popped up and text appeared.

'YOU'VE BEEN A BAD BOY, DEAN.'

The adrenaline made Dean shake. The back of his neck felt cold, and hairs became erect from goosebumps. He took his hands off the keyboard, bolted up, and turned for the door. Running to it he found the operating handle. He cranked it. The handle refused. Dean pulled and pushed the door. The door replied with solid immovable stability.

"Shit!" Dean cursed. He clenched his teeth. Dean glanced back at the screen. Words and sentences were forming.

'LEAVING ALREADY? WE BARELY HAD THE CHANCE TO MEET.'

Dean's frustration and anger at himself grew, making his body hot.

'DON'T WORRY DEAN, WE'RE NOT MAD, YOU DID EVERYTHING WE THOUGHT YOU WOULD DO.'

Dean looked around the room for a possible escape route. The ceiling was too high and too solid. The room was small, the door metal. A perfect place for seclusion, but also a perfect place to trap someone. He created a jail for himself.

'RELAX DEAN, THERE IS NO WAY OUT, BUT REST ASSURED WE DON'T PLAN ON KEEPING YOU HERE.'

Dean picked up the control board and slammed it down on the desk. A hiss came from a small ventilator in the side of the wall. White smoke started flowing into the room. After a few seconds it poured in.

Dean felt the Sig Sauer pressing against his skin. He was desperate and had to do something. Dean took it out, racked it, and fired at the door lock several times. He tried the handle, and it turned but not enough. The white smoke was reaching his face, but Dean held his breath. Firing more shots into the lock, sparks flew, and it severely damaged the lock. He tried the handle again, and it turned. Kicking the door with as much force as he could muster, it sent a massive shock-wave through his leg. The door whipped open. It surprised him. Yellow flashing lights followed loud alarm sounds. Dean burst out of the room, looked left, then right. Before he could even assess the situation, a massive amount of electricity went through his body, paralyzing him. The gun never went off as Dean fell to the ground losing all control of his body.

---#---

The pathwalker named Dennison stared at the screen with the cubicle operator. Silence filled the room. He watched as the scene unfolded. Dennison had his arms crossed. The ending was adequate, but a key issue would need to be resolved.

How did you get a gun in here? Dennison chewed on his cheek working to solve the issue. He made sure he would bring this up at the next corporate meeting. Dean made a valiant effort to escape, but in the end the company always wins.

The cubicle operator had typed a message that asked if the captives were having fun yet. As expected, no response popped up, but it was still fun and the facial expressions of the participants were priceless.

Dennison watched the screen and updated the corporate officer through a headset device. He informed him that Dean was captured, sedated, and would be brought to holding room seventeen. Silence on the line hung for a few minutes. As he waited, he thought about how he admired this Dean's attempt to escape; he had fight in him, which was good for entertainment.

A reply came from the headset. The officer vibrated the speaker saying, "Nice work. You know what to do." The response was flat and succinct.

"Yes sir."

Dennison thought about Tim, John, and Nick and how they came to be participants in the games. He smiled at the memory of recruiting them. Even Jone's story was sweet.

--#--

Several floors up in a building, Tim watched law enforcement officials talking to representatives of the company. Tim was nervous. His co-worker friend John was with him.

"Man, I don't like this," Tim said.

John nodded as he watched the group. "I hear ya. What do you think's going to happen?"

"Nothing." He rolled his eyes. "The company gets away with everything."

"Well, we'll see how they like my evidence. It's hard to sidestep facts," John said, referring to the information he provided authorities anonymously.

The group of officers and company personnel walked into the building looking like little ants from that high up. Once the officers disappeared in the building, the two observed the crowds outside. Immense in volume, the people looked like millions of bugs moving around on a dead animal. The streets were so crowded they could hardly be seen.

In front of the entrance to the building, there were protesters holding up their signs of disapproval. It was a brave thing to do. Past experiences like these meant being man-handled, beaten up, or even taken, and erased.

"It's too bad there aren't more of them," John said, "But they keep this up and it's the beginning of a large resistance."

Tim spoke. "Be careful man, what if they find out it's you?"

John shrugged and raised his eyebrows. "Let's hope this plays out my way."

"Got a Plan B?"

Staring out the window a few minutes more, John answered, "Yeah. My brother."

"Good luck," Tim said.

"For all of us," John had a good position in the company. It was fantastic for the resistance. He was a mole and decided to try and bring some attention, hopefully to make a positive difference. Maybe even raise more eyebrows to shut this place down.

Instead, it raised the eyebrows of the company. They took immediate and decisive action.

Tim would eventually see John later, but it would be in the complex, participating in the games.

Upon John's disappearance, Tim sent a message to his brother, Dean for help. Then, he was erased from his current life too.

---#---

Nick held his sign high above his head. He waved it, shook it, and shouted. The crowds were like a rock concert. However, most of them were for the company, not against it. He was part of only a small group of protestors. The protesters would build up little by little and then almost vanish, only to repeat the process.

A small group of personnel came out of the company wearing full body suits and masks. They had gas guns and fired them into the crowd of protestors. The grenades launched in the air leaving smoke trails showing the arc as they banged and clanged into the crowd. Everyone was so tightly packed that Nick couldn't move. The smoke erupted and poured out everywhere and Nick was in the middle of it, along with several others. The outer perimeter of the crowd started running in different directions. Some got away, many tripped and fell while others hid behind obstacles. The smoke hit Nick's face, he started coughing and his eyes stung. He was crowded in and still couldn't go anywhere yet, so he had to breathe the smoke. Lightheaded and weary, Nick made several steps before his legs gave out. He fell. Blinking a few times he noticed another couple went down next to him. He stared at them, unable to move. Nick was so tired all he wanted to do was sleep, but he knew what was going on. He watched the couple blinking at him trying to move but neither could budge. Nick tried to speak, but only baby gibberish vibrated out. His eyelids got too heavy to keep open, and he sank into a deep sleep.

Nick would later wake up in an unfamiliar place, his mind clouded of memory. Little did he know a killer would come after him, and kill him.

---#---

Jones was laughing hard as a few of his friends died.

"You son of a bitch!" one friend said with a full-face helmet on. There was a plastic but real looking gun in his hand with buttons on it. Video sensors surrounded his body articulating his movements perfectly. He was standing on a padded carpet that had many boxes and arrows on it to control the movement of the avatar.

"Yes," Jones laughed loudly. "That makes me the top killer."

The boys were playing 'Death-match,' a game built in the virtual reality world. It was a costly product that only few possessed, but Jones had a friend with the equipment. On that day, it was one of the only situations where kids and friends got together face to face.

"Damn, I have no idea how you got so beastly good shithead!" His friend said.

"I'm just a natural born killer!" Jones mused.

"Yeah, yeah. Monster is more like it. If this was real life, you'd be toast Jonesy!" Another friend laughed while taking off his gear.

The friends sat around talking and played various other games. After a while the friend with the equipment proposed, "Hey, you guys want to see something cool?"

The other two glanced at him with curiosity.

"Check this out," he looked devious, like it was taboo. He navigated his game database.

After a few moments of opening files, typing in fields, and back coding fields, the screen lit up.

The boys stared at it. The image showed a tunnel. It was dimly lit and long. Pipes, rubber coated wires, traveled the length of the tunnel that seemed to go on forever. The tunnel glistened with humidity and the wetness reflected off the floor.

"Looks like an empty tunnel. Big deal," said Jones.

"Yeah," he said, "Just watch, and this other channel will keep you entertained while we wait." He opened another screen so they could watch them both. It was a girl brushing her teeth. She was wearing a bathrobe which hung slightly open. Enough to see cleavage. She was pretty.

"Aw, you pervert." Jones said. The other boy laughed. The friend smiled with delight.

"You know it," he said. "Please open that robe, babe." Pornography was so common it was almost hardwired into people. Yet there was sometimes a thrill in the unsuspecting girl. It was an obvious joke as there were many full 360 degree virtual models for young men to play with.

"How'd you learn to do all this?" one friend asked.

"My older brother's friend Kevin taught me. You've met him once. Now watch close," he said, meaning the tunnel image as he turned the female display off. He didn't want them to be distracted.

After several minutes Jones saw a figure running down the tunnel.

"Is this the game?" Jones said.

"You bet."

"So what's the big deal? Everyone watches this." Jones was referring to most of the population, at least in the cities. Jones didn't partake in it, but many others did. "So you tapped into their feed, you get it for free," He shrugged his shoulders.

"Oh okay buddy, watch this," he said. A few minutes later, the friend pulled up a few files. Opening one, he started laughing as he changed the name on it. The new name read "Jones Anderson."

Jones' eyes grew wider as he saw his own name. "What the hell are you doing?" He wasn't laughing. These were files of the games, participants, players.

"Holy shit," said the other friend. "You tapped into the company's files?" His face was wondrous.

The other boys laughed at the joke.

"Put it back!" Jones commanded.

"Oh take it easy, they can't do anything."

"I don't care, put it back."

"All right, all right." The friend erased Jones' name and put the original name back on it, 'Tommy Knight.'

It wasn't long after that, Jones actually met Tommy…in the games.

66

"Nothing more we can do here," Tim said, staring at the now blank computer, disappointed. "But at least Dean told us how to get out of here."

It didn't look good for Dean. Tommy knew they might have caught him, it was obvious everyone had that same conclusion.

Tommy sighed, looked at Dahria and then Alexa.

"Hey, he said he saw them, so that means someone's alive, somewhere," Tim said.

Tommy was full of doubt, but tried to hold onto hope. "Let's go then."

"No. Not yet. You all should get some rest."

"What? We can't just stay here and…" Tommy protested.

"Trust me." Jake wasn't worried about getting out of here as much as killing Phoenix. In order to do that, he needed to make sure he and everyone else was properly rested. He found a nice spot to rest himself and left that up to everyone else to decide. "There's no sense in doing anything until we are all alert, and fresh. Phoenix will exploit any weakness we possess."

So that's his name. Tommy looked at Tim and Kevin. They nodded. He trusted them. Jake was an expert, but that didn't mean that Tommy didn't have a choice. He didn't know whether to trust Jake, but for now he had to. No one performed well under exhaustion.

Tim noticed Tommy's uneasiness. "Go ahead kid, it'll be all right. I'll keep watch." He turned his attention to Kevin, "You okay?"

Kevin's long face nodded.

It wasn't easy, but Tommy had to let go and rest. His eyelids sank like a black curtain as soon as he sat down.

---#---

After some time, Tommy popped awake. Another awful nightmare, his heart was racing. His nerves were firing and his body agitated. Calming himself, he took deep breaths and glanced around. *Just another dream, take it easy. It wasn't real.*

Jake was lying back, his head against a ball of clothes using them as a small cushion. His arms were crossed over his chest like he was cold. His stomach lifted and sank rhythmically. The instant Tommy moved, Jake opened one eyelid to a slit watching him. As soon as Jake realized it was Tommy, he closed it back up again.

Geez, Tommy thought, wondering how Jake did that. He never made a sound.

Tommy had his arm around Dahria, and he rubbed her and gave her a gentle hug. She stirred and they fell back asleep.

After a nudge from Jake sometime later, they all took time to pull themselves up.

Alexa was up and stretching out her limbs from the unforgiving excuse for a bed. She was talking to Kevin who rubbed his own back. Alexa glanced at Dahria and gave her a small smile to say good morning.

Tim was sitting against the wall and looked like he was keeping watch for as long as he could, but he rolled his head around and massaged his neck. Dahria walked over to him and placed her hand on his broad shoulder.

"Come here," she said. Her voice soothing, "you look so uncomfortable." She knelt down and rubbed his neck for him.

"Thanks," he said, "I'll be alright."

Tommy watched Dahria and admired her generosity.

Within the next five minutes everyone was awake and sore, but alert.

"Tomorrow we need to sleep in a bed," Tim was holding his shoulder and rotating it around.

Kevin responded, "Tomorrow, hopefully we all sleep up there." He looked at Tim and smiled.

Tim gave him the same response. He turned to Jake for advice, "Jake. What's the plan?"

"I think we stick together and search for anyone else alive, if we run into Phoenix, he's mine."

Tommy still wasn't sure how he felt about Jake. On one side he sounded like he was being heroic, but he felt like he was hiding something.

Jake continued. "Phoenix will most likely be setting traps. He doesn't want to kill quickly or kill too many people at once. He likes to savor the moment and spend lots of time with each one."

Tommy glanced at Dahria. She glanced at Alexa, knowing that must be hard to hear.

Tommy felt a small adrenaline rush, reminding him of what could have happened. Alexa was stone-faced, Tommy couldn't read it, but there was something different there.

"Where do you suppose we start?" asked Tim.

Jake thought for a moment. "Right here. We sweep this complex from south to north, then east to west. We end up in the living cells west block."

Tim shook his head. His body language suggested that it would be a large task. "Jesus, I wish we could split up. This is gonna take a long time."

Jake glanced at Tim, "Unless everyone would like to hunt Phoenix? I could take him out, and then we can look for your people." Jake was giving them an option, he didn't care either way. "Or I can hunt Phoenix, and your group can do what you like."

"No, I guess we should go with option A. Don't you think?" Tim's question was for anyone but Jake.

"Yes, I agree," replied Kevin.

"Same here," Alexa concurred.

Tommy nodded.

---#---

The team swept the tunnels and halls, checking the offices and rooms as they went. Jake was in front. Tommy watched him and studied his steps while being alert, trying to learn anything he could. They checked the south block hall, and power center number two. Next, up north through the tunnel they headed toward the conference area. As the team was getting closer to the conference hall, Tommy noticed a smell in the air. It grew stronger as they kept walking.

Unpleasant was an understatement. The smell of urine that sat for long periods of time mixed with diarrhea and putrescine reeked in the air. They were trapped with no means of escaping the rancid smell. Dahria coughed. Tommy had a hard time breathing in, like he was choking on ammonia gas pouring into his lungs.

"Jesus," Tim said disgustedly. "We need to dispose of the bodies." He didn't like saying this out loud, but it needed to be said.

"Breathe in through your mouth, it should dull it a little," Jake didn't seem bothered by the stench and kept moving to the conference hall.

Dahria took the back of her hand placing it under her nose trying to filter the stench. "Ugh." She was having trouble breathing. A twisted look of nausea contorted her face, which changed a few shades of color.

Kevin tried to be efficient. "We can burn the bodies when we get the chance."

"Ewuh," Tommy replied, not meaning to react out loud. The thought of that made him gag. He looked back at Alexa, she was wincing but seemed to deal with it.

"Come on, let's move." Jake entered the conference hall. The smell was overwhelming now. The bodies have had time to decay and the ventilation could only handle so much. "Don't look at the bodies, just focus on the destination, go!" Jake urged them on.

Dahria heaved but didn't let it stop her pace. Tommy gagged, but managed to control a vomit session. Tim spit on the ground, his mouth dry. Alexa seemed to take short breaths.

The small band crossed the conference hall and Jake scanned around searching for a sign of anything unusual. With nothing strange, they exited the hall and traveled down the long tunnel toward the power center number one. After nothing was found, they crept into the next tunnel that led to the command center. The smell faded the further they traveled.

It was Jake who found it. "There's a locked door, be ready. There is a chance the door's rigged, so find a rope or long cord of some kind."

Tim nodded, "Tom, you go over there," he pointed in the direction, "and Kevin, you over there." Tim went elsewhere to look.

After a few minutes Kevin found something. "I've got it." He brought back a long electrical cord.

Jake tied it to the wheel and turned it. When it stopped he said, "Get back."

They moved several feet away and Jake pulled on the cord. It was tight, but the door squeaked and it grinded open. Nothing happened. The door stopped on its own friction.

No sound.

Tim was the first to call, "Anyone in there?"

Tommy's eyes looked back and forth. Nothing.

Jake eased to the entrance of the office, the others following in behind him. Jake was poised and ready for a surprise. "Stay back, give me some room."

Jake glanced around the small office. Right away he found something unusual, he spotted a man lying on the ground. Still in combat ready stance, he eased over to him and checked with his boot to verify if the person was dead. There was no smell, which was a good sign. His boot shook him. The man moaned and rolled from his side to his stomach. Jake could tell it was not Phoenix.

"Man down," Jake said.

The small group entered carefully.

"Who is it?" Dahria asked.

Tommy's eyebrows were raised in a questioning look himself. He didn't know who it was. Neither did Alexa or Dahria.

"What the hell?" Tim said he was perplexed also, although there was something familiar about the man. He wasn't sure what it was, but he felt like he had seen him before, somewhere. He thought and thought. A Picture. A funny picture. A trip. Clouded thoughts.

As the man moved his arms around, he rubbed his eyes with the palms of his hands. It was a clumsy effort, like a baby.

A noise came from somewhere else. The sound was clouded and muffled but thudded, from a distant wall. Before anyone could even ask Jake spat out, "Watch him!" he said to Kevin and escaped the small office to investigate.

Tim, ripped from his thoughts, felt like he was remembering something significant. He vacated the room after Jake. Alexa and Dahria looked at each other for support and stayed here, but Tommy rushed after Tim without thinking.

There was a banging sound. It was somewhere in this center but from another office. The three got closer and they heard a cry for help.

Tommy thought the voice was familiar. He listened again and recognized it, "Jones! Is that you?"

Even muffled, the voice was unmistakable.

"Tommy?" It was Jones.

After unbarring and opening the door, Jones' eyes shined and his face had a big smile across it. He hugged his friend and two more men came out, Damon and John.

"Ho man, Tommy! You're alive! Holy shit, I'm so glad to see you guys!" Jones said.

As Damon walked out, his face went from happy to immense fear in less than a second. He saw Jake.

John noticed also and flinched. It was like he thought a baseball bat was going to hit him when he saw Jake. "What's he doing here?" He said, covering himself with his arms.

"It's okay," Tim reassured them. "He's helping us."

"Helping us?" Damon asked, confused. "What? Right after he clubbed John?"

"Hold on, hold on," Tim tried to ease the situation. "I know how it seems, but I want you to trust me. There's much more to the story."

The two men didn't relax their guard, but let Tim explain.

Jake, knowing he couldn't help this situation, stepped out to go back to help with the unknown person.

After a few minutes of explanation, the two of them grasped the situation with Jake. They were on edge, but dealt with it. The three of them strolled to the other office. The man was struggling to get up. He supported himself with his hands pushing on his knees. His face was revealed.

As John came up, his eyes went wide and his face showed excited recognition.

"Dean!" he said as if it were a dream.

67

The last name triggered Tim's memory. *Dean.* Tim now saw them together. John and Dean. Memories came flooding back like a river. John used to speak with fond memories of his brother at work.

John would show photos and talk about fun experiences he and his brothers had. Tim liked his character just as most people did. Fun loving and friendly.

Oh my God! Tim thought. *I was an employee at the company! Yes! Yes! I remember.* His eyes flicked back and forth as his mind was rendering images, like a computer loading information for an application. Tim was staring into a void concentrating. He remembered the company, John who worked with him, his life before the complex.

Kevin, the first to notice, "You all right?"

Tim looked up. He didn't know if he could share the information with anyone yet. He needed time to sort it out. "Yeah, yeah," he said, "just daydreaming." He stared at John talking with Dean. John was a friend at the company, but John didn't remember him...yet. He had to keep it under wraps for a while longer.

Tommy and Dahria were excited that Jones was okay. The two boys clasped palms in a reverse handshake like buddies in a competitive sport. Dahria grabbed each boy's arm and pulled Alexa in. They huddled and looked at each other with hope.

"Thought you were dead," Tommy told Jones.

"I thought the same for you both too."

"I'm glad everyone is okay," Kevin said.

Dean was groggy but seemed to remember everything. He was reacquainting with his brother. John was talking so fast Dean could hardly keep up. It was like John's memories were dormant and now released. He couldn't recall everything, but enough to make him realize that lots of things in his mind had been missing.

After more conversation, John stopped in mid-sentence and looked at Tim.

"Tim!" His smile was broad. "Tim! Holy shit! You! You worked with me at the company!"

Tim joined them. He nodded. "Hey buddy, it's good to know again," he said, patting John on the back.

Dean focused on Tim and squinted his eyes. "You're him right? You sent the message?"

Tim stared back, his face had a message on it. Yes.

"Nice work, thank you."

Tim nodded back. "Well. You're welcome, but it didn't seem to improve your situation."

Dean nodded and chuckled. He knew something, Tim could tell somehow.

"Damn man, what are you doing here?" John asked Dean.

Dean sighed loudly. "It was a poor attempt at a rescue brutha." Dean had a look in his eyes that suggested he had more to say, but wasn't the time or place to say it.

John noticed it. "What is it?"

Dean just put his head down, "I'm sorry man. Got caught."

Damon, along with Jake, were somewhat excluded from the group's conversations. They both watched from a short distance and Damon felt distant. He watched the others interacting with each other and realized just how much he hated being here. He was a doctor, a respectable man by trade, but he had shown a cowardice character all too well. Damon had feelings of regret and bitterness. He tried not to be this way, but he couldn't help it. He had separated himself from everyone. When it was someone else's life, he could handle the pressure, but when it was his own, it scared him to death.

Once most of the separate conversations came to a close, they highlighted that Townsend handled their capture and confinement. Kevin glanced at Jake.

Jake, oblivious to Kevin, watched them and had something in his stomach he hadn't felt in a long time. Envy. It had been a long time since he had a relationship, a friend. For as long as he could remember, he worked alone and lived alone, but it wasn't always like that. Memories of his life stirred.

---#---

"Jakey!" his mother called for him. It was dinner time.

Yes! Jake thought as he ran down the stairs.

His mother smiled as she could hear little boy footsteps booming down the stairs. Jake was seven. He was playing cops and robbers in his room with some of his toys. His mother, Victoria, interrupted him in the middle of the climax where the showdown was happening, but he never minded being called to dinner. He loved good food.

"Hey mom!" His curious and delighted face ran up to the counter. The air smelled like a sweet home cooked meal. Flavors from the full dishes engulfed the air, making Jake's mouth water involuntarily. "Mmm." Jake's eyes grew wide.

"Mm," Victoria smiled at him mimicking his tone. She moved closer to give him a kiss, but he was too quick and moved away.

Jake ran to the table.

"You can't escape me!" She chased him with her hands up. "I will give you the tickle from fingerland!"

While he was running to the table, a wall stopped him in his tracks, only the wall had arms that wrapped around him.

"Gotcha!" Ned, his dad, said.

"Ah!" Jake screamed. He struggled to get away so Victoria couldn't catch him. "Dad! No fair!"

Victoria, still chasing Jake, caught him with the road-block. She tickled him and laughed.

Jake released an uncontrolled belly laugh in response. He squirmed and his dad let him go. Jake fell to the floor to get out of range of Victoria's magical giggling fingers. She paused for a second to look up at Ned and smooched his lips.

"Smells good," he said after they separated.

She smiled from the compliment and shook her head as if a warm sun touched her face. Her brown curls bobbing like springs. She went into the kitchen and served everyone. Towards the end of dinner, as Jake was playing with his food, he imagined being an authority. He liked being in charge and bringing justice to situations. He would watch them on devices and it looked fun and intriguing.

"Why can't we live in the city?" Jake asked.

"Jake, we've talked about this before," his father said, "The cities are extremely dangerous, out of control, there's a lot of bad stuff."

"But don't you want to fix it?" Jake asked in earnest.

Ned admired his son for wanting to bring justice to bad places, but the cities were a lost cause. Fear entered his gut when they talked about these things. He didn't want his son to be a part of a situation no one could win. At this age, he knew Jake was ambitious and well beyond his years in maturity.

"When you're out on your own one day, you can do what you want, but in this house, you'll stay my happy little man. Some things can't be fixed, Jay." He got up and walked over to Jake and tapped him on the head with a wrapped up paper, "don't try to grow up too fast." He smiled and left.

---#---

Jake wasn't even aware that he was smiling. His eyes were glossed over with his mind being lost in memory of his family.

"Hey Jake," Kevin put his hand on his shoulder. The touch snapped Jake out of his trance. "What's wrong?"

Jake shook his head and blinked his eyes. "Oh, nothing. Just thinking of something."

Kevin waited for Jake to talk, but nothing more came out. Kevin nodded and let Jake be, even though he could see extra lubrication in Jake's eyes.

As Jake watched Kevin walk away, his eyes went to the ground, remembering what happened to his family. The murders led him into being an authority. It was hard, yet fulfilling, but there was one big problem. The job just didn't pay enough. Life became harder and more precarious. It came to a point where he couldn't sustain a healthy living. That was when the company got a hold of him.

Jake couldn't resist the benefits, pay, and what seemed like a form of justice. He didn't have much choice. Once he did the job, he found that even killing hardened criminals wasn't easy for him to swallow, but getting out of the company seemed to be even harder than getting in. Every job had its good and bad moments.

Over time Jake developed a different personality of himself he never knew he had. He taunted and even enjoyed getting confessions. Jake needed the justification, but in the back of his mind there would always be apprehension. When he found out the company was using innocent people, that was the turning point. It was finally clear to him. For the first time in his life since the company, Jake felt good about what he was doing, one hundred percent. These people needed him for a good purpose, his help to survive, and he would do everything he could to give it to them.

68

"Well everyone, what do you say we get the hell out of here?" Tim suggested.

"Hell yeah," Jones agreed. "I can't wait to smell the fresh air of freedom." His nose perked up and sniffed like he smelled orange blossoms in a garden. His smile showed a big white grin.

"Can't argue with that," Kevin said, but he had a pressing thought. "But Jake said this was a game." Empty stares wanted him to finish. "If this is a game," he continued, "they are watching. I wouldn't think they're just going to let us walk right out of here."

Dean was glaring at Kevin wanting to say something, but he remained silent.

"What choice have we got?" Tim asked. "We hunt this killer together or we get out. We take a risk either way."

"You guys go. My mission is to take care of Phoenix, I can't let him live." Jake said.

"What of the dead?" Dahria asked the group.

Their smiles and hope deteriorated as they sympathized with the deceased. No one spoke for a moment.

"I'll take care of them," Jake broke the silence in a genuine voice of concern. "It's the least I can do, I owe it to all of you. Get your people out of here." Jake had immense regret from his participation in all of it.

Damon was upset at himself. He dreaded staying here, but choked down his pride. "I'll help you," he said. "I know where the incinerators are and how to work them." He put his head down and sighed. "I owe it too. I've been a coward." He clenched his fists straining from his own personality.

Tommy gained a little respect for Damon at that instant, so did Tim. They looked at him as if to say thank you.

"Me too," Alexa joined the group.

Dahria raised her head in a look that signified Alexa was crazy.

Alexa never even looked back at her. She stood her ground and held her head high. "I need to make sure that Phoenix is over."

"All right," Tim said. "We need to vote who goes and who stays." Tim glanced at the others. No one spoke a word yet.

Dean clenched his teeth.

"We stay together," Tommy said, risking speaking for the others. Dahria closed her eyes and took two deep breaths. "We finish together, we leave together. That's the way we survive," he finished.

Dean kept his silence, *Dammit.*

---#---

Sweat dripped down the temple of Tim's head as he and Damon heaved Nick's body onto the metal slider drawer for the incinerator. An unnatural gaze looked in different directions on Nick's dead face. Tim did his best to hold it together, but it was difficult for anyone to handle. He made himself look away from the corpse and focus on the task.

Cremation caskets weren't available which yielded the people being stacked in grotesque positions so several bodies could be incinerated at once. However, to complete cremation for all remaining bodies, several hauls would need to be done. It was a time-consuming task.

Jake and Kevin grabbed both ends of another body and lifted it onto the table, and then John and Dean placed another. Jones, Alexa, and Tommy were helping move bodies into a line for them to access them easier. Dahria clenched her teeth together and helped them. She threw up once and gagged almost continuously.

The smell was pungent and overwhelming. It was like the contaminated air was raw shit being shoved down their throats. No escaping it, but they were all part of this and had a compelling determination to contribute.

Damon and Jake were the only ones who seemed to be able to either ignore or deal with the situation the best.

The incinerator made the room hot. Everyone was sweating and grunting. Coughs echoed, dry heaves sounded, and spitting were vibrating in the room.

No one spoke. It was a grueling task. Everyone was focused on getting it done as fast as possible.

Damon broke the silence succinctly, "Okay, that's it."

The others moved away without a word as Damon slid the table of corpses into the incinerator. The main door closed and Damon turned up the heat.

"About two or three hours," he said

Everyone stood staring at Damon with no response.

"Shouldn't someone maybe say something?" Dahria asked, peering around. She wanted to escape the aroma of death more than anything, but the sympathetic emotion won over the stench. These were people she knew, human beings.

No one wanted to speak and everyone looked at Damon who remained silent. He was a doctor, not a man of the cloth conducting a eulogy.

Taking it upon herself, Dahria spoke. "While I didn't know many of you that well, I am truly sorry you suffered this fate. You didn't deserve to die this way. I hope you are now free. Rest in peace."

A few muttered some semblance of goodbye or Amen.

"Thank you Dahria," Damon said. Kevin nodded.

A few moments later, they headed out for another incineration.

---#---

Several hours later, exhausted from lifting, dragging, and positioning bodies, they searched everywhere within a reasonable distance of the conference hall. They gained most of the population, about fourteen more bodies. Jake made it a point to locate Theod. He didn't want Theod just rotting in the tunnel. Jake owed him that much.

They burned another several bodies, but there were still nine bodies left. Most of the work was done, they just needed to wait for the incinerator to complete a full cremation before they could process more.

"I'll stay here and finish the burn," Damon suggested, "but I need at least one of you to help me lift."

Jake shook his head. He didn't like that it was taking this much time. "I need to hunt Phoenix. The longer I give him, the more he can prepare."

"But that might be what he wants. With you gone, then he can attack us," Kevin stared at him, pleading. He knew with Jake they stood a much better chance at survival.

"You should be safe here. Besides, I think I know where Phoenix might be," Jake said.

Everyone stared at Jake. It was clear what his intentions were, and it sounded dangerous.

"and I want to give him back his gift. I'm going with you," Alexa was serious.

Jake didn't question it, he could see she was sincere, and he decided it was her choice, so he let her make it.

"What?" Dahria asked in disbelief. "What the heck are you saying?"

Alexa turned toward her friend, "I've got to," she had a pleading look yet an unbreakable determination. "I'm sorry Ria, It's who I am now. I have no choice."

Dahria was awestruck. She couldn't believe it. "Of course you have a choice!" She pleaded. "Look!" Dahria pulled her away. "I know...I know what must've happened," her voice was quiet. "It almost happened to me. And I'm...I'm sorry." She cried.

Alexa stared at her, but her tears dried up, replaced with vengeance. After many moments she replied, "I'm so happy you got away, I really am, but this is who I am now. I can only try to make it right. I *need* to make it right, for myself."

They had a chance to leave this place and start over. Dahria realized even after all that has happened, her anger, fear, regret, one emotion beat every other. Love. Love for the free future. Love for a life with Tommy, with her family again. She couldn't wait to get out of here and forget this place. It beat any anger she had. At that moment she knew she was traveling a different path than Alexa. She looked at Tommy for help.

"Alexa..." Tommy said.

"Don't." She held her gaze, unrelenting. "I've made my choice."

They both stared at her with nothing more to say.

"I would have loved to get Townsend, that piece of shit." Jones interrupted, catching some of the conversation. He felt betrayed and cheated.

"You and I both kid," said John. "But finding him might be hard, and I hate to look for him when Phoenix is running around. I know Townsend locked us up, but he didn't kill us."

Jones nodded, "Yeah, I guess, but he tried to feed us to the lion." He was disappointed.

Tommy didn't want to be a coward and run in the face of danger, but he wasn't stupid either. He looked at Dahria, who was looking up at him. Tommy's main concern was reinforced. It was her. He hated what this killer had done, but they had their lives to live. Tommy then glanced at Jones, who received the message and nodded his head to signify that he stays with them. It relieved Tommy.

"The three of us will go with Damon and help," Tommy announced. He was referring to him, Dahria, and Jones.

Dean realized he could do nothing until the task was done. He had to wait until everyone was ready to leave, together. His fear subsided, the company would not interfere in the showdown.

"Let's get some food," Jake said. "Then Alexa and I will go hunt and you all can finish."

All of them agreed and followed him.

69

Phoenix watched the small screen of his device. He was mobile and just finished setting up. He watched the image dance around and show many of their faces. The boyfriend Tommy was talking to...there she was.

Mm, he thought with lust. Dahria. He smiled with excitement. Phoenix tingled with anticipation from thinking of his future artwork with her.

Among the faces that displayed, there was one person he didn't recognize. The man stayed silent most of the time. It didn't matter who he was, but Phoenix was curious how he got here.

Phoenix had watched them move and incinerate a bunch of bodies. He was elated about the extra time that gave him to prepare 'fun' packages. It was like his purpose was destined. Phoenix was careful of their movements as he wandered the halls and tunnels, stopping in a few precise locations to set up some new toys.

As he watched, he saw all their faces, except Alexa. She was still wearing his scintillating gift around her neck with the camera built in.

He laughed out loud to himself, amazed at how many things were going his way. "Thank you baby. I can't believe you still have my heart." Phoenix took out his radio transmitter box. It was small, one switch and one red button were located on the top.

"And I shall have you again, my love," he kissed the box.

He watched the group. Excellent. His wound was there, but held together nicely and didn't bother him. He checked it carefully and it was mending fine. No leaks.

Phoenix relaxed until the group moved.

70

As Jake led the group to the cafeteria, Dean pulled him aside and had a private conversation with him. It took several minutes. They kept it quiet. Jake shook his head several times but it looked like Dean was pleading with him.

"What the hecks that about?" Jones asked.

"You've got me," Tommy thought.

Once Jake was done, he walked over and informed everyone that it was time to finish the burn and start the hunt. "Grab something to eat quickly, and let's go."

When they finished eating, they all used the respective restrooms. Tommy looked up at the ceiling and the lights were shining bright. Keeping his eyes from glancing around in an unwanted area, he could hear the liquid hitting the urinals from the other two emptying their bladders.

"Sounds like Niagara," Jones smiled at the ceiling. It picked up a laugh or two.

The bathroom areas in the complex had higher quality finishings. Paneled ceilings like an office, LED lights were bright, walls with texture or tiles, and light switches. It seemed like locations around the command center were more luxurious. This restroom was pretty spiffy. Of course, everything was savage in this complex compared to the outside world. Bare minimum standards to survive.

Dahria And Alexa relieved themselves in their stalls in the women's room. They were talking to each other through the partitions and Dahria went on a tangent about her experiences. After several moments, she finished. It was quiet. Too quiet.

"Alexa?" She called out.

No answer.

Dahria's heart sank.

"Alexa!"

Nothing.

No!

She screamed, got up and banged on the stall door.

Jake, hearing the scream, was cursing himself for not being more aware.

"Damn it!" he said, running toward the door. It seemed so casual to just use the restroom, then he pondered. *Partition stalls. Shit!* "Restroom!"

The door to the restroom burst open and Jake ran in. He grabbed Dahria and moved her to kick the stall door open. Nothing. No sign of Alexa.

"Oh my God," Dahria was hot with anger. "Not again!"

Jake cursed himself for waiting so long, giving Phoenix time to set up traps, but he never thought it could be so quick.

Jake found some type of broken bulb on the floor and wafted it. "Urgh!" He turned his head away and threw it down. "Fuck! She's been knocked out with gas." Without waiting for any reactions, Jake looked at the ceiling. It was the only way. Jake climbed up on the toilet and removed one panel. He looked up into the rafters. Jake saw a winch. He lowered his head and shook it, his face grim.

"What do you see?" asked John, who couldn't view anything from everyone blocking him.

"He used a silent winch to take her up into the rafters," Jake exclaimed.

"What do we do?" Jones was confused.

As this was going on, Dean was gritting his teeth so hard they almost broke. He knew what he had to do, but had to wait until the proper time. They would be watching. *Play the game,* he thought. "We need to get her," Dean said. He wondered if the risk was worth it. He needed a terminal.

Jake peeked where the rafters went, only one way Phoenix could have gone. He jumped down and said, "follow me!"

Dean had to risk it, he couldn't let her die. "No! Follow me!" Everyone stopped and looked at Dean. "Trust me, we don't have much time."

Just as the group exited the restroom door with Dean in the lead, the lights went off.

71

Alexa bolted into awareness but her eyes were still closed. Something smelled terrible, like ammonia. There it was again. Her eyes opened and she moved her head to get away from the awful smell. She tried to focus, but nothing came into detail.

Darkness.

Her heart beat faster as she noticed the silence. A voice broke the silence.

"Hello my love," a soft voice penetrated the dark.

His voice was all too familiar. She knew this tone. Him, Phoenix. Her heart sank in disbelief, yet there was anger, a fight in her yearned. But there was also fear. She found she could move freely, which shocked her. She was groggy, but could sit up. Did she have the nerve to face him? Her awareness of an inevitable death beat into her. If she was going to go, it would be *her* way, not his.

She turned right into his gaze. Her eyes did not waver. There was a dead stare in them. He was at least fifteen feet away, sitting back on a padded office chair. Alexa could see an evil smile stretch across his face. She looked at herself, her clothes were all on.

"I figure we can go a little slower this time. Fall in love, I don't want our relationship to be based only on sex." He laughed. "Gosh, I've missed you so much." His voice soothing, but to Alexa it was like the hiss of a venomous snake. Beautiful in color, elegant in its smooth undulations, but deadly in its bite.

Alexa didn't know exactly what to do. She was defenseless and knew she was dead if she fought him, but when that happened, she would fight until the end. So be it. He was toying with her, playing a game. She decided to play too.

"And I've missed you," she replied with the same tone. Alexa surprised herself holding up so evenly. Then, she changed her tone and blurted, "I've wanted to cut off your dick and shove it up your ass!"

"Wow!" Phoenix responded laughing. "That was colorful! I see you've changed!" He relaxed and said with a serious sound, "I like it." He stared at her with his penetrating eyes and smiled big. His groin was churning with lust and blood. "So where shall we start this time?" he said with a casual arrogance, like this was a second date with a prostitute.

Alexa was thinking of what to say to him. A man like this had faults. She couldn't reason with him or kill him, but maybe she could give him a good sting. She couldn't play too nice otherwise he would catch it. Resisting to some extent might be enough. Alexa knew he was lustful and she played it. She needed to make him so overwhelmed with desire he wouldn't think straight.

"Well?" Phoenix prodded. "How about a dance for me?"

She thought of many responses, but didn't want to piss him off too much either. She wanted to make him lose control *her* way. Playing hard-to-get seemed to excite him.

"I could try a different point of entry," he said with a smile as Alexa didn't answer. "Shutting you girls up is fun. Girls love to ramble on and on and on," he mimicked a puppet talking into his ear with his hand, "but it's much harder to talk with something down your throat."

She became nauseous with that image. "That'll sure be a good way to get it bitten off," she threatened.

Laughing, "Yeah, I better put it where there aren't any teeth, huh?" His laughing stopped as an idea struck him. "Or…" his eyes moved up and to the right, accessing the creative centers of the brain, "I could rip them out. Try to bite me and it'll just be tighter. Ooh." His face lit up like a street light thinking of the pleasure.

That's it, she thought, but in reality it scared her to death. She winced in pain thinking of it and replied. "Yeah, if you would like me to be unconscious from the pain, moron! It wouldn't be as much fun unless I was awake, right asshole?"

His laugh was huge, "You got me there, it's better for the game absolutely, but you *do* need to be silenced with that dirty mouth you have now." He stood up abruptly and tried to push his fist into his mouth, mocking her. It didn't fit, and he pretended to choke. He laughed again.

Alexa stood up. She scanned around the room for any place to escape, but the only way out was through Phoenix. Alexa did the unthinkable, but it was the only option now, she unbuttoned her pants.

Phoenix froze as if his blood became concrete. He didn't know if this was reality. Intrigued, he watched.

She hid her embarrassment well and pulled down her pants only enough to show the top of her developed lines.

His eyes fixated on it. He felt his gums and glands hurt as they produced saliva.

"Commando. Wow. Who's the lucky guy that has your panties?" Phoenix teased knowing full well who had them.

Alexa had no reaction. While still watching him she turned around and slid her pants down seductively a little further exposing her round buttocks. She put her hands on the wall and pushed out her rear end to him. This made her insides burst with displeasure, but her outside was teasing. She hoped it worked. One hand caressed her own curvy rear in a playful gesture.

Phoenix marveled over the wonderful sight. He located a point of entry and his manhood hurt with maximum engorgement. Phoenix lost control. Moving closer, he was fixated on the sexual organs of Alexa.

She listened and watched as he struggled to open his pants as he couldn't get it open quick enough. Sliding down his drawers bending over, his member flung stiff as his underwear was pulled to his ankles.

As Phoenix waddled up and grabbed her cheek, Alexa made her hands into rock hard claws, turned with lightning speed, and engulfed as much of his testicles and sack as she could. Alexa drove her fingers in as hard as she could, rolling and pulling with all the energy she had. Her nails were like blades.

Phoenix released a piercing high pitched sound of pure pain, but Alexa held on like a pit bull. Twisting more, loving the sound of agony from his guts, she grinned. Her face was wild. Phoenix wasted no time punching her in the face, desperate to get her off.

"You fucking bitch!"

His punch was solid, enough to daze her. The force from the blow knocked her back, and she used this inertia to pull harder, but she lost some strength. She couldn't take another hit and had to let go, but pulled hard and ripped. She tried to make a run for it. Bolting for the door, she pulled up her pants that were left just under her bare buttocks. Getting to the door without looking back, she grabbed the wheel and turned it. It blurred with speed and banged to a stop. She pulled with force to open the door and felt a hard grab on her shoulder.

"Come here!" Phoenix was fumbling with one hand getting his uncooperating pants back up while the other tried to grab her. The two actions while running forward made it clumsy. The circus act granted Alexa some leeway. She was able to scramble from his grip, but the door shoved her into the wall as she held onto the wheel.

Something caught Phoenix's attention, and he glanced through the open door and stopped the attack on Alexa.

Alexa used the distraction and ran at him. Throwing her arms forward. She intended to push him back enough to allow her to exit. Phoenix turned full circle out of reflex. Alexa's arms were deflected around his motion. Her momentum kept her going, and she wasn't able to stop herself. She tripped and fell hitting the opposite wall away from the exit door. She grunted from the pain of her skin and body impacting the floor and skidding. Alexa looked back and noticed that Phoenix wasn't pursuing her. He was backing up. His motion was calm and precise. Alexa glanced around Phoenix to see a wonderful sight.

Jake's face.

A smile of disbelief made her cheeks tight, but Phoenix had speed. He moved across the room, closing the distance to Alexa on the ground.

In that motion Phoenix realized he had made a grave mistake, one that could cost him everything. The room was sealed, he had no escape. They outnumbered him. Under normal circumstances, he might have been able to fend off several attackers with excellent odds, but not when Jake was present. He changed the game. But Phoenix had an edge, he had Jake's knife that he took from Nick. That was good enough leverage for Phoenix to talk his way out. He needed to get Jake into a private battle.

Jake could see that Phoenix appeared calm and well controlled. He couldn't rush him as Phoenix would kill Alexa too fast. "Phoenix," Jake spoke.

"Baka!" Phoenix played and smiled. "How are ya?" He sounded like two buddies who hadn't seen each other in a long time.

Neither of them moved, but the others kept filing in the room.

"Bahkah?" John asked.

"Come on," said Phoenix to Jake, "your friend here isn't Japanese either? Stupid!" He used the dialogue to position himself and pressed his foot on Alexa in a vital area to injure her if needed. His weight pressed on her and she moaned in pain.

Jones envisioned what he thought might have happened and lost it. "You son of a..."

"Get back!" Jake moved toward Jones. He didn't want Jones in Phoenix's range and become a liability.

Jones paused.

In the misdirection, Phoenix slipped down to Alexa's side and held the knife at her throat. He pulled her up, and the group watched.

"Interesting predicament we have here, eh Jake?" Phoenix laid out. His tone, friendly again.

"You're not going anywhere Phoenix. They are not part of what we are, let her go, and we can give the players a good show. Let's have some fun. What do you say?" Jake was laying down the rules or making an offer. Hopefully, Phoenix couldn't resist the challenge.

"Wrong." Phoenix replied. "The game ends when the last one dies." His stare was hard at Jake. "I was saving you for last. The big showdown! Whoo hoo! Can you imagine the bets being placed by the players!" His eyebrows rose in wonder. Then, frowned. "Now you go and fuck it up!" He shook his head, "No matter, this will be even better! We now have an inside audience as well as an outside one."

John was getting agitated. "Give her up," he said.

Phoenix continued to be cool and calm. His attention would not flounder off Jake. "No, I don't think so." A stream of blood formed and ran down Alexa's neck. "I want to taste that lovely pussy again." He licked the blood off the back of her neck and enjoyed the taste. Phoenix smiled. It was sinister. He caught the movement from John, his baiting working on him.

Come get some!

John went for him. "Let her go!"

"He's trying to get a rise out of you, don't..." but it was too late. Jake was too far away to get to John in time, so he moved forward toward Phoenix. But Phoenix glided away to John to deal with the easy threat.

Dean grabbed his brother, "No! John!" In doing so, he pulled his brother back behind him, and that pushed Dean forward, in range of Phoenix.

Phoenix didn't waste any time and quickly exchanged hostages. He threw Alexa toward Jake, giving her a small incision to disorient and weaken her, grabbed and held Dean in the exact same manner as Alexa.

"Back off shithead!" Phoenix spat out to John. "Or I'll turn him inside out!" He had wanted to keep Alexa as a hostage and kill the fool John, but things didn't work out that way.

John watched in horror. It happened so fast. *What have I done?* John couldn't believe how quick and precise Phoenix was.

Tim took Alexa and ripped part of his shirt to apply pressure on her wound.

Tommy couldn't believe the situation. He felt helpless.

Dean inhaled a deep breath through his teeth. He was in pain from the point of the blade pressing hard into his neck. Dean was standing on his tippy toes trying to gain height over the point of the knife pushing him up.

"I said back up." Phoenix said. "Or I'll put him out of commission too. Soon I'll have you all out of order one at a time."

Unless we all rush you at the same time. No! I can't risk anyone one of these people getting killed on my watch. Jake motioned for John to back up with his hand.

"All right Jake. This is how it's going to play. We go to the equipment center where I had my lovely run-in with my first painting, the girl Jen."

So it was him, Tommy thought. *Bastard.*

"Everyone watches from the outer area looking through the chain fence." He grew excited. "It'll be a cage match!" He howled like a werewolf does at a full moon. "Now that's entertainment!"

Jake said nothing. He would have his chance to end the evil. *Him and me. Good.*

"The only catch...this guy here," he wiggled Dean in his grasp, "must remain in the cage tied up, just in case anyone outside gets any funny ideas. A little insurance policy."

"What?" John said. "No! You can't use my brother as a guinea pig! You'll just kill him in the cage!"

"Exactly!" Phoenix roared. "I'm going to kill them *both* in the cage, that's the idea, dickhead! And you will come just a bit later!" Phoenix pounded.

"Just you and me." Jake said.

"That's not how this works Jake," Phoenix said. He was adamant. "If you come at me, this guy dies right away, and we'll still fight, and you don't have a knife, do ya?" His lower lip pushed out like a pouting three year old kid.

There were some confused looks on John's and other faces.

Phoenix noticed it and proceeded. "Awe, he didn't tell you? Shoot. Yeah, *I* have all the knives." A small laugh echoed. Without letting it sink in, he continued using his leverage. "At least in the cage, if you win, I'll be dead, and there is no way I can kill this guy then. He lives. That's the only way."

There was no point in deflecting. Phoenix took this round.

Jake had no choice. "Whatever man. Let's just get this done." The only game left for him was to end it. Jake turned his head and looked at John. His face read 'this is the way it has to be.'

---#---

Arriving at the equipment center, Dean was standing on a table with a noose placed around his neck inside the combat area.

"Ya'll watch it now. I don't want to have to knock out a leg and have him fall." Phoenix's voice was humorous, but he was the only one who thought it was funny. He looked at them outside the cage and smirked. Then he saw Alexa. "How's my love muffin?" He blew her a kiss.

"How're your balls asshole?" She replied.

"Aching for more!" He laughed.

Her stare was fierce, but he wasn't looking at her anymore.

"And you," he said looking at Dahria, 'We have some unfinished business."

His smile caged her heart in fear, but said nothing.

Tommy couldn't help but tighten his fists and clench his teeth.

Phoenix stretched his arms, bent down, touched his toes, and sighed. "All right baka, you ready?"

Jake had been mentally preparing himself for the fight. He kept his head cool and focused. Jake knew how dangerous he was, and wouldn't let himself underestimate him.

"Come on Jake," Jones encouraged, his voice so soft only people close to him could hear it. He was nervous. Their lives depended on him.

Tommy watched intently. Dahria was behind him. She held Tommy from behind and peered around his shoulder.

Dean shifted on the table, being careful not to tip it over. He looked up at the rafters wondering how strong they were.

John watched the two men in the cage. His nerves firing made his skin feel like prickers were everywhere. He wanted to get his brother out of there as fast as he could. John couldn't believe he didn't put up more of a fight for him, but realized it probably wouldn't have done any good. It should have been himself up in that noose. Instant regret filled his mind that he hoped wouldn't come back to bite him.

Tim was next to Alexa, Kevin, and Damon.

Damon watched with one arm around his waist while the other elbow rested on the arm and his knuckles against his lips. Nerves were getting the better of him too.

"Ahoo!" Phoenix howled up into the air. "Let's party!" His arms outstretched like he wanted a hug. Two knives were in each of Phoenix's hands, but before anyone could protest, he threw Jake's knife at the table leg that held Dean. It flipped a few times and stuck perfectly and Jake pulled it out. Phoenix had a smirk on his face that Alexa wanted to gouge that same way she did his groin. She was feeling weak though.

The two faced each other. Their arms went into different fighting positions and they took their stances.

They went at each other.

An incredible display of footwork advertised an immense array of training. Back and forth they moved. One was the aggressor while the other retreated and vice versa. The blades whizzing through the air.

Kevin and Damon winced from behind the cage several times as it appeared like someone would inevitably get hurt. They just hoped it wasn't Jake. Kevin grew to respect and even like Jake, who turned out to be their protector, their avenger. He observed Jake had incredible skill, but Jake's opponent was also adept.

The first slash was made. Phoenix stepped back to check the damage. Being minimal, he rushed back in with a straight jab. Phoenix's side started to hurt, and the wound re-opened and leaked, but the adrenaline made it almost unnoticeable. Grunts from both men erupted here and there. The first two feet of the fighting area was hazy from the kicked up dirt.

Phoenix connected with a solid kick that knocked Jake back against the cage. The fence rebounded Jake into the fight and he used the momentum for a forward kick. It went right past Phoenix as he moved out of the way. His knife came down and connected somewhere in Jake's quadriceps area.

"Argh!" Jake yelled in pain. His leg dropped, the weight too much for it and he fell. As he hit the ground he rolled and swiped his knife parallel with the ground. It connected cutting both Phoenix's lower front shins. That made Phoenix jump back.

"You bastard!" Phoenix yelled out and came down on Jake with a stabbing motion aimed for his heart. Jake rolled out of the way and Phoenix's knife plunged hard into the dirt ground. Jake kept rolling a couple more times and sprang back up, fast on his feet. The pain in the leg was bad, but a small amount of weight could be supported. Jake realized he was wounded enough to fight at much less than full capacity.

"Come on Phoenix! You got me! Finish it!" Jake taunted him.

Anger shot through Phoenix and he rushed him. He wasn't expecting the dirt to enter his eyes as he stepped forward.

Jake flung it with precision and Phoenix's momentum kept him moving forward at Jake. Blinded, the only action Phoenix could perform was swing and slash where Jake had just been, but Jake wasn't there anymore when he arrived. His knife raked back and forth but only connected with air. Then, he felt another wet wound from his stomach. *Fuck!* It took his breath away. Phoenix tripped and was still moving forward. He hit something hard with his shoulder and it broke. Hitting the fence with his face, Phoenix rolled over, sat down on the ground, blinked, and wiped his eyes expecting a quick attack from Jake. He thought his shoulder broke. The attack never came and realized his shoulder never broke.

Screams were heard from outside the cage, and the fence rattled as Phoenix looked up, blinking with dirt in his eyes. He had crashed into the table and broke its leg. Dean fell and was being hanged. No one could get to Dean but Jake. Phoenix smiled. *Good insurance.*

Jake climbed up on the fence and sawed the rope. Dean's face was dark purple from the constriction and he looked around frantically.

Phoenix used the opportunity.

·Jake finished the last chunk of rope and Dean fell to the ground hitting it hard. Dean spread out flat, and didn't move.

Jake released his grip and as he jumped down, his weight made Phoenix's knife plunge deep into his gut.

"Ugh!" The sound was like pain that needed to get out, but only a soft sound emerged. Jake couldn't breathe. His weight was too much, and he fell backward with Phoenix following him down.

Phoenix looked into Jake's eyes. Triumph. "You fought well," his eyebrows rose signifying courtesy respect, "but the better man won."

Jake could only let out gasps of air. His face contorted in pain as he looked pure evil in the eyes. He couldn't do anything but lay flat. His energy depleted. Jake's mind swam with many thoughts; Regret about not being able to see this killer gone forever, thinking he should have done more from the beginning, fear of the unknown, and love for these people. He wished he could've saved them. He needed to right the wrong he committed in some microscopic way. All of that was washing away now. The dirt and grime remained. He failed.

"No!" Tommy yelled, stunned.

"Jesus Christ!" Tim yelled.

Others were shouting disbelief of what happened.

"And we have a victor!" Phoenix got up and raised his hands. He stepped over Jake and did a victory lap giddying up like he was riding a bull. His wounds were bleeding and needed attention, and the new wound made him speak a little softer, but wasn't mortal.

Dean was on the ground and wasn't moving. John was freaking out. "Dean! Dean!"

"Whoo hoo!" Phoenix yelled in a great mood. Blood ran down his stomach from his wounds, but he didn't seem to care. He was breathing heavily from the exertion, pumped full of adrenaline.

John was trying to get to Dean but Tim was holding him back. "Let me go!"

"John! John! Come on! We can't help him!" Tim said.

Phoenix stopped his commotion and looked at everyone around him outside the cage. He over-exaggerated his sashay to the chain link fence like he was the bravest man who ever lived and grabbed hold of the links, peering through like *they* were the animals in the cage. "Oh, my. What a good time this will be. I have you all to myself." He smiled.

"Shit!" Tommy said. "We've got to get out of here!" He pulled Dahria, and she pulled Alexa.

Phoenix walked calmly over to the lock and was about to become free. There was nothing they could use to keep him from escaping.

It took muscle and yelling from Tim to pull John, but he came with them. They ran.

"Wait! Wait! My babies! Don't leave me in here all alone!" Phoenix urged them. He looked at the unmoving Dean and Jake. Jake was still alive, but in grave condition. "I'll be back Jake, it's been fun. You take care now you hear?"

Jake could only look into his eyes with regret and fury.

"To the iron door!" Tim said. "Fast!"

---#---

The iron door was in front of them. Out of breath, Tommy, Jones, and Tim worked on the process for opening the door. After performing a couple of actions, green lights turned on and a hiss of gas pressure equalized.

"That's it!" Tim said with excitement.

Dahria jumped up and down impatiently for the door to open. She kept looking back down the hall for Phoenix.

"Come on, door." Jones said.

John was staring off into space thinking of his fallen brother while Kevin was looking behind them to check if

Phoenix was coming. Alexa was holding her neck looking pale. Damon wanted to puke.

Four giant door locks unwound all on their own, like giant screws rotating and unscrewing. Anxious sounds came out of the group. A loud hiss exited from around the door signifying the seal opened. It was immense.

"Open it!" Jones said.

Tim grabbed the door, and it swung open.

The smiles and excitement stopped.

Shock.

Tommy's gut felt like all its contents had just been sucked from it.

"What!" Jones shouted. It took only a second or two before he went berserk.

Everyone stared at the wall behind the iron door.

Solid wall.

No exit.

It was a fake.

Jones pushed at it hoping it was an illusion.

It wasn't.

After several seconds of beating at the wall, Jones sunk down against it and sat down and started giggling. He put his hands into his face, frustrated. Everyone was stunned.

"Oh my God," Dahria's hope diminished.

"Son of a bitch! What the hell are we going to do now?" Damon asked.

Pure frustration made John shake his head back and forth in bewilderment.

Tim put his head down and concluded a harsh realization.

"We better hurry if..." Tommy suggested, but didn't get to finish his sentence.

"You hoo!" Phoenix's voice echoed down the hall some distance away. "Where are you guys? I'm getting lonely!" Phoenix called out. "Anyone know of a good doctor around here? I'm hurt! Show some pity for a poor old wounded fool!" He finished the last part laughing.

"Too late kid," Tim said. Hope ran out. He knew this would mean death. Death for some, but maybe even all of them. The situation was beyond dire. Phoenix had the only weapon, but he had to try. "Look everyone," Tim said, constructing the situation. "We can do this. There's no choice now, anyway. We need to fight him at the same time, together. Find something you might be able to use. Look around, move!" He didn't wait for any replies.

Everyone scattered like roaches and came back with something. Tommy ripped out the wires from the computer and gave one to Jones.

"Dahria, I want you to stay back, you hear me?" Tommy said to her.

"You need me too!" Dahria protested.

"Of course we need you, but Alexa's wounded, take care of her!"

Not wanting to argue, she found Alexa, who was a few shades paler, and they both hid as best they could.

Tim picked up the screen of the computer. John grabbed the metal chair. Kevin and Damon had nothing, so Tommy gave them each a wire.

The group had nowhere to go. There were no hiding places, no doors, only the entryway to the tunnel. It was large enough to fit everyone with plenty of room. They could form a half moon surrounding Phoenix.

Tommy felt dread, fear, and hopelessness knocking on his brain trying to get in. He tried to push it out, but it was difficult. He focused and was as ready as he could be.

"Spread out and form a half circle, but stay close, just out of arm's reach. Remember, we need to work together as a team, at the same time." Tim said.

"Jesus Christ," John said. His heart was beating fast enough it felt like it would shake out of his chest. "He can't be *that* good, can he?"

Kevin didn't want to say anything to make matters worse, but he saw how good Jake was. And he watched the two of them fight. Phoenix *was* that good.

Damon looked scared out of his mind.

Footsteps approached the small group. Only emergency lights shined down the long tunnel illuminating sporadic areas. They were spaced apart at equal intervals. A shadow phased into appearance. Footsteps were the only sound heard as Phoenix walked the line of death towards them. Then, the light made Phoenix fade into view and then fade back into darkness when he passed the spotlighted area. He was smiling. The sequence repeated, another light, evil face, then turned to dark again. His wondrous blade shined when the light reflected.

"Hello my angels," he said with welcoming condonation.

"Wait for my signal," Tim whispered to the group.

"Geez, thanks a lot for just leaving me there," Phoenix's tone was cool. He moved closer to them but stopped well out of range. "Wow," he said, "you've got some serious weapons there," he chided. "I'm not sure I want to engage myself with such professional athletes."

Tommy looked at Phoenix's mid-section. It was bloody. This area would be what he would try for. Maybe Phoenix was hurt enough for them to win. It was a far reach, but it was hope.

"Where's my mates?" He sniffed the air, his face suggesting that he smelled a sweet fragrance while basking in the sun on a warm day with a cool breeze. "They're close. I can smell pussy."

No one moved.

"Of course...it might just be *you* guys!" The laugh was huge. "Oh my God!" He grabbed his stomach, "don't make me laugh! It hurts!" He kept laughing loudly against his own wishes.

No one fell for his ruse. He knew Phoenix was smart and didn't want to deal with everyone all at once if he didn't have to.

"Now!" Tim hoped Phoenix's hysterical laughing was a distraction for himself.

This is it! Tommy thought. *We charge to our death!*

Phoenix was so quick to adjust into seriousness it astounded Tommy. No one in the group was even close to Phoenix, who was already poised. It was like Phoenix knew the attack would come at that precise moment.

Phoenix slid to one side and stepped forward. Kevin was the first one he encountered. A quick kick to Kevin's knee and he dropped like a stack of free standing bricks.

Tommy saw Phoenix's position and tactics. It meant he could encounter them all in a line. That was no good. Tommy watched Tim go to Phoenix with his computer screen right in front of him.

Phoenix took his left hand and with a ridiculous smooth action, lifted the screen up exposing Tim's midsection. His knife sliced clean and Tim went down. Tommy and Jones arrived at the same time along with John. His attention swung to John, who was older than Tommy and Jones, so he was the obvious more formidable opponent. Tommy noticed something strange, Phoenix held out his wrist, offering it to John. Falling for the bait, John grabbed it, and Phoenix knew exactly what to do with it. In a polished motion, he took John's wrist and flipped it over with force and snapped it.

"Agh!" John spouted in pain.

Phoenix used John's momentum and spun him around right into Jones, knocking him over.

Tommy was not expecting Phoenix to be spinning as he arrived. He tried to tackle him, but it was like trying to hold on to a spinning turbine. His energy went right around Phoenix and landed him face first on the concrete floor. His wrists took a beating catching his fall as he skidded to a halt. Skin and blood were written on the floor like kids drawing with chalk.

"Olé!" Phoenix chanted and turned toward Damon, who was late in his attack. At this point, Damon didn't bother. He stopped and backed up.

Phoenix laughed. "Way to help your fellow companions doc." He was clapping. "Gosh, these kids are more brave than you." He focused his attention on Tommy and Jones.

"Awe, kids. I'm sorry it had to come to this, but, hey. If it were any other circumstances, I'd bet on you." He walked over to Jones who was getting up from the fall and Phoenix stepped on him. Jones couldn't move. "However, I've got a quota to meet and girls to get it on with."

"No!" Tim said while Tommy turned his head to look up.

Phoenix wasn't playing games anymore. It was time to call Jones to the light.

"Stop!" Tommy shouted.

Jones' eyes grew big. Death was standing above him.

The blade was glistening in Phoenix's hand. His eyes were dead, cold. It was over.

Jones put up his hands to block the attack in reflex, but knew it wouldn't do any good.

Phoenix raised his knife high, but it never came down. His eyes grew wide. A gut sound came out of his mouth like he had just been punched in the stomach. It looked like he lost focus with the attack on Jones and tried to grab his back but was unsuccessful. Phoenix was stunned and hobbled to turn. Tommy was shocked to see the hilt of a knife sticking out of his back.

Phoenix's face turned into a grimace. He lost some control of his body as he stumbled two steps to look down the hall.

One spotlight illuminated Jake's face. It had anger, his eyes held revenge. Jake could barely stand, but he had the help of another man. Dean.

"Dean!" John was happy his brother was alive. He pulled himself up the best he could, holding his snapped wrist.

Phoenix said nothing. He was in shock. Making the mistake of overestimating the wound to Jake, and failing to make sure Dean was dead, he realized his fatal error. Too much adrenaline made him not think clearly. Pain trickled in much more intensely now. Already hard to breathe, his muscles felt like the signals allowing him to move were interrupted by something blocking the communication.

Jake expertly threw his knife in a spot to have brutal consequences and to incapacitate.

Phoenix lost strength in his legs and fell to his knees. He was breathing deeply, like he couldn't get enough air.

Tommy grabbed Jones, "You okay?" he said, helping his friend up.

Not smiling, his face shiny from sweat, Jones nodded. "Yeah." Jones knew he came too close to death. "Thanks."

Tommy then turned to Kevin and Tim. He helped them up. Tim was bleeding. "How about you two?"

Kevin hobbled on one leg, "I'll be fine."

"I'll make it." Tim released pressure, checking his wound. It was bleeding, but didn't seem to be critical.

Damon slid over to John and Tim. John moaned from the pain, but it gave Damon a sense of worth. He needed to stitch up Tim, but it could wait for a little while.

They all moved in front of Phoenix and watched.

Dahria grabbed Tommy's arm.

Alexa slowly walked over and knelt down.

Phoenix eyed her, breathing heavy.

She slowly removed her necklace, her restraints of metal and jewels no longer her prison. She held it out in front of him and dropped it on the ground. His eyes followed it then slowly rose back at her. She wanted to say and do many things to him, but realized it wouldn't matter to her. She wasn't like Phoenix and didn't want to be. When he would die, her fear would go with him. The fear was a part of her that *needed* to die so she could live again.

Jake hobbled closer and looked down at Phoenix. Thoughts flowed through his head, but only two words were important to him.

"Game over," he said.

Phoenix's eyes shifted to Jake and stared at him with an unknown expression. Maybe regret, pride, or just acceptance. No one would ever know for sure.

Phoenix gave them a large grin and even giggled. It fell short as his laugh was choked off by blood. Soon his eyelids grew heavy and white slits were all that could be seen. He tried to lie down but instead fell to the side. In turn, his breath stopped. His life escaped and would never re-enter his body.

Alexa stood up. She and Dahria embraced.

Kevin stepped over to Jake and put his hand on his shoulder. "Thank you, Jake."

Jake gave him a warm smile. A sense of fulfillment and success enveloped him. He had righted his wrong, maybe not fully, but he had made a difference. A positive difference. Jake thought about all the points in his life that meant anything to him. He knew *this* task was the most important thing he had ever done. He had avenged, beaten evil at his own game. There had been only a handful of memories of success in his life, but he now had a feeling that left all those moments behind.

Happiness and contentment.

Jake had gone full circle. Accomplished. Then exhaustion ruled his body and he closed his eyes. He sank into rest and never opened them again.

72

They stood over Jake and mourned.

"Thank you again Jake," Kevin murmured. His memory of the moment of Nick filled his head. If he had been allowed to judge, Jake would've been dead, in turn probably killing everyone else in here. *Interesting in the choices we make.*

"We've got to get going. They're watching," Dean whispered.

"What?" Tim asked.

"We have to get out of here. Now. They'll be coming for us. I'm sure this didn't go as well as they planned," Dean replied.

"We can't get out," said Tommy. Sorrow echoed his voice. "The iron door opened to a solid wall. We're trapped."

"I know," Dean said.

Confused expressions plastered everyone's faces.

"What do you mean?" asked Kevin.

"I saw the plans from the computer terminal. I knew it was too easy, but had to play along if I was being monitored, which I was. That was when I realized the only way out was to find a way in." His voice was hoarse from the rope, but everyone could understand.

John's jaw dropped. He realized what Dean was saying, "Yes! That's my bro!"

The rest of the group was dumbfounded.

Kevin said, "so you planned…"

"When they took me from the company office," Dean continued, "I had already implanted some pretty expensive technology to record what happened to me."

"Holy shit," Tim said. "So that's how you were able to figure out how to get in…to get out," he said mostly to himself, astounded.

"So what do we do?" Dahria asked him, eager to get things going.

"Come on." Without wasting any more time, they hurried to the command center.

Damon persuaded them to cut through the medical center, so he could quickly dress Tim and Alexa's wounds, and set John's arm. He made a sling so he wouldn't injure it further. Kevin limped but was getting better and Damon said he would be fine. It didn't take long at all.

While waiting, Jones had mentioned he would have liked to get his hands on Townsend. Many agreed that he probably removed himself a while ago. The thought of him getting away burned a hole in Jones.

Tim was afraid of what the company would do, already wondering if they were positioning themselves for their escape attempt.

Tommy looked at Dahria with hope. She returned it hugging his arm. Tommy grabbed Jones, who helped Alexa and pulled them into the group.

Kevin was glad to be alive.

After they left the medical center, the group entered the command center, Dean spoke, "Here we are."

Tommy was nervous. He shook with anticipation. The excitement and agitation bubbled over like boiling water too full for the container.

They entered the same room that they first found Dean in. After piling into it, Dean stayed by the light switch. Dean took the plate of the light switch and slid it up. It revealed a small device that looked like a control pad. Dean pushed a code into the keypad along with an up arrow. It lit.

The room shook and Tommy felt his weight increase. He was looking at the open door they had entered from. A wall from the top of the open door started closing, moving down. The door was now blocked off by a dirt and rock wall. Tommy realized the optical illusion and it tickled his brain. The wall wasn't moving down, the entire room was moving up.

It was an elevator!

"Holy shit." Tim said in amazement. "This was here the whole time?" He shook his head.

Tommy wondered what their new lives would be like. *Where're we going to go? What about everyone else? What're they gonna do?* The thoughts excited him, but scared him too. Tommy choked down his thoughts not wanting to be overzealous.

A few minutes later, the ground vibrated and shook, then stopped. The exit door was black, like a void. Tommy couldn't see anything until lights attempted to turn on. Buzzing and flickering, the lights illuminated parts of the long tunnel.

The group walked the long tunnel until they reached a door. Everyone stared at the handle in wonder, but Dean knew where it went. He turned it and opened the door. A blinding natural light beamed in, like a doorway to heaven. Taking a few steps forward, the sun hit their faces.

Tommy closed his eyes and felt the warmth. The golden glow painted on his face. Tommy wasn't sure if he was dreaming or awake. He smiled as the cool breeze touched him.

No one spoke, awestruck, allowing the moment to infiltrate their senses.

Tommy noticed something unusual about the smell of the air...it wasn't muggy or pungent. It was fresh from earth. Tommy thought it was the best smell he had ever tasted. He opened his eyes and took in the scene. Amazing.

"Welcome back home my friends," Dean said.

Tommy smiled. He gazed at Dahria, Jones, and each of the others, all looking at the fantastic sight.

"Wow," someone said.

For what seemed like an eternity, something hit their eyes. A sparkle from *natural* light.

ABOUT THE AUTHOR

James Thomas hit the Arizona desert when he was a baby. He lives with his wife and two great kids.

www.ingramcontent.com/pod-product-compliance
Lightning Source LLC
Chambersburg PA
CBHW031252170626
46807CB00001B/99